EMILY'S LIST

SEAN PLATT

DAVID W. WRIGHT

STERLING & STONE

Contents

For Anna

EMILY'S LIST

ONE

Just Blink And Unthink

I REALLY DON'T *WANT* to blink, but there are rules to these things.

If I don't blink, Mom will die.

But I don't just blink to help me un-think the awful thoughts. I do it when I get anxious. And right now, my anxiety is making me want to scream as we pull off the highway and head into the town that's about to be our new home. My second one in sixteen years.

Mom's watching, *observing,* to see how I'm handling this.

And God, I don't *want* to blink. I want her to think I'm handling this fine, that I'm not regressing.

But, there are rules, and I have to follow them — or bad things will happen. Again.

My logical mind knows the bad things probably won't happen. But Obsessive Compulsive Disorder doesn't care about logic. It's all about emotion and fear, and right now I feel the panic swelling in my chest, demanding I give in to the compulsion.

Or else.

I close my eyes, tight, figuring maybe she'll just think I'm tired, or squinting from the morning sun. Maybe she won't see me blinking.

I cover my eyes with my hands, lending to my "Oh, the sun is too bright!" excuse.

Four times.

She's not going to die.
She's not going to die.
She's not going to die.
She's not going to die.

Four times and things will be back to normal. Four times and all the horrible things my imagination has conjured will return to the depths from which they come — at least until the next time I think something.

Four times.

I open my eyes.

Mom is looking straight ahead as she drives, but I can tell by the slightest downturned curves teasing the corners of her mouth she knows exactly what I was doing.

And I can almost feel her disappointed sigh, despite her holding it back.

I'm such a freak.

We pass a giant sign that reads, *Welcome to Pine Hollow, Washington. Home of the Fighting Lions.*

I'm guessing that's their high school football team, though the idea of actual lions fighting makes me giggle.

The sign is surrounded by lush landscaping and a fountain, the kind of thing I imagine the town spent a small fortune on to welcome newcomers in an attempt to attract local businesses. Mom says it's a beautiful little town with a crap economy since the lumber mill closed a few years back. We got a great deal on a cheap house, the best place we can afford at the moment, and her new job is only an hour's drive to Tacoma.

"Isn't it beautiful?" she asks.

I know what I'm *supposed* to say. Because, objectively, it *is* beautiful. It's a little town in a valley between two small mountains with even larger mountains looming beyond them. The sort of scenic place you might expect to see on a postcard. The kind of place most people would love to call home.

But it's not my home.

"It's different." That doesn't sound too negative. Mom says I'm always such a downer. As if telling me might change my mood or turn me into a miniature version of her, Mrs. Positive Polly. My mother's name is Mary, but people call her Polly. I'm not sure why.

Sorry, Mom, I don't do the whole Positivity Mindset thing. I can't just push a button and change how I think or how my brain works. I wish I could.

"I thought you'd appreciate *different*. It's not like you ever cared for Los Orillas. You hated it there. Consider this an upgrade. A small town where you actually know your neighbors and everyone is nice to each other. And just think how beautiful it'll look at Christmas."

"Yeah, but Los Orillas was home."

She laughs. But it's a frustrated chuckle. "Come on, Cora. *Please*, just give it a chance."

Trading city life, beaches, and the nearly constant sunshine of Southern California for a cold, rainy, small town in the middle of a mountainous nowhere is not my idea of an "upgrade." But I can't complain to Mom. After all, I'm the whole reason we're moving — to give me a fresh start.

As if changing locations can magically make me forget what happened.

Driving down the main street, two things hit me at once. First, there's a lot of small, old-timey shops close to the street, the kind that feel like they've been here for at least a century, nothing at all like the sprawling shopping centers back home.

Second, there are no big signs for fast food restaurants, malls, bookstores, or movie theaters. None of the signs of culture I'm used to.

"Doesn't this place have any good stores?"

"There are stores all around. See? There's a clothing store there, a secondhand shop there, and oh, look, there's a bait shop!" She laughs at this last one.

"Serious, Mom. Where are the *good* stores?"

"Maybe they don't have the big chain stores you're used to, but I'm sure they have plenty of awesome local shops. We'll look around after we get settled."

I cross my hands over my chest, sink deeper into my seat, and glare out the window while wondering what kind of backwoods stuck-in-the-past place she's dragged me to.

The people walking along the main street are almost exclusively white folks. Not the mix of cultures and colors I'm used to back home, where I fit in, and nobody looked at me any different for being bi-racial. Sure, they treated me different for other reasons, but race was rarely among them.

Here, I feel like my light brown skin will seem even darker, my curly hair even curlier. If I'm the only one like me, I'm going to stick out for sure.

And I *hate* sticking out.

I know I'm only going to make Mom feel bad if I keep sulking, but I can't help it. My entire world has been upturned — again.

No, I wasn't happy in Los Orillas, but at least I had my best — well, my only — friend, Kris. And there were places I could go to take my mind off of things. There was a bookstore where I could spend hours sitting in comfy chairs, reading, and drinking iced coffee. There were also great restaurants and a multi-screen theater with reclining seats. Places that reminded me of when things were good.

Places that reminded me of Dad.

And here, nothing but all sorts of nothing.

I hate it already.

We stop at a red light.

"Oh, look, that place looks popular." Mom points to our right where a group of teenagers are hanging out at a cluster of tables in front of Nan's Ice Cream. The kids are all laughing and goofing around.

Three boys are tossing a football. A beautiful blonde with blue eyes is sitting at one of the tables. She looks like she belongs on TV. The girl, and her good-looking friends, are surrounded by cute boys.

The blonde looks up and straight at me.

Feels like I just got busted staring.

I quickly turn away, look ahead, and sink lower in my seat, begging the traffic light to turn green.

Is the girl still staring at me? The temptation to check is strong, but I don't dare give into it.

I hate myself for being so awkward.

The light turns green, *thank God*, and we go.

"They looked like they were having fun," Mom says.

"So, the hot spot in town is Nan's Ice Cream? Awesome! Can't wait to hang out by myself and get fatter."

"Stop it. You're *not* fat. You're a normal, healthy weight."

I don't say anything. Mom doesn't see my body the way *I* see my body. I'm too tall, so I always stand out. And in all the wrong ways. Even more when I'm fatter. I'm finally down to a weight I don't entirely loathe, but still not as thin as I want to be. The last thing I need is Mom thinking I'm going to stop eating again. Then she'll start forcing me to eat more.

We drive in silence, turn off the main street, then take winding roads through what seem like nice enough neighborhoods.

I *do* like that most of the homes have huge yards. Back home, you had to be stinking rich to have anything more than a patch of brown grass because the water cost too much to keep it green. Here, everyone seems to have enough yard for four houses. And they're making great use of them — kids goofing around together, parents playing with their kids, a mom pushing her little girl on a tire swing. People are even playing ball in the road, something you could never really do back in Los Orillas without getting hit by a car or a stray bullet.

We pass by people walking their dogs and teens riding bikes or skateboarding. One of the skaters, a cute boy with long dark hair, smiles at me as we pass.

I smile back before turning away, feeling butterflies.

"Was *that* a smile?" Mom teases. "And here I am without my camera! Aunt Alicia will never believe me."

"It wasn't a smile," I joke. "Just gas."

She laughs. "You're going to like it here, Cora. We both will. I know it's hard moving from the only place you've ever known, but this is a nice town with nice people. It's going to feel like home before you know it."

"Maybe." I feel a little bit better, though I'm not entirely sure why. Sometimes Mom's enthusiasm can be contagious, though I'd never admit it to her.

"I can't wait for you to see the house!"

Mom came out here two weeks ago with her sister, Alicia, to get the house ready ahead of time. She lives in Tacoma, about an hour away, where Mom will be working as a neonatal nurse. There's talk that a hospital is opening a little closer next year, so if she can get in there, maybe she won't have to drive so far.

"And, here we are," she says, turning onto a cul-de-sac with fifteen houses, seven on each side and one at the end. "Want to guess which house is ours?"

I look at the houses. They all look nice, or at least okay, except one — a run-down, creepy looking place with chipped paint and a yard overrun with knee-high grass and gnarled weeds. The windows are boarded, and it looks days away from being condemned.

"Please don't let it be *that* house," I say.

"Yep, it's that one."

"For real? That'll take *forever* to fix up!"

"No, not for real. Guess again."

I look again.

Then I see it — a two story house, an old looking one, at the end of the cul-de-sac, freshly painted a bluish-gray. The color might remind me a little too much of a battleship if not for the deep red door and the bright white fence. A sprawling yard opens into the woods.

"That one?" I ask, pointing. Though it's probably older than our last house, it looks nice.

"Yes."

"Wow, how'd we afford it?"

"Houses are cheaper here. This one's been on the market a while, and the bank wanted to unload it."

I consider making a sarcastic comment about the prices in Nowheresville, where no one would ever choose to move unless they had to, but I refrain — for now. "Sweet! Looks nice."

Mom smiles.

"Do I get to pick my room?"

"Well, there are only three bedrooms. And you're *not*

getting the master. I figured you'd want the next biggest one. The third one is tiny."

I get out, sling my backpack over my shoulder, pull out my phone, then snap a photo for Kris.

Within seconds, she comments, *Nice! I'm packing my bags.*

Kris lives in a tiny house with three brothers she hates, a mom who never takes her side, and a dad who is a sexist, controlling jerk. She fights with him and her brothers all the time. Basically, she's a rebellious badass whose parents refuse to let her blossom into who she really is. She's often talked about running away to come live with me. I'm hoping one day she'll actually follow through. But I know she's too scared to actually do it.

You come, you've got a room.

"Can Kris come live with us?" I ask, after the text is already sent.

"Sure."

She's kidding, I think, but if things went bad with Kris and her father, I'm pretty sure Mom actually would let her live with us. She thinks of Kris as a second daughter. Once we're eighteen, I'm hoping we can live together.

Two more years.

I won't miss much about Los Orillas, least of all the bad things that happened. But I will miss Kris. I already do, and it's only been a day since I saw her.

Love you, I text.

Love you too, Apple.

Apple is a play on Cora. Well, core, as in apple core. One of her many quirky names for me. Apple, Core, Coral, or, when I'm sick, Quarantine. I hated Core at first, so naturally, it's the one she loves calling me most.

I slip the phone into my jacket pocket and follow Mom to the front door.

She hands me the keys. "You want the honors?"

I take the keys then slide them into the lock. As my fingers touch the doorknob, a chill runs through me.

And another bad OCD thought comes to me.

YOU'RE BOTH GOING TO DIE HERE.

I blink four times, and *un-think* the thought before I open the door.

We're not going to die here.
We're not going to die here.
We're not going to die here.
We're not going to die here.

TWO

Welcome Home

THE HOUSE IS NICE, though it's weird seeing our furniture in a new place.

The L-shaped leather couch that fit perfectly in our old living room makes this smaller room feel claustrophobic. The dining room set, a circular table that was perfect for the nook in our last house, is too small here. And the old kitchen table we have clashes with this more modern kitchen full of stainless steel and bright colors. It's like someone took our home and is trying to shove it somewhere it doesn't belong.

Everything looks out of place, just like me.

Mom leads me upstairs to my bedroom. One of the only things I'm looking forward to about the new place is that she got me all new furniture. I never liked my old bedroom set. I had it for way too long and it always felt like a little kid's room.

She looks at me with a nervous smile.

I open the door.

And I love it.

My bed is now queen-sized, with pink, white, and

gray bedding, several overstuffed pillows, and a sheer canopy of white tulle. Fairy lights are strung along the ceiling. The white bookshelf, nightstand, giant dresser, and vanity desk are a matching set from Ikea — the thick, chunky style you see in the rooms of beauty YouTubers and book vloggers. Mom even decorated with vases full of colorful flowers. Even if they're not real, they sure are pretty.

I turn to her, tears in my eyes, and give her a big hug. "I love it!"

"You haven't even seen the best part." Mom opens the closet. It's full of my boxes, but it's also a walk-in. "I didn't unpack your stuff, figuring you'd want to decide what goes where. Once you unpack, you'll have tons of space in here."

"Thank you, Mom!"

I sling my backpack on the bed, open it, then pull out Sneezy, my stuffed giraffe. My dad gave him to me when I was young, and he's one of my most treasured possessions. I find him a spot between some pillows.

Mom smiles at me, surely remembering how Dad would read me stories at bedtime, using Sneezy to act out stories and even adding on to them. Sometimes he'd play me songs on his guitar and ask Sneezy what he wanted him to sing. Sneezy had super bad taste in music and only asked Dad to play songs from the eighties — the cheesier the better.

"Okay, one last room," Mom says.

I'm wondering what she did with the space. Back home, she and Dad had their own offices. Mom did scrap-booking and some other crafts in hers. Dad, who was a writer, worked in his.

The way Mom looks excited, I imagine her new room has giant tables and drawers for all her supplies. Maybe she'll let me use the space to draw in when she's not using it.

This room is also upstairs, right over the front door.

"Close your eyes." Her big smile makes me wonder even harder. Maybe she made it into an art studio for me. That would be cool, though right now I only draw. I don't paint or sculpt or anything that requires a studio.

Still, the way she's smiling …

I close my eyes.

She opens the door and guides me in.

"Okay, open them."

I do.

And see my father's office from back home, almost perfectly transferred to this house. All the bookshelves are in the same place, same as his desk. Even Dad's collectables line the shelves, just like they did in Las Orillas.

"You brought Dad's office here?" Surprised tears sting my eyes.

"Yeah. I know how much you miss him and that you sometimes go into his office in the middle of the night to feel close. I wanted you to have some part of him here."

I'm full-on crying now.

Mom hugs me.

"Thank you, Momma."

"I love you, Cora. Thank you for giving this a chance."

"I love you, too."

AFTER DINNER, I get my clothes ready for school. I don't want to start tomorrow, but Mom thought it would be better to start on Friday than Monday. Best to get it over with and not be anxious all weekend.

She knows how I am.

Despite this, as I lay out my clothes on top of my dresser and think about starting over at a new school, the anxiety crawls across me like spiders.

THEY'RE GOING TO HATE YOU.

JUST LIKE AT YOUR OLD SCHOOL, EXCEPT NOW YOU DON'T HAVE KRIS!

I wish I could turn off that inner voice, that negative monster forever lurking inside my mind, wanting to tell me all the things that could go wrong.

I stare in the mirror, cycling through a list of all the things I hate about myself. I'm too tall. I'm not skinny enough. I've got a baby face. My hair is too curly. My feet are too big. My thighs are colored with scars, old burns from self-harming.

And that's just the surface flaws.

Look under the hood and you've got all sorts of crazy — anxiety, depression, OCD, and, oh yeah, I sometimes see freaking ghosts.

I'm one more suicide attempt or breakdown from Mom giving up on me and throwing me back in a mental hospital.

WE ALL KNOW WHAT'LL HAPPEN THERE!

I try not to think about it. Try to counter it with positive thoughts, like Mom, and the therapists, told me to do.

I'm not going back. I'm not crazy anymore. Just take the pills, follow the program, and don't return to old habits.

Like burning. I want to feel the damage blooming on my skin, dragging me out of my dull stupor to remind me I'm alive. Make me feel it in a way I haven't since all that happened with Dad.

It's been ten months since I burned myself. Some days are easier than others. Tonight, the more I think about all the unknowns ahead of me, the more I need the heat of release.

Don't do it.

You can't lose ten months at the first sign of anxiety.

Take your pills and follow the program.

All six bottles are tucked away in the front pocket of my backpack. I line them up on my nightstand, making a mental note to take them before bed.

But first, I need to shower.

I reach into the pouch in a hidden pocket of my backpack, grab the lighter and safety pin, stick them in my jeans pocket, then head to my bathroom.

It's nice, with a big whirlpool tub/shower combo. The lights are operated by a dimmer, and I turn them down to a soft glow. Mom has bubble baths, fancy soaps in dishes, and pretty bottles of shampoo and conditioner lined along the edge of my tub.

I make a hot bubble bath, get undressed, then grab the lighter and safety pin from my pocket. While I sit on the toilet, I stare at them, desperate for agony's release.

Unreleased anxiety is like a hammer hovering over my toes, waiting to strike them.

The pain of the flames is better than waiting.

I look at the scars on my inner right thigh (my preferred leg because it's more sensitive.) There are about forty there from the times I'd burned too long without icing the wounds quickly enough. Even after I learned about it reducing the chance of scarring, I still burned too long.

Sometimes I wanted the reminders. They're not too bad, and you can only see them when I wear underwear, a bathing suit, or shorts that are too short.

But my attention turns to the areas on my legs I've not yet scarred — clean canvases begging for paint.

I think of Mom's face the first time she saw them. She was confused. Once she realized what was happening, she turned furious. Then she sobbed and asked why I would hurt myself like that. Why I'd want to do permanent damage.

She didn't get it.

All I know is the pain brings a release when things get really bad. Maybe it's because it's the only thing I can control. Or maybe it's some other messed up reason I don't understand. Whatever the case, Mom would be irate if I did it again.

I can still remember her weeping at the foot of my bed, head in her hands.

Her anger didn't bother me much, but it was the first time she realized how badly I wanted to hurt myself, and she was devastated. And knowing I'd broken her heart gutted me. Since then, I've seen that look too many times.

I never want to see that look again.

Plus, if she saw I was self-harming again, she'd probably want to commit me. Or, at a minimum, not trust me to be on my own. That's the last thing I need.

YEAH, BUT YOU CAN BURN YOURSELF ONCE.

SHE WON'T NOTICE ONE LITTLE TIME. YOU CAN BURN YOUR ARM AND SAY YOU DID IT COOKING.

JUST THIS ONCE, TO GET YOURSELF CALM BEFORE TOMORROW, BEFORE GOING TO A NEW SCHOOL WHERE EVERYONE IS GOING TO HATE YOU. WHERE YOU WILL NEVER FIT IN.

COME ON, JUST ONCE.

The lighter and pin tremble in my hands, my compulsion growing.

Soon it's all I can think about.

I'm blinking like crazy, tears welling up in my eyes.

JUST ONCE. COME ON, CORA.

DO IT ONCE, THEN THE COMPULSION GOES AWAY.

YOU'VE DONE IT HUNDREDS OF TIMES, WHAT'S ONE MORE?

ONE LITTLE SCAR AMONG MANY.

NOBODY WILL EVEN NOTICE.

I get up, shove the lighter and pin back into my pocket, then throw my jeans across the bathroom where I can't easily reach them.

After climbing into the tub, I grab my phone then text Kris.

You around? Need to talk.

I wait for her to see the message, but she doesn't seem to be online.

It's almost nine. She has to be home. Her father doesn't let her stay out past eight on a school night.

SHE'S PROBABLY MAKING NEW FRIENDS.

YOU WERE HOLDING HER BACK, REALLY.

NOW SHE'S FREE TO HANG OUT WITH THE COOL KIDS.

I keep waiting.

AFTER MY BATH, I put the lighter and pin in a secret spot in a box under my nightstand's bottom drawer then head downstairs, desperate for anything to take my mind off of my compulsion.

Mom is pacing on the back porch, talking to Aunt Alicia on the phone. She's smoking, which she never does in front of me, so obviously she's stressed.

I check my phone again, still no word from Kris.

So I head upstairs to Dad's office, close the door behind me, then sit in his big chair behind his old oak desk. It was custom made by his father before he died. A beauty, save for a single imperfection — a white ring from a glass of iced water I drank at his desk when I was nine. Dad didn't usually yell at me. When he was mad, he got quiet. But that time, that time he yelled and asked how I could be so careless.

Bawling my eyes out, I ran to my bedroom, shut the door, then threw myself on the bed. I'm not sure what was worse, that I'd ruined his desk or that he never came to comfort me.

Now I sit at his computer, the same Mac he'd written most of his books on. The same computer housing all his unfinished work organized in a folder I haven't been able to bring myself to open.

I can't bear to see the stories he won't ever finish. The stories I killed along with him.

KILLER!

YOU GOING TO KILL MOMMA NEXT?

I blink, four times as I un-think the thought.

I'm not going to kill Momma.

I'm not going to kill Momma.

I'm not going to kill Momma.

I'm not going to kill Momma.

I turn on his computer. His wallpaper comes up. It's a photo from our last family vacation — a camping trip six years ago. I don't remember any of us enjoying the outdoors, yet seeing this photo of us makes me nostalgic for the bit of happiness we shared.

The folder of unfinished work tempts me. I consider opening one of the many documents, but I'm not sure Dad would want me to read them. He was fiercely private about his unfinished stories.

YEAH, BUT HE CAN'T FINISH THEM NOW — THANKS TO YOU.

MAY AS WELL READ THEM ALL.

My gaze trails down to the ring on his desk.

"Sorry, Dad." I trace the ring, wishing I'd never ruined his desk. Resentment rankles like a splinter because he never came to comfort me.

A loud bang nearly gives me a heart attack.

I look around for the source, thinking something big must have fallen over, or maybe the window slammed shut. But it's locked, and everything appears to be in place.

Then I see it, a book on the floor.

Dad's giant hardcover Bible, one of the biggest, heaviest ones I've ever seen. A gift from Grandpa, in hopes it'd convert him.

I don't think it worked.

"Mom?"

No answer.

I don't think she came in the room and knocked the book down. First off, she's not in the room. Second, she doesn't usually play jokes like that. Third, she's too superstitious to knock a Bible onto the ground. And lastly, she'd never disrespect Dad's stuff.

The book is in the middle of the room. Even if it somehow fell, the Bible wouldn't fall that far.

It looks like someone pushed it.

Or it jumped.

"Cora?" I hear my father's voice behind me, as sure as I'm standing here.

I turn toward the corner but don't see him anywhere in the room.

A chill runs through me, same as it does when a spirit is near.

"Dad?" I keep my voice low, partly out of fear Mom will hear me. Partly out of fear that he just might answer.

I spent most of my life seeing ghosts until the doctors found a medication that "fixed" me.

The one ghost I've *wanted* to see has yet to appear.

"Dad?"

Still no answer.

Yet I feel ice cold.

DID YOU TAKE YOUR PILLS YESTERDAY, CRAZY?

I can't remember.

Though I haven't seen him since his death, I've heard him a couple of times. Once at the funeral, and another the night I swallowed a bottle of pills hoping to follow him into the grave.

Both times he'd said only my name.

BOTH TIMES YOU IMAGINED HIM.

YOU NEED TO TAKE YOUR PILLS!

I pick up the Bible, find its spot on the shelf, then slide it back in, tapping it four times before leaving the room.

I consider going back to his desk to turn the computer off, but I don't want to go near that corner. Not if there's a spirit there. I haven't seen any since I started this new pill regimen, outside of what I saw in the mental hospital. But that doesn't mean there isn't a spirit in here.

As much as I want it to be Dad, this doesn't feel like him. It feels like a stranger, and I don't want to be anywhere near it.

I turn off the light, close the door, and ignore all the chills in my body.

THREE

The First Day Of School

OF COURSE it's raining as we pull up to Harrison High School — *Home of the Fighting Lions!* We're in a line of other cars waiting to drop off their kids. Cars pull up, kids get out, the parents leave, then the line rolls forward and the cycle begins again.

It's taking forever.

The longer we sit here, and the longer I watch the other kids get out — teenagers who have probably known each other since they were toddlers and now laugh, talk, and greet each other in front of the school — the more I feel like I don't belong.

The second I step out of this car, their eyes will be on me — The New Girl.

Watching, making judgments, deciding my social fate in milliseconds without ever getting to know me.

They'll see me and think *Freak.*

I'm blinking uncontrollably, my heart racing, and stomach in somersaults. If I don't calm down, I'll puke all over my brand-new T-shirt and jeans.

Oh, God. No.

I focus on my breath, slowing it as I close my eyes and count backward from one hundred in twos while trying to quell my panic.

Maybe I didn't take my pills last night. And now I'm going to be even more anxious! Crap!

Mom's hand touches mine. In her uniquely calming voice, she says, "It's going to be fine."

"You sure my hair doesn't look stupid?" Normally I wear it down, and it goes a few inches past my shoulders, but today I did two braids on either side with pink bows. "I don't look like a little kid?"

"You look great, honey."

We move forward another couple of spots.

"Maybe we should come back on Monday. Who even starts school on a *Friday?*"

"Come on, Cora. We agreed that delaying the first day would only make it more difficult because you'd be dreading it all weekend. It won't be any easier if I turn the car around and go home. Best to get it over with."

I know she's right. Avoiding stressors I have to face always make them worse.

We move forward again.

My stomach lurches.

"Focus on the present, Cora. Just you and me, in this car, and nothing can hurt you. This is a good school, one of the top rated in the state. I'm sure it has a few jerks, but there will be nice people, too. Teachers who care, who will be there when you need them. Everything is going to be fine. A new school and a fresh start. For all of us."

"Easy for *you* to say. *You* were pretty and popular. Everybody loved you."

Forward again. We're about ten cars back from the spot where I'll have to get out.

What had been taking forever is now going by entirely too fast.

I need more time to gather my courage.

"You are beautiful, Cora. Don't ever forget that or let anyone make you feel less than. And believe me, being popular is not all it's cracked up to be. Most people only liked me because they thought I was something I wasn't or because they were trying to fit into some group I lucked into. But only a few people really knew me. Those were my friends. Just remember not to worry about the people who might not like you. Focus on just being yourself, and you'll attract the right people into your world."

The way she spits all this at once, I feel like she might have been working on the speech all morning. On one hand, I'm touched she cares so much about me. On the other, I kind of hate being so weak I need pep talks just to do normal stuff everybody else does without a problem.

BECAUSE YOU'RE PATHETIC!

YOU'RE NOT NORMAL, CORA.

YOU'RE A FREAK!

We move forward.

Just two cars back now.

Ugh.

I look at the other kids. Just another routine day for them. *They're* not on the verge of a panic attack. *They* don't need their mom giving them a motivational speech.

They just do it.

BECAUSE THEY'RE NOT FREAKS!

I need to stop thinking. Get out of my head and out of the car.

We move forward.

I feel everyone's stares — both the kids hanging out in front of the school waiting for the first bell to ring and everyone in the cars behind us, waiting for my door to open.

Do or die time.

"Thank you." I lean over and kiss Mom on the cheek, forcing myself to act despite the fear.

She hugs me.

"I love you."

"Love you, too." I grab my backpack off the floor then climb out of the car and into the rain.

I don't dare meet anyone's gazes. Not yet. Instead, I turn back and wave at Mom as she pulls away.

Now I'm alone, standing in front of my school. I turn around, feeling everyone focus on me, but I look past them all and move forward, focusing on the school itself as the bell rings and the doors open.

I thought I would be afraid to see a school that looked like the one we just fled. That place where everyone hated me.

But this one looks different, and that's even scarier. It looks older. Despite it seeming almost quaint, with slanted roofs and smaller windows, it also somehow feels angrier.

My skin must be several shades darker.

Somehow I manage not to puke all over myself.

FIRST PERIOD IS ENGLISH, one of the few subjects I'm naturally good at. Maybe it's that I've always been a voracious reader. Maybe I inherited some talent from my father. Either way, it's a nice easy class to start the day. Last year my first period was Algebra. It was like rolling out of bed tired and having to do rocket science before being alert.

The English teacher, a pudgy balding man with big glasses named Mr. Jennings, takes my papers from the front office and tells me to grab the only open seat — right up front in the middle.

Ugh.

I hate sitting up front.

If given a choice, I always sit in the back, where I can blend in. And not feel like people are watching me.

There's the blinky girl. Wait. Watch, she'll start blinking any minute.

And they'd giggle.

Sometimes they'd even throw paper balls at me.

I avoid eye contact with anyone and take my seat.

I wish I'd left my hair long so I could hide behind it. Then only the teacher might see my blinking. I rest my head in my hands like I'm tired or something, cover as much of my face as I can, and blink four times.

As other kids file in, I pull out my spiral notebook and doodle so I don't accidentally engage anyone.

Drawing is one of the few things that calms me. When I put effort into it, I'm not half bad. It's also a good thing to do when you want to disappear in a crowded cafeteria or classroom.

But it's harder to blend in while sitting in the front row.

I can feel the other kids looking at me and hear their whispers.

Who is she?

If I just stay busy, maybe nobody will say anything to me.

I wish I wasn't so scared of meeting people. I wasn't always this way. I was once extroverted. In seventh grade, all that changed. That's when my OCD, depression, and anxiety blossomed all at once, like some horrible side effect of adolescence. I was suddenly this anxious, blinky, tic-riddled mess.

My father had suffered many of the same symptoms

for most of his life. That fact provided me a small amount of comfort. Very small, but it was something.

Doctors searched for the right cocktail of drugs to "fix me."

Three years later, I'm still broken.

The bell rings.

Mr. Jennings closes the door as a lanky boy with long brown hair — the kid I saw on the skateboard yesterday — rushes in.

He smiles.

I think he recognizes me.

Then he takes a seat in the back.

I put my notebook and doodles away, fold my hands on the desk, and pretend to pay attention as Mr. Jennings clears his throat.

"Good morning, class. We have a new student joining us."

Crap. So much for blending in.

"Her name is Cora Gray, and she comes to us from California. Won't you stand up and tell us a bit about yourself, Cora?"

Stand up?

Time has slowed to a crawl. I tug on the bottom of my shirt, self-conscious as my mouth starts before my brain has conjured words to fill it.

"Hi, my name is Cora."

"Not to me," Mr. Jennings says, making a motion to turn around. "Talk to the class."

I want to die. But I do as he asks.

No surprise, everybody is looking at me. I see them all, though I don't really see any of them.

Too much data to take in.

My mouth is speaking one set of words as my brain screams another. *Don't blink, don't blink, don't blink, don't blink!*

I'm not even sure what I just said, but now the class is staring at me and everyone is quiet.

Did I blink?

Did I say something stupid?

Oh, God.

"And what's your favorite color, Cora?" Mr. Jennings asks.

What? My favorite color? I'm not seven!

"Um, pink?"

It's a stupid answer. The thing most girls probably say. I feel like half the class is judging my choice. I should've said something different.

Don't blink, don't blink, don't blink, don't blink!

My chest is tight. My heart is racing. I might drown if I can't blink soon.

Everyone is looking at me like I'm a zoo animal brought in for show-and-tell. Maybe a sloth. Even Skater Boy is looking at me weird. A jock dude with perfectly coiffed hair smirks beside him. The girl in front of him, a pretty blonde who must be popular, leans back and whispers something.

I think she was the girl eating ice cream at Nan's.

SHE'S TALKING CRAP ABOUT YOU!

"Okay, thank you, Cora," Mr. Jennings says.

I quickly turn and take my seat, venting a breath that had been throttled too long.

Mr. Jennings starts talking about today's assignment, and I can finally lower my head into my hands.

I start blinking, praying that no one can see me, until the compulsion is relieved and the tightness in my chest finally eases enough to return my heartbeat to normal.

And once I'm back to normal, the shame returns.

I'm such a freak.

FOUR

The Invitation

I'M SITTING ALONE in the cafeteria eating pizza and drinking a Coke, even though Mom told me not to waste my lunch money on junk. She says I shouldn't think about my weight and that I don't eat enough, but she still gives me grief when I eat unhealthy food.

She's never said as much, I know she judged me when I was heavier. Wished I wasn't chubby. Wasn't happy about it when I starved myself, either.

I have my notebook out and I'm doodling more than eating, because I'm a nervous wreck and my appetite's gone.

Between doodles, I spy on the other kids, trying to figure out who is whom, what groups run the school, and, of course, where I fit in.

I never had a group of my own, even when I had friends. I was kind of with the Artsy Kids, sorta with the Emo Kids, and a bit with the Drama Kids. I got along with them all well enough but I never truly felt like I belonged in any particular group. They tolerated me. Until seventh grade, when they decided to hate me along with everyone else.

This is my chance to start over. I'd love a group to call my own — people who got me and who I understood. Friends I could create art with or just hang out and have fun with.

From what I've seen so far, Harrison High School seems like it's run mostly by the jocks. Hell, *The Fighting Lions* is plastered on the town's welcome sign. High school football is huge here. They walk around tall, proud, and loud, making stupid jokes, eyeing girls like meat, and being giant douchebags.

They run the place. Everyone else gets to exist on the fringes. But that's okay, there's plenty of room for others to thrive in their athletic shadows.

Tables in the cafeteria seem split along group lines. From first impressions, the school is made up of at least ten groups.

The Jocks are first-tier, of course.

Then the Basics.

The Drama Kids.

The Artists.

The Exchange Students.

The Skaters.

The Emos, Goths, and Scene Kids.

The Nerds.

The Gamers.

The Furries and Weeaboos.

And last, the Awkwards.

I'd love to introduce myself to the Artists, to hang out with them and talk to them, but I've never felt good enough. They're always so much more talented than I am, so I always feel like a fraud. When artist-types compliment me, I'm always sure it's driven by pity.

Fashion is a little different here, too, and I'm sticking out. Most of the girls are wearing light jeans. Mine are dark blue. My shirt says *Doctor Who* and has a picture of the TARDIS. And nobody is wearing graphic tees except for a few Awkwards, Skaters, and Gamers.

I wonder if today's outfit will consign me for the rest of my high school career to a group where I don't belong. A part of me hates that I'm worried about insignificant things like this. I should be strong and independent, not fretting over what other people think.

Easier said than done.

I think about what my Mom said about being myself. Of course it's easy to be yourself when you're beautiful and everyone likes you. Not so much for freaky me.

The sound of people talking, laughing, and having fun makes me feel especially alone.

I keep doodling as kids continue taking seats at pretty much every table but mine. Like there's this giant sign on my table that says, "Don't sit with the New Kid."

Just keep doodling and don't think about it.

Again, easier said than done.

A group of girls gets up from the Jocks' table to take their trays to the trash cans. They'll have to pass by me, so I keep my head down and focus on the intricate line work on my ink drawing — a girl with long curly hair extending to a tree behind her and becoming one with the trunk.

I try to act like I don't even see them, though I can see them in my peripheral vision as they approach.

Suddenly they stop, right in front of me.

Maybe they'll go away?

I can feel them looking down at me, maybe judging my drawing.

YOUR DRAWING SUCKS!

YOU ALWAYS DRAW THE SAME CRAP OVER AND OVER!

THEY'LL KNOW YOU'RE NOT A REAL ARTIST.

I have to look up, or it'll be obvious that I'm ignoring them.

There are three, a beautiful blonde with green eyes and perfectly on-point makeup wearing ripped light blue jeans and a deep red long-sleeved shirt. She is the one from my first period class who was whispering something to the jock. She's flanked on either side by twin brown-haired girls, one with a pink stripe in her hair and the other with a bright blue stripe. Both are dressed in light jeans and hoodies that match their dyed streaks.

They're all staring at me like I'm some new creature they've discovered.

The blonde cocks her head sideways, "Wow, that's good."

"Thanks." My cheeks flame.

"First day here?"

"Yeah."

"Where you from?"

"California." I don't mention the town. It's not like I lived in San Francisco or Berkeley. Silicon Valley, Hollywood, or San Diego. Just boring Las Orillas.

"Cool," she says. "My name is Kaycee. This is Amber and Alice."

Amber with the pink stripe, Alice with the blue.

"Hi," I say. I'm not sure if I'm supposed to offer my hand to shake or what. I feel like a kindergartener on her first day with no clue how to make friends.

I can hardly look at them, they're so pretty, but I do my best not to flinch away like an Awkward.

YOU ARE SUCH AN AWKWARD!

GOD, YOU SUCK SO MUCH, CORA!

"I *love* your hair," Kaycee says, reaching out and touching one of my braids. "It's so cute."

So cute drips with insincerity.

Touching my hair is a *huuuuuge* pet peeve, especially with white girls who think they're giving me a compliment by remarking on my "exotic" looks.

Maybe she doesn't know better. Not like there's many brown people here. Maybe she's genuinely admiring me or trying to be nice. Try to judge her by her intention, not my perception.

"Thank you." I smile to hide my discomfort.

"Why are you sitting by yourself?" Alice asks.

I start blinking.

Damn.

FREAK!

I squeeze my eyes tight, hiding them behind my hand like I have a headache, hoping they didn't notice.

When I pull my hand away, I open my eyes wide, maybe too wide, and look at my drawing. "I don't really know anyone yet. But that's okay. It gives me time to draw."

I can't decipher Kaycee's smile. She's either super friendly or totally fake.

But the most popular and pretty girls are never very friendly unless you're in their clique. And they can always tell whether you belong within milliseconds of seeing you. Even when you fit in, they can be vicious.

But maybe that's not a universal truth. My mom is pretty and she's the sweetest person I know. I shouldn't assume the worst. After all, it's my first day and I don't know anyone. The social cues might be different in a small town like this.

"Cool T-shirt," Kaycee says. "So, um, you into *Doctor Who?*"

"It's okay," I say, though I freaking love it. Dad turned

me onto it and we marathoned every episode from the Tom Baker days through the most recent seasons. But I'm pretty sure saying I like *Doctor Who* would make someone like Kaycee think I'm a huge nerd. And while there's a contingent of cool nerdy kids in California, that doesn't seem to be the case here. Here, nerds are ostracized to one or two tables filled with sad looking kids. "Do you watch it?"

Kaycee give me a little half-laugh which the twins practically echo, then she's looking around the cafeteria as if her interest is already waning.

Her eyes widen as she turns to the girls. "Hey, we should totally invite New Girl to hang out at the mall with us tomorrow, you think?"

"Totally," Amber says, looking at me. "You wanna meet us at the mall?"

Kaycee says, "It's probably not as awesome as the malls in Cali, but it's a'ight."

"Sure." I try not to appear *too* enthusiastic. "I didn't see a mall when we were coming in. Glad to know there *is* one."

"What's your LiveLyfe?" Kaycee asks as she pulls out her phone and starts swiping the glass.

I give her my username.

Seconds later the phone buzz in my pocket. I pull it and accept her request.

"Cool, I'll send you the deets later."

"Cool."

"Nice meeting you, New Girl," she says before leaving. As the twins follow, Alice looks at my drawing. "You're really good."

"Thanks." A stupid smile spreads across my big, dumb face, way too happy that someone cool complimented my drawing.

She holds my gaze for a moment, and I know her compliment is genuine.

Maybe she's an artist, too.

Alice looks at me for a second or two longer than feels comfortable before quickly looking away like she's done something wrong.

Then she leaves in a hurry as I watch, confused.

Well, that *happened.*

FIVE

Saturday At The Mall

I'M in the food court sitting at a table in front of Pretzel Palace where Kaycee told me to meet her.

It's been twenty minutes and my Coke is ice and water. Still, I sip it for something to do. The place is crowded, and people are watching me.

I'm wearing my favorite dress, a pink one I got for a dance I never got asked to go to. This is the first time I've worn it, and now I feel inverse to how I felt yesterday at school — way overdressed. Like I'm trying too hard.

All I want is to go home and change into something less obvious. Scratch that. All I want is to go home. Period.

I look at my phone to check the time. Consider calling Mom to have her come get me.

The girls were supposed to be here at noon.

Maybe there's another Pretzel Palace and I'm sitting in front of the wrong one. But, of course, I know there isn't.

THEY STOOD YOU UP, DUMMY.

It's hard to ignore the ever-present voice. As hard as not giving in to my compulsion to blink.

I approach the old man working the counter. "Is there another food court in the mall?"

"No, ma'am." He looks at me odd, probably because now I'm blinking too much. "You waiting for someone?"

"Yeah, some friends told me to meet them here. I might have gotten the time wrong. Thanks."

I head back to my table before he can ask what's wrong with me. Sitting, I idly tap apps on my phone. Having something to do makes me look less like I'm being stood up. Unfortunately, I didn't bring my art pad.

Blink, blink, blink, blink.

I want to scream — as if that would silence my need.

I scroll through Kaycee's photos on LiveLyfe. She has tons of them — her pretty friends, her good-looking family, and all the picturesque places she's been. Not to mention the hundreds of shots showing off her attractive food and fancy coffee drinks. Is it possible to both hate someone and want to be like them?

God, I'm such a hypocritical mess.

She seems like the kind of basic girl me and Kris would've laughed at, but only because those girls were narcissistic bitches who laughed at us.

I take a screenshot of some of Kaycee's photos and send it to Kris.

My new BFF, I type, joking.

A few minutes pass before she writes back: *Wow. Really?*

Nope, you're still my bestie.

Good. She looks like a total Barbie. WYD?

At the mall. Meeting Barbie and her Barbie friends.

For real?

Yeah, they asked me to hang with them.

I watch the dots as she's typing. But then they vanish.

They reappear and I wonder if she's typing something

super long, or typed something before deleting it. And if so, what had she typed?

I can almost feel Kris's disappointment swelling. She's all about being "real" and would probably think less of me if I hung out with this crowd. But I like the idea of hanging with the cool girls. Or at least not feeling like an outcast. Having friends again.

More dots before they vanish and reappear.

Then she finally sends it. *K. Have fun with Barbie.*

Is she mad at me? Or did she genuinely have to go? I stare at her response, examining it for clues to her intent. She usually says something sweet when we sign off.

Love ya!

See ya, Apple!

Or something.

This feels like she's left in a huff. Like she's mad at me for hanging out with someone she doesn't even know. What right does she have to judge Kaycee based on her photos?

Maybe Kris is jealous. Or mad that I moved and was hoping I wouldn't replace her — not that I could. She's the only one who really knows what I went through. Or most of it.

No one knows my deepest secret.

SHE PROBABLY THINKS YOU'RE A BIG FAT HYPOCRITE.

YOU MAKE FUN OF THE COOL KIDS BUT THEN YOU JOIN THEM THE FIRST CHANCE YOU GET.

But I invited it, sending her the photos knowing she'd laugh.

HYPOCRITE!

But I didn't send the photos to make fun of Kaycee. Did I?

And if so, why? Was I feeling so insulted at being stood up that I had to take a shot at her?

Great, now I'm mad at my bestie and feeling guilty for being a judgmental jerk.

Kaycee and the twins enter the food court holding heavy-looking bags from Forever 21.

There they are!

The sense of dread is fading, replaced by a bud of joy. I hate the volatility of my emotions and how much others can control them. How stupid I felt for thinking they might have stood me up. This isn't the past. Mom was right. This is a fresh start. My old life will only haunt me if I let it.

I sit up straight, look down at my phone to get off of Kaycee's page so she doesn't think I'm some kind of stalker, and wonder if I should stand or sit as they head towards my table.

Don't be too eager. Play it cool, like you always hang out with cool girls.

I stay in my seat.

They're about twenty feet away, laughing and talking about something. I wonder if they've even seen me.

They finally look my way.

Then continue right by, never breaking from their conversation.

What the—?

Are they headed to one of the restaurants to grab something before they sit with me?

The answer is a slap in the face. They keep walking, right out of the food court.

Oh, God.

They never had any plans to meet me.

They did this just to blow me off!

My heart is racing and my breath short as my mind vacillates between anger and confusion. Anger, because why would you do this to someone you don't even know? Confusion, because … maybe they didn't see me?

NO, STUPID, THEY SAW YOU.
THEY DID THIS ON PURPOSE.
A CRUEL JOKE.
YOU ARE ONLY A JOKE TO THEM!
They were talking to each other, though. Maybe they were so lost in their conversation that—
NO.
THEY DON'T JUST HAPPEN TO WALK THROUGH THE FOOD COURT, THE VERY PLACE THEY TOLD YOU TO MEET THEM, AND THEN JUST KEEP ON WALKING.
THEY BURNED YOU.
BAD.

I feel so freaking stupid.

Hot tears well in the corners of my eyes.

And I'm about to become a blinking, crying mess.

I get up and practically run to the bathroom.

It's empty, thank God. I duck into a stall, close the door, lock it. Then I stand there, burying my face, letting the tears flow into my palms, feeling like this is all just some cruel repeat of life in Los Orillas.

I hear voices.

The bathroom door opens.

Girls talking. Laughing.

No, not just any girls.

It's *them.*

Without even thinking, I climb onto the toilet seat, hiding.

What am I doing?

"OMG, did you *see* her face?" Kaycee asks. "Priceless. Just staring like we took her ice cream or something."

One of the twins laughs. "At least she stopped blinking for a second."

More laughter. Then, "Seriously, what's her problem? Who blinks like that?"

"Hey, don't judge her. She can't help it. She clearly has mental issues. Look at that dress."

"Don't forget her stupid pigtails," Kaycee says. "Seriously, what's her deal?"

More laughter.

And the sound — people I don't even know laughing viciously — is like strangers assembling to stab me.

Same hell, new coat of paint.

Kaycee asks, "I'm not sure what's worse, the dress that looks like a prom gown or the Doctor Who T-shirt."

"For sure," one of the twins says. "Maybe she *likes* being a virgin."

"As if anyone would want to get with that blinky, twitchy nerd!" Kaycee says.

More laughter.

I can change my location and the people around me. But I can't change the one constant — *me*.

Why are they being like this? They don't even know me. I didn't do anything to them. Why?

BECAUSE YOU'RE A FREAK, YA' FREAK!

GIRLS LIKE THEM ARE NEVER FRIENDS WITH PEOPLE LIKE YOU.

I wonder if they'd seen me blinking in the halls earlier that day before approaching me at lunch. Maybe Kaycee saw me blinking in class and decided to hate me on the spot.

It doesn't matter how or why they chose me, the results are the same. I'm crying and hiding in a bathroom stall while they laugh at me.

Nothing ever changes.

SIX

Pretending Nothing Happened

AN HOUR after the bathroom incident, I'm sitting outside the mall waiting for Mom to pick me up. I waited that long before calling for a ride so my eyes wouldn't be puffy.

I can't tell her about this. She'll pity me. She'll want to get involved, call the girls' mothers or something that would only make everything worse. Mom loves me, but sometimes her love can be suffocating.

She pulls up, smiling as I get in the car.

"So, how'd it go?"

"Good." I open the bags and show her the clothes I got with the money she'd given me — a pink hoodie with a unicorn, a blue shirt, and some light jeans.

"Those are nice. Did you have any money left over?"

"Ten bucks or so."

"Keep it for next time. So, tell me about your new friends."

We pull out of the parking lot, and I can barely look at her. It hurts to see that smile and the light in her eyes as she hopes things will be different this time. Hurts more that I'm lying to her face.

"It was okay."

"Just okay?" A note of concern creeps into her voice.

"I dunno. Super gossipy, talking crap about other kids. A lot."

"Ah. Were they mean to you?"

"No."

I wonder if she can see through my lie. Or if she thinks I'm too picky. Mom's never come right out and said it, but reading between the lines, I'm certain she thinks the reason I don't make friends is because I'm too negative, too stuck in my depression. Too closed off to give people a chance and let them in.

She's never understood how hard it is for me. Never realized its other people who don't give *me* a chance. She's never had a problem making friends or managing difficult people.

"I mean, they're okay, I guess. But they're not Kris."

"I'm sure you'll make another BFF soon. The kids here are nice, I hear."

"Yeah."

"And the important thing is that you went out. Didn't stay all cooped in your room."

"Yeah." But I wish I'd done exactly that. At least nobody can ridicule me in my room. And I can get lost in my books, TV shows, and art.

Mom turns up the radio and starts to sing.

I sink into my seat and stare out my window as we pass the school, wondering what will happen on Monday when I see Kaycee and the twins.

How many people had they told about what they did to me?

I don't think I can take this again.

MOM HAS BEEN CALLED in to work a night shift at the hospital. That's fine for me. I'm tired of pretending that earlier stuff didn't happen.

With Mom not around, there's nothing to stop me from burning.

The lighter and safety pin are begging me to draw them out of their hiding spot.

I've resisted — so far.

I spend most of the night in my room waiting to hear from Kris, but she hasn't seen any of my messages. I wonder what she's doing and wish I could be with her.

Kris is the kind of person you can chill with in your bedroom, talking for hours without getting bored. It's not often I find someone I'm comfortable enough with that we can sit in silence for long stretches, yet feel completely at ease in one another's presence.

I miss that.

I need that.

So tonight, I'm extra sad I moved here and left my only friend behind. Sure, we promised to chat on video, but how long before she finds someone else to occupy her time?

How long before she forgets about me or we have nothing in common anymore?

What if I never find another Kris?

Being an outcast sucks, but having at least one close friend makes all the difference in the world. And as bad as things got back home — and they got about as bad as things *can* get — at least I had Kris's shoulder to cry on.

Now I've got unread messages staring back at me.

I go to Kaycee's LiveLyfe page to see if she posted anything making fun of me. *Hey, look what we did to the new girl today.* Maybe took a photo or video and posted it.

But I don't see anything.

I can't remember if any of them had their phones out.

I remember their horrible words in the bathroom and wonder what Mom would say to make this better. She seems to think you can get along with anyone if you can just figure them out or find some way to make them like you.

Maybe that works for people like her.

But people like me are hated, no matter what we do.

MAYBE YOUR MOM IS RIGHT.

MAYBE THESE GIRLS PICKED UP ON YOUR NEGA-TIVITY, HOW YOU WALK AROUND WITH SLUMPED SHOULDERS, FACE BURIED IN YOUR SKETCHBOOK LIKE SOME KINDA VICTIM!

WHAT DO YOU EXPECT TO HAPPEN?

ACT LIKE A VICTIM, YOU'LL BE A VICTIM.

EXPECT THE WORST, GET THE WORST!

That's not true. I was looking forward to being friends with them. I wasn't expecting the worst. I wasn't acting like a victim!

NOT EXPECTING THE WORST, EH?

WHY WERE YOU CALLING THEM BARBIES, THEN?

I was kidding!

MAYBE THEY PICKED UP ON YOUR NEGATIVE ENERGY.

No, they planned to do this from the moment they met me! It had nothing to do with my energy. I was sitting in the back of the cafeteria minding my own business.

MAYBE THERE'S STILL A WAY TO FIX THIS.

SHOW MOM THAT YOU'RE NOT A VICTIM.

SHOW HER YOU TURNED POTENTIAL ENEMIES INTO FRIENDS.

Do what, ask them to meet again so they can sell me out?

NO, NOTHING THAT STUPID.

BUT PLAY IT COOL, ACT LIKE YOU WEREN'T BOTHERED.

SHOW THEM YOU'RE NOT A WHINY LITTLE BITCH AND LEAVE AN OPEN DOOR.

It feels stupid. Counterintuitive. After all, they targeted me. I did nothing to deserve this hate.

STOP DWELLING.

MOM WOULDN'T DWELL.

SHE'D FIND A WAY TO TURN THIS AROUND.

I bring up Kaycee's name on my phone and click to message her. I figure I'll play dumb like I didn't see them, maybe give her a chance to reconsider her hatred.

I type, *Hey, I must've missed you at the mall. Hope to hang out some other time. Just hit me up.*

It feels weak. And stupid. Like I'm giving Kaycee more ammo against me, something she and the twins can laugh about. *Oh, this poor girl thinks we actually wanted to hang out with her. Wow, buy a clue, dumbass!*

I click SEND.

And instantly regret it.

I go downstairs to get a Coke. Except this time, she bought diet soda.

Okay, Mom. Gotchya. Gotta watch the sugar.

I stop in front of Dad's office on the way back to my room, then step inside.

It feels weird calling it *his* office since he's never even been in this house, but it is his office recreated here. And while it's not the same as back home, there's something about being in here that makes me feel comfortable, last night's weird spirit-thing aside.

I grab his jacket from the door hook and wrap it around me. I close my eyes, inhaling his scent and the bittersweet nostalgia.

I eye the corner where I sensed something watching me, but I'm alone now. Maybe I was last night. Hard to separate reality from my imagination or some possible side effect of the pills.

Sitting in Dad's chair, I pull my knees up to my chin and set the Diet Coke down — on a coaster — on top of the ring.

I open up his laptop and look through photos of us. Most are of me and Mom, taken by him. Or ones Mom took and sent to him. Not a ton of us together because we rarely did things as a family. Dad's work kept him busy. That and his anxiety kept him indoors.

But there are a few with the three of us. Tall and handsome with curly hair, dark brown skin in contrast with bright blue eyes. In some photos he's smiling, but even in those something seems off. Like he's sad perhaps, a far-off expression that always made him look so much like the writer he was.

So many times I wondered what was going on in his head. Was he thinking about his stories or being haunted by the demons of his anxiety and depression? I wonder if he ever truly felt happy, or was that a mask he made only for us?

I trace my fingertip over his face and across the lines around his eyes, all the while wishing I could go back in time to ask him. Or to warn him about what was going to happen. Stop him from dying that night.

The worst part about losing someone you love isn't them being gone. You never get completely used to it, but your mind finds a way to adjust to the New Normal. No, the worst part is when you momentarily forget they're dead. Waking up from a dream or lost in thought, back in a moment of How Things Used to Be, where they were still alive.

Then the moment snaps, reality crashes, and it's like losing them all over again.

I check my phone, then check Kris's LiveLyfe page to see if she's posted any updates. Can't help but wonder if she's ghosting me. Maybe she's mad I was hanging out with a Barbie — not that it even happened.

She was never the jealous type, but there's a bit of history with the Barbies, particularly a girl named Devon — my best friend before Kris. Devon turned on me, then recruited half the school to do the same. Kris was the only person who came to my defense. Protected me against all of Devon's friends, and pretty much any Barbie who dared to mess with me since.

I'm sure there's a part of her that thinks I'm being naive or stupid to meet these new Barbies at the mall. Maybe she's giving me the cold shoulder to show me how stupid I'm being? Maybe I should confess, tell Kris what really happened, and let her know she was right.

I put my phone down and look at Dad's folder of unfinished stories, mouse pointer hovering over it as I think about opening it.

YOU WANNA READ HIS STORIES NOW, BUT COULDN'T BE BOTHERED TO READ HIS BOOKS WHEN HE WAS ALIVE?

Dad had hit the best sellers' list with a young adult post-apocalyptic trilogy seven years ago called *The Lost Ones*, but then depression got the better of him, making it hard to consistently write. The more he struggled, the worse it got, and the more difficult he found his job. The cycle ruined him. He'd only published three books since the original trilogy.

I used to be jealous of the books that occupied so much of his time. I didn't even crack them open until a month after he died.

He'd dedicated all of his books to Mom and me.

I immediately felt horrible. What kind of daughter

didn't bother to read her father's work? Certainly one undeserving of a single dedication, let alone multiple ones.

I felt even worse after I read his novels. He wasn't just my father, he was an incredible talent who'd created people and worlds that were now gone forever, that his readers, of which I was now one, could never return to.

It's hard not to wonder what he would've done had he lived.

HAD YOU NOT KILLED HIM!

I click open the folder.

Forty documents, each with a unique title. I haven't opened any of them, so I have no idea how much is here. Could be drafts or outlines or just brainstorming ideas. So far, I see only stolen potential, stories that will never be realized, and it's all my fault.

I'm startled by a loud SLAM!

Another book is on the ground. Not the Bible this time.

A hardcover edition of the first book in *The Lost Ones* trilogy.

Did Mom come home early and is just messing with me?

Except she isn't due home until around two.

MAYBE SOMEONE ELSE SNUCK IN.

OR MAYBE IT'S THE GHOST!

Dad's office door is open. I'm pretty sure I closed it.

The hallway outside is ominously dark, and I feel suddenly exposed.

I slowly reach for the desk drawer, pull it open, find the heavy metal scissors with the big black handles that Dad always kept there.

I grab them, hold them tight.

As I approach the doorway, my heart races.

A cold chill runs down my spine — the same sensation I used to get when I sensed a ghost.

Hair stands on ends on my arm.

I'm blinking, hard.

A sound splinters the silence — the floor creaking just outside the room.

Ghosts don't make any noise when they walk.

Someone is in the hall.

SEVEN

Discovery

"Mom?"

I cautiously approach the open door, bracing for someone rush at me.

Could I stab them if they did? I'm not wondering if they'll overpower me before I can hurt them so much as if I can actually shove a blade into someone's gut or heart.

What if it *is* Mom messing with me?

What if I accidentally stab her?

Should I go back to the desk to call 9-1-1?

Another creak of the floorboards.

If someone *is* out there, I don't have time for a phone call. They'll be on me before I can get the words out of my mouth.

Dread builds as I creep towards the door. I brace for anything.

Heart racing, eyes blinking.

YOU'RE GONNA DIE!

I'm not going to die!

I'm not going to die!

I'm not going to die!

I'm not going to die!

The hall's darkness seems to grow denser, and the temperature feels like it's dropped twenty degrees.

If I wasn't holding my breath, I'd probably see misty condensation.

Then nothing but silence as I stand on the other side of the door.

NOBODY'S IN HERE OR THEY'D ALREADY BE RUSHING YOU!

STOP BEING SUCH A WIMP!

I yell, rushing into the hall, scissors in a death grip, praying Mom doesn't impale herself on them.

But there's nobody here.

And there's no way somebody left the hallway this quickly without making more than a pair of creaks on the floor.

I flick the switch, bathing the hall in light. No sign of intruders or even Mom looking to scare me — something she's not prone to doing.

"Hello? I'm calling the police."

No response.

I finally exhale, and there *is* mist.

Another sound, this time scratching. It's coming from somewhere down the hall. Faint but constant.

The house is old. Maybe it has rats. I'm not scared of rats, but I certainly don't want to get bitten by one. Or risk getting rabies.

OR, WITH YOUR LUCK, YOU'D CATCH THE BLACK PLAGUE!

There are three other rooms on the second floor — mine, Mom's bedroom and bathroom, and my bathroom.

I follow the scratching to my room.

When I open the door and flick on the light, the scratching stops.

I don't feel a ghost in here. And the temperature is back to normal.

It's got to be a rat.

There aren't too many places for a rat to hide, basically under my bed, behind my dresser, or in the closet.

After slipping the scissors into my back pocket, I grab the wastebasket next to my bed then pull out the empty bag. Clutching the basket, I raise it high, ready to slam it down on whatever might be in here.

I kick at my bed and yell.

Nothing comes scurrying out.

Silence.

And then scratching, coming from my left. The closet.

I carefully grip the basket with one hand, open the closet with the other, and wait for something to come running out.

Nothing does.

The scratching stops.

There are still a dozen or so unpacked boxes sitting in the closet, awaiting my attention. Is the rat behind one of them, or maybe inside?

I *really* don't like the idea of a rat eating my possessions or pooping all over them. But I also don't feel like going through all my things right now.

I grab the top box and shake it.

Nothing moves.

As I'm about to grab a second box, the scratching resumes. Not in a box, but above me.

When I flick on the closet light, I notice an attic door. Whatever is scratching is doing it faster, as if desperate for escape.

My mind conjures an image of a trapped cat, too weak or thirsty to meow, clawing for someone to find it.

I look around my room for something to open the

hatch without lifting it myself and having something jump on my head. If that happens, I *will* flip the heck out, maybe fall and impale myself with the scissors. I'm *just* klutzy enough to manage that.

Thank God I didn't get rid of my hockey stick when we moved. I only played a total of three games when I was thirteen, but for some reason, I kept it. And it was more useful to me now than on the ice. I use it to pop the door out of its housing, knocking it up and into the darkness as I sidestep away so nothing can scare me.

Nothing does.

Nor is anything scratching.

"Oh, you get shy now?"

I'm determined to see what's making the noise, more determined to get it out of my attic. There's no way I can go to bed knowing there's something furry scurrying around my room. And if it *is* a cat, I want to save it.

Mom won't let us have a cat because she's allergic, but I'm sure she'd let me nurse one to health. And then maybe I could keep it in my room.

I take my vanity chair to the closet, then grab a flashlight from my nightstand drawer. It's big and heavy and belonged to my father. Sometimes I keep it under my pillow in case someone creeps into my room in the middle of the night.

It could crush someone's skull if I swung it hard enough.

I'm about to stand on the chair when I remember to take the scissors out of my pocket and put them on the nightstand. Don't want any accidents. Then I climb up, heart racing as I anticipate something jumping into my hair or down my shirt.

I make a lot of noise with the flashlight, hoping to

scare whatever it is farther from the hatch. Then I peer inside the darkness.

Nothing in the immediate area.

The light flickers as I pan the crawlspace past wooden beams and insulation, scanning for beady or feline eyes shining back at me.

I see any number of dark areas where a small animal could easily be hiding. I wish I'd not made all that noise to drive it away from the hatch.

"Here, little fella, I won't hurt you," I say, sending a *tst tst* through my lips.

Silence.

And there's no way I'm crawling into the attic to further search. It's too creepy and God only knows how old the insulation is. Or if it's filled with asbestos.

I'm about to grab the door to pull it closed when my hand touches something cold.

Yelping, I snatch it back from the space.

But my sleeve has caught onto something.

I'm freaking out, patting at my shirt, thinking for sure that a rat has crawled up my sleeve and is about to scurry up my arm and start biting my armpits or worse.

I jump off the chair, yanking at my shirt to tear it off, before I see the thing I'd touched fall to the floor with a dull metallic thunk,

A necklace.

I bend over, pick it up. It's gold with a pearl brooch, a black and white painting of a young blonde-haired girl's face and what looks like a coil of white thread beneath an aged but otherwise clear crystal, or maybe glass. The crystal is encircled by engraved lilies of the valley intricately carved into the pearl face.

It feels old and mysterious, and I wonder how long it's been in the attic. The house isn't ancient or anything, but this painting looks like something from the early 1900s. I bring the brooch closer and study it.

The girl is so realistic, I think maybe it's not a painting but an early photograph.

She's wearing a white dress, looks to be around six or seven. And something about her feels weirdly familiar, though that's impossible since I've never seen this necklace or the girl.

I stare at the picture, wondering who she is, then turn it over and see a name engraved on the back.

DEAREST ADA.
October 9, 1812

ADA.

Then I realize that the white thread is probably a lock of her hair. The entire piece feels both tragic and beautiful.

I want to research the necklace and brooch, and whomever this Ada person was, but I'm not even sure where to start.

I put the hatch door back in place, not even caring about the rat that might be up there any longer, then head to my father's office to start researching the necklace.

Sitting at his desk, I see my phone has messages. Kris finally got back to me.

Call me when you have a minute. Got soooooo much to tell you.

I'm glad to know she's not ignoring me. I set the necklace down and open FaceTime on Dad's computer.

"Oh, my God!" I blurt.

She's finally done it — gone from jet black to purple.

"Your dad let you do it?"

"I kinda didn't tell him until after it was done."

"Oh, wow. Did he kill you?"

"Yes, and you're now speaking to my ghost. Boo!"

I laugh and we slip into conversation just like we've always done. Despite the miles and how afraid I was that things had changed, it all feels like the warmest sort of echo.

But then Kris gets to the thing she wanted to talk about, and it isn't her hair.

She's back together with her ex, Tyler the Terrible.

"What? I haven't even been gone two days. Why?"

"He's changed."

I roll my eyes. "No. He hasn't. He will never change. He'll always be a drug addict jerk."

Kris is quiet, her lips pursed.

I'm blinking.

"You know I'm right, Kris."

"You always talk about other people not giving you a chance, but you're just as bad."

"What? Sorry, I tend not to give abusive assholes a second chance."

"He's *not* abusive."

"But you're not gonna argue the asshole part?" I tease, trying to lighten the mood.

But Kris is still staring at me, without a hint of a smile.

I can't believe she's letting this jerk walk all over her. Taking him back after he cheated on her — with her friend Kelly.

Former friend Kelly.

"He hit you."

"One time. He was drunk. And it was barely a tap."

I'm blinking, frustrated, unable to do anything but wonder who I'm talking to.

"You weren't even there," she adds.

"If I was, I would've kicked his ass. Hell, if *I* was dating him and he did that to me, *you* would've kicked his ass. No way you'd let me get back with him."

Kris is quiet.

I hate how she's making me feel like I'm overstepping my boundaries. There have never been barriers between us, not when it came to boys. It was us against the jerks of the world. And we always spoke our mind.

We didn't let the jerks get the better of us. Well, not a second time, anyway.

She's still quiet.

I don't know what to say and I hate the gulf between us — physical and emotional.

I feel like she wants to disconnect. Doesn't want to talk to me if I'm only going to make her feel bad about the big stupid mistake she's so obviously making.

"What do you want me to say, Cora?"

"That you're joking. That you've come to your senses and you refuse to ever see him again. That would be a good start."

"You don't understand. He's going through a lot."

"Ugh! I *do* understand, more than anyone. Who was there for you when he cheated on you? When he hit you? When he treated you like crap?"

"He apologized. And … he's trying."

"Yeah? Like your dad tries?"

She stares at me.

Her eyes well up. She *hates* crying in front anyone, even me. "I've gotta go."

She hangs up before I can stop her. Or apologize for being too blunt.

Then she signs off. Or hides her status.

I want to punch something.

Instead, I bury a scream into Dad's jacket.

Why did I push her so hard? Tyler has always been her

sticky spot, the one area where she throws logic out the window and becomes a slave to her worst intentions. I should've known I could never compete against him. Not in any straightforward way. Especially long distance.

Damn it.

Now I'm crying.

GREAT!

YOU PUSHED AWAY YOUR ONLY FRIEND!

BRAVO, CORA!

YOU DID IT AGAIN.

I stare at the screen wishing I could rewind the clock, unsay the words I used to push Kris away.

My heart is racing.

My chest is tightening.

The walls are closing in on me.

I scream again, this time not burying it.

But the scream isn't enough.

YOU KNOW WHAT TO DO!

I go to my nightstand, pull out the bottom drawer, grab the box.

Head downstairs for a glass of ice.

Return to my bedroom, lock the door, take off my pants.

I get the safety pin and lighter, then I thumb the metal wheel until I'm met with that familiar flame.

I shouldn't do this.

Mom will be so disappointed.

MOM ISN'T HERE.

MOM WON'T SEE ONE LITTLE BURN.

YOU NEED THE RELEASE!

I hold the pin in the flame until it hurts.

Then I find a spot high on my inner thigh. A place Mom won't see.

I press and hold until I'm lost in the pain.

EIGHT

The Girl In The Woods

THERE ARE USUALLY two times I look forward to in any given week. Friday night, because it's the end of a long school week and I get to stay up late without any real bedtime. And Sunday morning, or, more specifically, noonish, when I typically wake up, staying in my warm bed even after I open my eyes, bundled under my warm faux down comforter for as long as I want, checking social media, watching videos, or anything other than getting out of bed. It's my cozy happy time.

But today I'm not feeling cozy or happy. I'm hating myself for succumbing to the pin.

I sit up and look at the burn. A bit darker than I thought. Guess I left the pin on too long or didn't ice it enough.

I run my fingers over the mottled flesh, glad that Mom won't see it.

My pills are still lined up on my nightstand. I get a sinking feeling as I try to remember if I took them last night or not.

I really should write these things down, but when I

used to keep track, I always wrote that I took them even when I didn't, just so Mom couldn't use that against me. Which really isn't helping me now! I should develop a system so I can tell when I really took them or not.

If I didn't take them, it might be two nights in a row I missed them. But if I did take them, I don't want to double up. I'll be a freaking zombie.

I don't feel like I usually do when off of my meds, which can range from extremely depressed to horribly manic. I feel sad because of how things went with Kris, but not worse than the usual sorrow.

I'll take them tonight.

I should be fine.

I check for messages from Kris but find nothing. She's still showing as offline. Her status doesn't even say when she was on last, which means that she's gone invisible. She's never done that before. So now she's avoiding me.

Why did I push?

BECAUSE YOU RUIN EVERYTHING AND EVERYONE IN YOUR LIFE!

I hate that we're not talking. Not just because she's my only real friend, but also because I can picture her bitching about me to Tyler and him comforting her, telling her I'm toxic and she's better off cutting me out of her life.

With me out of the way, he'll be able to totally manipulate her as he pleases. At least until he breaks her heart again.

Maybe he'll knock her up and leave. Or even worse, marry her then keep her prisoner in some trailer park and force her to keep spitting out loser kids from his demon seed while he does drugs and wastes whatever money she makes from her three jobs.

I hate him so much.

I click on Tyler's LiveLyfe page. We're not friends, but

his account is public. His status reads, *In a relationship with Kristine Patterson.*

Barf.

I put down my phone and look at the necklace, still hanging from the lamp on my nightstand where I left it last night. Inside the brooch with that lock of hair, the portrait of Ada stares back. Thanks to everything that happened with Kris last night, I forgot to research the necklace. Maybe I'll start after I shower.

There's a stillness in the house It's a feeling I've come to know more since Dad died and Mom works more hours.

Downstairs, I find a note from Mom telling me she had to work at noon, despite last night's shift. I feel bad for her. Dad had what had seemed like a reasonable insurance policy, but it barely covered the mountains of debt we went into with medical bills following his accident and those weeks in a coma before he finally died.

I refuse to feel sorry for myself and mope.

This is a new town and a fresh start, after all.

I'll put the past couple of days behind me, grab my phone — which has an excellent camera — and wander the neighborhood. Dad and I used to do explore every Saturday morning — the one time of the week he always made sacred for us. Or, almost always. Whenever he was way behind on a deadline, nothing mattered more than finishing his book.

When I get ready, I put on the necklace then look at myself in the mirror.

I've always been into antique styles, stuff you can pick up at a thrift store. I love the look of fashion from the 20s. Flappers were cool, with those straight, short dresses. But I also like the lacy stuff from the early 50s, that makes me think of my grandma, and even retro stuff from the 70s and 80s.

I put on a sundress that seems slightly older than my mom, grab my phone and key, then head out.

A cool crisp autumn breeze blows leaves across my yard. We're surrounded by trees, and they're just starting to turn. Seasons barely existed in Las Orillas, same for all of Southern California.

I kneel down and get my phone's camera close to take a macro photo of a red maple leaf sitting atop an orange one, zooming in to focus on the thread of lighter colors running through each like veins.

After a few shots, I think of Kris, the one person I most want to share the photos with. But I can't. Not until we get past whatever's going on.

Assuming we can.

What else can I shoot? There's nothing much of interest nearby. Then I remember the path leading into the woods I spied last night while looking into the back yard.

I walk around the house, delighting in the sound of leaves crunching beneath my feet, tapping into some nostalgic half-memory from childhood, a time Dad and I were exploring the woods. He brought me to a creek to show me different rock types. He chose a smooth, dark gray stone with flecks of black then gave it to me. I don't remember what it's called, but it sits in my Box of Memories, one of a few treasures I have of our Saturday sojourns.

I wish he was here to see this place. I bet there are all sorts of cool rocks, plants, and animals here that he'd appreciate.

Los Orillas has the ocean, and it's beautiful, but there weren't snow-capped mountains or trees with fiery oranges and reds. I'm sure he would've loved this place.

The woods behind my house are dense, the trail

leading uphill seems to go on forever. I could get lost for days if I went too far, but I'll stick close to the path.

As I walk the path, I snap photos of unfamiliar trees and birds I don't recognize. A reddish-brown squirrel scampers right by me. Despite all that happened yesterday and how it felt like more of the same, today feels like a revelation. This place is so wonderfully different.

The people might suck, but the area is beautiful. I've never seen snow in real life, so I know I'm gonna be as giddy as a little girl when I finally do. I'll send Kris enough photos to make her want to leave Tyler and come live with us immediately.

The wind picks up, the air turns colder. It's a reminder of last night and how quickly the temperature dropped inside my house.

Gray clouds churn, threatening a storm. I wouldn't mind walking in the rain, but I'm wearing my black Converse, which have already taken a ton of abuse.

A branch breaks to my right with a loud SNAP! that makes me spin around.

Something is just out of sight behind a thicket of trees — a dark shape moving fast.

Two thoughts come to mind, and neither are pleasant. A bear or a wolf.

I've done zero research on the wildlife in these parts and don't have anything I can use as a weapon. Dad would be disappointed. He always stressed the importance of being prepared for anything on our walks.

He carried a walking stick that doubled as a weapon and a fully-stocked backpack — water bottles, a first-aid kit, granola bars, a flashlight, a knife, a tarp, and always at least one book to read. Dad seemed to have everything. He jokingly referred to it as his bag of tricks and told me about some cartoon cat named Felix.

All I've got is my phone.

Maybe I can get the battery to explode on a bear.

I'm about to turn around when I hear another sound I don't expect — a girl singing.

What?

It's coming from around the bend.

Careful to not make any noise, I follow. But I have no idea what I'm walking into.

I stop just before the path widens to a small clearing where a triangular treehouse is suspended between three large trunks. It has a ladder, door, black-shingled roof, and windows. There's even a deck, where the source of the singing sits with her legs dangling over the edge.

Her dark hair hangs to the middle of her back, and she appears to be around my age. She's wearing all black, from her long dress to her leather boots with thick purple laces.

I don't recognize the song, but her singing is achingly beautiful.

"And the darkness said to me don't cry,
It's not for us to ever know why,
The world will do to us what it will,
Nothing is forever but the way you—

A fat, cold raindrop hits my face. I let out a yelp, then freeze in embarrassment as the girl stops singing and looks down at me.

There's this feeling I get when I see specific people, a thing that's difficult to describe as anything other than a recognition of something within them. A sorrow, an energy, or a shared knowledge between us. I don't get it often, but it short-circuits my other thoughts whenever I do.

And I feel that as I look at her. As if I've known her forever.

I get a better look at the girl's face — porcelain white

skin, big brown eyes beneath thick eyebrows, round cheeks, and full lips painted black. She's also wearing a black choker. At school, she'd be sitting at the emo table.

The sky opens. Rain starts pouring.

I look back towards my house, though I can't see it through the woods, and try to figure the distance to see how wet I'd get if I ran back.

The girl calls out, "Up here."

I run to the ladder then climb up, laughing as I haul myself onto the deck. Then I follow her inside the treehouse.

She closes the door. The place isn't tall enough to stand without hitting the ceiling, so we both sit cross-legged across from one another.

I look around. There's a sleeping bag, empty soda bottles, energy drink cans, and a mess of cigarette butts, all of which look like they've been here a while.

The only sound is rain pelting the roof, twisting branches in the wind, and my loudly racing heart.

"Thanks," I say. "This your treehouse?"

"Nah, I don't know who put it here. Used to be other kids that hung around it, but lately, I'm the only one." She looks me up and down, then says, "You new around here?"

"Yeah, just moved in."

"Where?"

Normally, I'd never tell someone my address, but for some reason it leaves my mouth before I can think."

"Cool. What's your name?"

"Cora." I extend my hand, immediately thinking she'll give me a calculated disinterested look and wave it away. Girls like her are usually guarded. In my experience, it isn't because they're mean. Despite their attempts to dress scary, they're simply protecting themselves. Most of the goths and emos I've known, though not many, feel too much, so they try to shut it down. I can relate.

"Emily." She shakes my hand.

Her arm extends from the long sleeve of her dress, and I see the scars of a cutter.

HEY, SELF-HARM SISTERS!

I look away quickly, but not before she catches my stare.

Feeling stupid, I try thinking of something I can say to ease through the moment.

"Where do you live?"

"About five minutes that way." She nods back the way I came. "I'm trying to get away from my family. Who are you here to get away from?"

"I was just bored. Mom's working, and I don't really know anyone yet."

"You go to Harrison?"

"Yeah. Go, Fighting Lions!" I say with a sarcastic fist pump. "Just started Friday. You?"

"Homeschooled."

"Ah."

"Yeah, it sucks. My parents think public schools are filled with Satan worshipers or something. They were born with sticks lodged so far up their asses, I'm not sure how they ever sit down. What about yours?"

"It's just me and my Mom. Dad died."

Usually when I tell people that my father died, they respond with an apology of some sort.

Not Emily.

She asks, "How?"

I'm surprised, and wonder if she's always so blunt. Maybe it's a product of being homeschooled and not knowing how to act around other kids. I appreciate her candor, since the apology route always leaves me feeling uncomfortable and not knowing how to respond.

Why are you *apologizing, you didn't kill him, did you?*

"Car crash." I leave out the part about it being my fault.

"That sucks."

"Yes. Yes, it does."

Silence as we both look out the window at the rain which is now pounding harder.

"I hope there's no lightning," I say. "Being in a tree and all."

"There won't be any."

She says this with a certainty that I can't even question.

"How you liking it here so far? How was school?" She's still staring out the window at the thick sheets of rain turning everything a grayish white wall.

"The town is okay, I guess. School, I hate."

She turns to me. "Why?"

"It's just different," I say, still slightly on guard.

"Bullshit." Her eyes bore into mine. "Why do you *really* hate it?"

So I spill my guts, telling Emily everything from what happened at the mall to the fight with my best friend to Kris's crappy boyfriend. I didn't mean to tell her any of this, let alone *all* of it, but it pours out of me as if it's been pent up forever.

Oddly, it feels good, venting my confessions to someone who doesn't know me and won't judge me.

"Sorry," I say after what feels like fifteen minutes of ranting. "Didn't mean to unload all that." I laugh nervously, then start blinking.

Emily stares at me.

Self-conscious, I turn back to the window, forcing my eyes to open wide and stop freaking blinking.

"People suck. They'll always disappoint you if given half the chance."

HEY, I LIKE THIS GIRL!

"No." This sounds so much like a conversation between my Mom and me — and now I'm playing the role of Miss Polly Positive. "Not everyone. Just most. Which is why I try to avoid them." I laugh, thinking she's saying this stuff to be extra emo.

But Emily isn't smiling. She's quiet for a long moment, then looks me over, head to toe. "You seem all right, though." She looks down.

At first, I think she's looking at my chest, then I remember the necklace and reach up to touch it.

"Cool necklace. It got a story?"

I don't know why, but my first instinct is to protect the truth. Which is weird, because I rarely lie. "Family heirloom. I don't really know much about it."

She meets my gaze again. I feel like she's reading me, like she can sniff out my lie and is about to call bullshit.

Instead, she says, "Cool. It's pretty."

"Thanks. I like your dress and your boots."

"My parents hate them, which is why I'm wearing them."

I chuckle. "I'm surprised they let you wear it if they hate it so much."

"They've kinda given up on my clothes. It's enough for them to control every other element of my life. Believe me, this is the least of their disappointments."

Another nervous giggle burbles out of me, though I'm not sure if she's joking or hinting at dark things that I should treat more seriously. Judging from the other cuts I see on her other arm and leg whenever she moves enough that her dress or sleeve slides a bit, I'm thinking there's a lot lurking under the surface.

Maybe she needs a friend even more than I do.

"Well, if you ever wanna talk, I'm a good listener."

"Thanks." Then she looks out the window as the rain fades to drizzle. "I better get home."

I'm surprised she's going to leave so quickly. We were starting to click, and I want to talk longer. How do I ask for her number or when I'll be able to see her again without seeming needy?

"Okay. I should get back too. Thanks for letting me crash with you."

"I'll see you around, Cora," she says before crawling through the door, then descending the ladder.

I follow, watching Emily walk to a path opposite the one I'd come from, then disappear behind a row of bushes.

Light rain pelts me as I walk home, but it doesn't dampen my mood. I'm happy to have finally met someone, even if she's someone Mom wouldn't approve of.

NINE

The Boy Next Door

Mom ordered pizza for dinner.

She didn't get home until almost dark and is thoroughly wiped.

While we eat, she asks about my day.

I told about exploring the woods and meeting Emily, but I don't mention the necklace because I left it in my room and don't feel like going to get it.

"So, what's Emily like?"

"Quiet. She's homeschooled." I leave out the goth part. Not that Mom would judge the girl's style choices — she's cool about letting people express themselves. But she might worry about me hanging out with someone who is clearly depressed, someone Mom might deem as a threat to my mental well-being.

"Did you take your meds today?" she asks as if reading my mind.

"Last night, yes," I lie.

Mom seems to think if I miss a single dose I'll spiral into a depression and slit my wrists or something.

Truth is, I take too many meds. A pill for depression, another for

OCD. An antipsychotic — no, I'm not psychotic — pill for the hallu-cinations, and a pill for anxiety. Not to mention the supplements Mom buys from the vitamin shop. Some of the pills are big enough to choke a horse. They're supposed to help, and I guess they do. Especially since Dad died and after my time in the looney bin. But they also sometimes leave me in a fog. Too numb to feel anything, bad or good.

But whenever I ask the doctor if we can maybe change my meds or taper off a few of them, she always says, *Maybe in a few months.*

Now that we're in a new place with a new doctor, maybe I can finally pare down to one or two.

I ask Mom about her day. She pours a glass of wine and says she'd rather not talk about it. A baby probably died. She's routinely exposed to tragedies that would over-whelm most people. She'd disagree, but I think she's pretty heroic.

She asks me the routine stuff — the best part of my day, if I have any homework to do, what I'm looking forward to at school, and if I've gotten all my stuff ready yet. But I can tell she's dying for a long hot bath. And for a few more glasses of wine to put the day behind her.

I tell her I'll clean up and take out the trash.

"You sure?"

"Yeah. When I'm done, I'm gonna call Kris then read for a bit."

"Okay, thank you." She gets up and kisses my cheek before heading upstairs with her glass and the bottle.

I clean the mess then round up the trash. We still have plenty from unpacking, meaning several trips to the curb will be required.

I'm balancing several bags and boxes — trying to reduce the number of circuits and get it all done before the rain starts again — when I hear the garage door open next door. Because my house is at an angle, the house is more across the street then beside me. This cute blond around my age comes out then tosses a couple of bags into a giant green trash can on wheels. Cans and bottles clang as the sacks drop into the bucket.

He's wearing a tight tee, and though it's dark, I can see from the scant light in his garage that he has a nice body. It makes me hate mine even more.

I slow down so I can time our mutual approach.

He looks up as he's rolling his can to the curb.

And I trip.

Because of course I would.

FREAKING KLUTZ!

I scrape my hands on the driveway. Boxes and bags both scatter then tearing open, spilling trash and cardboard all over my driveway.

He rushes over to me.

I want to vanish into a hole, but it's too late, the boy is standing over me, hands out. "You okay?"

I take his hands as he helps me up, then I look down at mine.

So does he. "You're bleeding."

"I'm okay. Just a few scrapes."

"Go clean up. I got this." He starts gathering my trash, then puts it back into the boxes and bags.

"Thank you." I go inside and wash up in the bathroom. My right hand is bleeding, but not too bad. Easily fixed with a bandage. Then I grab the rest of the boxes and return to help him clean my mess.

Too late.

He's has already finished. All the bags and boxes are neatly stacked at the curb.

He comes up to me, now soaked, his wiry but muscular arms glistening in the rain. He takes the boxes, adds them to the pile, then turns to me and smiles. "Got any more?"

I want to melt into his big brown eyes. His face is boyish. His body lean and muscular. He reminds me of a farmer's kid, down to his southern accent.

"No, that's it."

"You all right?"

I hold it up, though he can't see through the bandage, so that was dumb. "Just a scratch. I'm such a klutz."

He laughs.

I love the sound of it.

"You're welcome. I'm Alex, by the way, Alex Marston." He offers his hand.

I shake it, and immediately my heart races above a stomach rolling with butterflies. It feels like he can see every last nerve.

Again, I want to vanish.

He lets go of my hand and stares at me, a smile teasing at his lips.

Is he smiling? Laughing?

Am I blinking?

Do I have pizza in my teeth?

"And you are?"

How stupid can I get? "Oh, sorry. I'm Cora."

"Nice to meet you, Cora. Where you from?"

"California. You?"

"Born and raised in Georgia. Came out here a few years ago."

Not knowing what else to say, I say, "Cool."

His smile widens.

"Okay, I best be getting back. I'll see ya 'round. Take care of that hand, eh?"

"Okay." I smile and nod like an idiot because I suddenly don't know how to act in front of a cute boy. Especially with my stomach still doing somersaults.

I check him out, admiring the way his shoulders flex as he moves, how his back tapers to a thin waist.

His nice butt.

He turns back and smiles at me.

Oh, my God. Did he see me checking out his ass?

He waves. "Goodnight."

I wave, then run inside, wanting to puke.

AFTER MY SHOWER, I'm in bed checking my LiveLyfe account to see if Kris has messaged me.

I need to know she's not mad at me. But there's no response since our chat, nor activity shown.

She's ghosting me.

I feel a pit in my stomach.

But also an anger.

I didn't do anything wrong. She's being stupid going back to Tyler, but I also know she's not thinking clearly, and I don't want to blow up our friendship over something like this. I'm her only real friend and if — no, *when* — things go sour with Tyler, I want her to be able to come to me without it being all weird.

Sorry about last night. Just really missing you and wishing I could be there for you. Hope you're not mad. Love you.

Then I wait a bit to see if she's received my text.

A bit turns into twenty-five minutes, and it's suddenly nine o'clock as my eyes tire and I rest the phone on my stomach.

As I'm drifting, I look at Sneezy and hug him, missing Daddy.

I wasn't an anxious child until middle school, though kindergarten was a rough start. I'd cry after Mom dropped me off, so Dad put my stuffed giraffe into my backpack. He told Sneezy to look after me then each evening report back to him about how my day went.

I stopped crying in class. And whenever I missed Mom or Dad, I'd look back to the cubby hole and find comfort in Sneezy being in there, imagining entire scenarios where he'd sneak out of my backpack and explore the classroom, playing with the other toys. I created entire adventures that stretched over weeks, then months. I'm not sure if it was my attempts to impress Dad with my storytelling abilities or if I just liked making him laugh.

Every night, I would.

And then, before bed, he'd take over Sneezy's voice and make up funny songs while playing guitar. He had the cutest Sneezy voice, way better than mine, and he'd often exaggerate with deafening sneezes at the best part of the song, then pretend to get angry at Sneezy for ruining it.

I wish we'd recorded Dad singing both the songs with Sneezy and the real ones.

Sneezy looks sad tonight.

I hug him tighter.

I WAKE up in a panic to an explosion of light and sound.

For a moment, I feel like the wall of my bedroom exploded inward and a giant helicopter was aiming floodlights at me.

Then I realize it's only thunder and lightning.

Through my open curtain, I see the tree branches outside my window thrashing in the wind.

The clock on my nightstand reads 3:33 AM.

Another staccato burst of lightning.

When I get up to close my curtains, my phone falls to the floor with a thud.

I pick it up then plug it into the charger on my nightstand, resisting the urge to check for Kris's response. If it's there I'll want to read it, then no way I'll get to sleep after that. And if she hasn't, I'll be wondering why not and whether our friendship is over.

Best to put it out of my mind, or try to, until morning.

Another burst of lightning, followed by a BOOM!

I cross my room to close the curtains.

As I pull them closed, something moves at the edge of my yard, just near the path into the woods.

My heart nearly stops as my mind screams, *What was that?*

I open the curtains then scan the tree line. But I see only darkness.

And of course, now there's no lightning to help illuminate the woods and behind my house.

Squinting doesn't help separate still shadows from those moving in the wind. I can't see anything but feel as if there's something in the storm, staring back at me.

I close the curtains then return to bed, my heart and mind racing.

Was it a wolf, a deer, or … a person?

No person would be out in this weather at this hour.

Right?

The thought consumes me, and I'm afraid I'll never fall back to sleep.

I take a sleeping pill then lie down, trying not to look at my phone or think about what might be outside my house waiting for my dreams to claim me.

TEN

Monday

I WAKE up with my stomach in knots.

Not only has Kris not yet read my message, I'm dreading first period where I'll see Kaycee for the first time since the mall.

Why does she have to be in my first class?

As I'm getting dressed in my new blue shirt, pink unicorn hoodie, and blue jeans, I look over at the necklace and brooch dangling from the bedside lamp.

Ada, the person I keep forgetting to look up on the Internet.

I debate whether I should wear it to school or not. This kind of necklace will draw attention. People will ask me about it. I already lied to Emily, for reasons I don't even understand. I don't want to get in the habit, and I defi-nitely don't want attention.

I decide to wear the necklace but put it under my shirt, my little secret — a comfort I can lean on when things get stressful — like I did with Sneezy.

I go downstairs where Mom is waiting, dressed for work.

"Want breakfast to go?" She's holding a toasted bagel

and looks hung over.

"No, thanks. I'm not hungry yet."

"Take it with you then." She puts it in a bag, along with a plastic knife and a single-serving of peanut butter in a small plastic tub.

"Thanks." But I can't imagine eating it.

"Text me some stuff you'd like me to pick up for your lunch this week and I'll get it on the way home."

"I can't just buy lunch at school?"

"No. That cost adds up quickly, and it's not healthy."

I feel like such a loser bringing a bagged lunch when most of the kids are buying. But I try not to argue when she's not in the mood.

"I'll be in the car." She grabs her bag and her coffee, then heads outside.

I feel like she's mad at me, though I'm not sure what I did wrong.

SHE KNOWS YOU BURNED YOURSELF!

I try to remind myself that she always gets like this the night after drinking too much. Then I remind myself how much stress she's under, raising a daughter on her own after her husband died. Mountains of medical debt and long hours to barely cover the bills, all while constantly surrounded by sick and dying babies.

And that's just the stuff I know about. She must also be incredibly lonely since Dad's passing. I can't even imagine the love of your life dying so young.

I follow her to the car.

As I get in, I see Alex and a man who I guess is his father — a blue-collar-looking, salt-and-pepper-haired guy with a beer belly and a cane. They get into the pickup parked in the driveway.

I wave.

Either Alex doesn't see me, or he's ignoring me.

His dad gives me a gruff look, the kind a racist might give when he realizes black people moved in across the street.

I get in the car and buckle up.

As Alex and his dad pull out of the driveway, he looks out his window and smiles at me.

I smile back.

MOM HAS to stop for gas before dropping me off. I'm thankful for the chance to stall. I tell her I need to use the restroom then sit in there for several minutes, trying to time things so we get to school as close to the first bell as possible.

The last thing I want is to deal with Kacey or the twins in front of the entire school.

Bad enough she's in my first class.

We arrive just as the kids are filing in. Perfect timing.

I kiss Mom goodbye, grab my backpack, then head inside.

As I walk into Mr. Jennings' class, I spot Kacey and the jock at their desks, whispering and laughing.

I know it's about me but pretend not to notice.

After taking my seat, I pull out my notebook and my sketchpad then start to doodle, keeping my head down, trying not to think too much. Or blink too much.

Four times. Just four.

I blink once, squeeze my eyes tight, then open them.

Don't do it.

Just ignore them.

More laughter from behind.

I feel the necklace against my chest, warm, comforting … like Sneezy. It brings a smile to my lips.

Mr. Jennings enters, closes the door, then sits as the bell rings. He talks a bit about the poetry they'd been studying, long before I arrived, and how he now would like us to try writing some.

Half the kids in the class groan as if Mr. Jennings had asked them to do advanced trigonometry.

I might have, too. But writing has always come easy to me. I could never author a book, but assignments like poems and short stories are simple enough.

But I'm not most people.

Judging from the kids I went to school with before and what I've seen so far at this school, most kids think reading is stupid.

Skater Boy says, "I don't know what to write, Mr. Jennings."

"Why don't you write about your mom," the jock replies. "That's what I'm writing about. Anyone know what rhymes with MILF?"

Kids start laughing as poor Mr. Jennings does his best to regain control. With his serious tone he says, "Well, Brandon, why don't you write about something you love or fear."

"So, his Mom?" The jock laughs hysterically at his own joke.

Kaycee and a few others join him.

Mr. Jennings finally says, "Okay, Trent, since you're such an expert, we'll have you read yours to the class."

More laughter, this time from Brandon.

"Aw, come on!" Trent gripes.

And then it hits me — does *everyone* have to read these out loud?

Oh, God. No.

HEY, EVERYBODY, IT'S TIME TO EMBARRASS OURSELVES AGAIN!

I don't mind writing something the teacher will read, or even something he reads aloud, but *I* don't want to stand in front of the class and leave myself open to ridicule.

Ugh.

Now I *really* don't know what to write.

"Okay, you've got five minutes. I don't care if it's four lines or forty, just write whatever comes to mind. And remember, it doesn't have to rhyme. Okay, time starts now."

Crap!

My mind races as I try to think of something that won't suck or make me stand out too much. The other kids don't know my dad is a writer, but eventually it'll come out.

Then, if past experience holds true, they'll have different expectations. They'll either accuse me of trying too hard or of not being as good as my father. I lose either way, which is why I hope nobody ever finds out who he used to be.

I start writing, not sure what it's going to be until I'm halfway into it.

"Pens down," Mr. Jennings says.

I stare at the words on the paper. They suddenly feel raw, too vulnerable. Why did I write *this* as my poem?

God, I hope I don't have to read it.

I start blinking.

"Since Trent was so eager to read, he'll go first. Front and center, Trent."

Trent sighs as the other kids erupt into twitters of laughter.

He walks with a swagger, his back straight and shoulders wide, brimming with confidence. He's the kind of guy who's probably rarely, if ever, anxious.

Mr. Jennings is sitting at his desk, hands folded on his lap, facing Trent.

Trent smiles at him, and you just know he's written something smart-ass.

He looks down at his paper, then starts reading.

"K for blue eyes that kill me,
  A for an ass that's poppin'."
  Students break into laughter.
  "Y for why are you so awesome?
  C for cheering that you do so well,
  E for everything you do for me,
  And another E for every time I think of you.
  Kaycee, I love you."

"AWWW, THAT'S SO SWEET," Kaycee says in that same fake voice she used to compliment me.

The other jocks in the class hoot, holler, and clap like Trent scored a touchdown.

I don't have to look back to imagine Kaycee's face, her big fake Look-At-Me smile. Nor do I have to look at the other girls in class to know they're also looking at Trent like he's the sweetest guy to ever pick up a pen and write a poem about his girl's *poppin'* ass.

Meanwhile, I'm trying not to laugh. I might projectile-vomit if I do.

"Thank you for that, Trent. We could've done without the A-word, but otherwise, a good effort."

"Thanks, Teach." He smiles, offering high-fives to the other dudes on his way back, giving Kaycee a kiss on her mouth before he takes his seat.

Mr. Jennings looks around the class for the next victim.

Please don't look at me.
Please don't look at me.
Please don't look at me.
Please don't look at—

And then, of course, he looks right the hell at me. "How about our newest student, Cora?"

I truly hate my life.

"Okay." I stand slowly, poem in hand, trying to keep the page from shaking, and doing everything in my power not to blink.

No such luck.

The moment I see everyone looking at me, the blinking begins.

Not a crazy amount, but noticeable all the same. I rub at my eyes as if they're dry, as if that might explain it all away.

I don't look back at the class.

I know they're all looking at me.

Kaycee is probably smiling her fake bitch smile.

THEY CREATE a treatment
Then create the illness,
If you're not sick yet,
They'll find an ailment,
Got a pill to wake you up,
Got a pill to feel something,
Got a pill to bring you down,
And another to feel nothing,
Got a pill so you'll fit in,
Got a pill to 'fix' your brain,
Got a pill so you'll stand out,
And another to ease the pain,
How many pills 'til I'm good enough?

How many pills to fix all that ails?
How many pills do you need to push?
To meet the quota of forecasted sales?"

AS I FINISH, a few kids in class give half-hearted claps.

But I don't care who. I just want to run back to my desk while trying not to puke.

"Wow, that was very good," Mr. Jennings says. "Do you write a lot?"

I don't want praise. Or to stand out. I just want to sit.

"A little bit," I say.

"Well, Cora, you certainly have a way with words, and you should keep at it."

"Thank you." I rush to my seat.

Now I get more unwanted attention. Jealous, judgmental stares from students who don't appreciate the teacher praising me. It's something I've dealt with enough times to recognize what's coming before it happens — the backlash for standing out.

"Now," Mr. Jennings says, "do I have any volunteers to go next?"

"I'd like to," Kaycee says.

I don't turn around, but something about her voice strikes me as way too eager. Something isn't right.

She gets up then walks by me, brushing against my arm.

I know it was intentional but don't give her the satisfaction of acknowledging it. I keep my eyes on my poem.

Kaycee clears her throat. "I call this one 'Blink.'"

My heart freezes.

The classroom is quiet, waiting for her.

The sound of blood rushes through my veins as my heart kicks into overdrive. I brace for what's coming.

Kaycee starts.

"TWAS ONCE A GIRL who blinked all the time,
    Nobody knew the reasons why.
    Was she broken at birth or dropped on her head?
    Maybe twas no reason or rhyme."

UNCOMFORTABLE LAUGHTER MINGLES with the cruel guffawing behind me. Everybody is staring at the back of my head, waiting to see how I'll respond.

I'm frozen, my chest tightening.

My eyes blinking even though it's the last damned thing I want to be doing.

I want to get up. I'm dying to run.

Kaycee looks at me, offering me the cruelest smile I've ever seen on another human.

I look at the teacher, hoping he'll see my distress.

But he appears clueless, looking at Kaycee, waiting for her to finish.

"SO SHE SAT BY HERSELF,
    at lunch every day,
    As she had no friends,
    least none who would stay,"

MY HEART IS RACING SO FAST and my chest is so tight, I might have a heart attack or die on the spot.

I get up, not looking at anyone, and say, "I need to go to the bathroom."

Not waiting for permission, I race out the door then

run down the hall, trying not to break down before I'm alone in a stall.

I'm hyperventilating. Not sure I'll even make it to the bathroom.

But somehow, I do.

I throw open the door then find myself sobbing in a stall for the second time since moving here.

There's no way I'm going back to class, and I don't care if I get in trouble. If anyone comes looking for me, I'll tell them I'm not feeling well.

I wish I could call Mom to come get me, but I don't want to be weak. I don't want to let Kaycee win. It's bad enough that I ran out of class blinking and on the verge of tears. Yet another embarrassing moment I'll never live down.

I check to see if Kris has gotten back to me.

No.

I clench my fists then scroll through LiveLyfe until I decide to find Alex. I'm not sure if he said his name was Marsden, Marsdon, or Marston. After a couple minutes, I see it's the third one.

A few public photos, most from a few years ago — Alex on a farm with a horse, with a little girl that might be a relative, and one of him at around ten-years-old or so with another boy, both of them making muscles and posing with goofy faces.

The pictures make me smile.

Something about Alex strikes me as pure and kind. In a world full of fake, he stands out as the real thing.

WHAT ARE YOU TALKING ABOUT?
YOU DON'T EVEN KNOW HIM!

Most of his profile is private, so I can't see how many friends he has, who they are, or any of his posts to get a feel for what he might be like.

WHAT IF HE ONLY POSTS RACIST MEMES?
WOULD YOU STILL LOVE HIM THEN?
I don't love him! I'm just crushing.
WHATEVER.
YOU FALL TOO EASILY.
NO WONDER YOU'RE EVERYBODY'S DOORMAT.

I hover my finger over the friend request, wondering if I should. It might seem weird that I just met him and immediately started stalking him online.

NO, DON'T DO IT.
JUST PLAY IT COOL.
WAIT FOR HIM TO COME TO YOU.
DON'T BE SO DAMNED THIRSTY!

Sometimes my inner voice saves me from making a fool of myself. Other times, it's too paranoid and critical.

I decide to ignore it and send a request.

YOU IDIOT!
YOU'RE GONNA SCARE HIM AWAY.

The bell for second period rings.

Yes, I can finally leave the stall!

I check myself in the mirror, dab away the smeared mascara, then make my way back to Mr. Jennings' class to retrieve my backpack.

The class is empty, *thank God*, except for the teacher. My backpack is on his desk.

I go to take it.

"Are you okay?"

I nod. "Just sick to my stomach."

He looks at me, clearly not believing me.

"Kids can be mean sometimes. I'm sorry."

So he *did* realize the poem was about me.

"I had a word with Kaycee after you left. That kind of behavior won't be tolerated."

"You didn't need to do that."

I start blinking, then close my eyes and turn my head, hair spilling over my face.

God, I hate myself.

"Well, I'm sorry I didn't say something sooner. I wasn't sure what she was doing until you ran out, then I put two and two together."

SO HE KNOWS YOU'RE A BLINKY TWITCHY FREAK TOO.

AWESOME!

"It's okay, really. Thank you." I turn and sling my backpack over my shoulder as his second period kids spill into the room.

I leave the class hating my weakness, and how totally pitiful I am.

Lunch

I DECIDE to skip lunch and sit in a hallway in the 400 building, doodling in my sketch pad.

A few kids pass by, a couple others sit on the far end of the hallway talking, so I don't feel like I stick out too much or look like I'm hiding.

My stomach grumbles and I wish for the very thing I was opposed to before — a bagged lunch. At least I'd be able to eat while hiding. But I didn't bring it, and I left my bagel in the car.

A book drops next to me with a THUD, loud enough to startle me.

"What the hell?" My gaze moves from the heavy *World History* tome up, fully expecting Kaycee and the twins to be staring down at me.

Instead, I see a friendly face.

"Alex!" I'm way too excited to see him.

He drops to a cross-legged position with surprising flexibility.

"What's poppin'? Why you sittin' here?"

"I forgot my lunch money."

"What? Well, come on, then, I'll get you somethin'."

"No, that's okay." I should've said I wasn't hungry instead.

"Don't be ridiculous." He picks up his history book, then stands and offers his hand to help me.

I stow my sketchpad in my backpack and take it.

He lifts me with ease, takes me to his locker — a few down from mine — trades his history book for science, then looks at me. "Let's go eat."

On the way to the cafeteria, he talks about his morning, telling me about falling on his face in gym class while trying to make this bad ass spike in volleyball. His funny story, or maybe his easy demeanor, melts away my anxiety.

As we pass other kids, I'm trying to determine what social group Alex fits in best. He's either saying "hey" to, or being greeted by, Jocks, Nerds, Gamers, Emos, and Awkwards. I can't tell if he's popular with everyone or one of those kids who kinda knows a few people from every group but belongs to none.

At my old school, when I existed on the fringe of a few, people never greeted me like this — with genuine warmth.

If he's so popular, why is he choosing to hang out with *me?*

We get in line. He orders a slice of pepperoni pizza and a Sprite. "Get anything you want. Though that's not nearly as impressive as if we were at some nice steak joint."

I laugh.

I order a slice of cheese pizza and a Coke.

There are plenty of tables to choose from. Most everyone's done eating and is now walking in the courtyard outside or meandering in the hallways before the bell rings for fifth period.

He picks a table in the back where nobody is sitting then pulls out a chair out for me.

"Thanks." I take a seat.

He grabs another, spins it around backwards in one quick move, straddles it, then sits across from me with his back to the wall.

"Thank you for lunch. I'll pay you back tomorrow."

"Don't worry about it. My treat."

"Thanks." I take a bite of pizza, wondering what to say. I'm pretty sure three thank-yous are my limit.

Turns out, I don't need to wonder too long.

"What were you drawing?" Alex asks.

"Just doodling, really."

"Can I see?"

"It's not very good." I take a drink of Coke.

"Cool. I love 'not very good' drawings. Good art is *soooo* overrated."

I laugh, nearly spitting Coke out of my nose. "Fine, but you asked." I pull my sketchbook out of my backpack and slide it across the table.

He opens it up and stops on the first page where I drew an intricately-lined and crosshatched eye with a ballpoint pen.

"Wow. I have to say I'm disappointed. You promised me 'not very good' but you give me this … this greatness? What am I supposed to do with *this?*"

My cheeks burn.

Alex turns back a page and is looking at a pencil sketch of a fairy. A partial drawing. I messed up the hands, so I erased them. I still kind of suck at hands. Fingers specifically.

He continues through the drawings, making a comment about each one. I don't think I'm nearly as good as he thinks I am, but his being impressed makes me feel like maybe I might not suck as much as I think.

YES, YOU DO!

I study him as he studies my work. It's difficult to keep my expression neutral while admiring the angles of his face, the look in his eyes as he looks at my creations, or the smile teasing his lips as he talks.

I wonder what he kisses like.

Footsteps sound behind us, getting louder. I turn to see Kaycee and the twins approaching.

My heart is in my throat as I brace for whatever she's going to say or do.

She smiles. "Hi, Alex, how are you?"

Are they friends?

I think I'm going to puke.

"All right." He looks up at her with an expression I can't quite decipher. "What's up?"

"I just came over to see how Cora is doing. Poor thing ran out of class looking like she was about to die. Are you okay?"

"I'm fine." I meet her gaze. "Just a little sick to my stomach."

I say this last part with the kind of unmistakable glare known the world over by girls who hate each other.

"Oh, you missed the end of my poem," she says with that same smile. "Let me know if you'd like a copy."

I don't know why Kaycee hates me. She doesn't even know me. But if she wants hate, I'll give it right back. I refuse to let her bully me into running away. Not again, or at least not right this second.

Who knows how my anxiety will respond next time?

But for now, I'm handling it.

My fist tightens into a ball beneath the table. I would never hit first, but if this is going to get physical, I'm aiming for her perfect little nose.

She wrinkles it as if sensing my intentions. "Well, I'm glad you're okay."

Then she smiles and turns to leave.

Amber gives me a nasty little smirk. But Alice doesn't even look at me. She just turns and follows them, as if she can't meet my gaze like the others. Maybe, of the three of them, she's the one who goes along with things without having any actual malice towards me.

"What was *that* about?" Alex asks.

I'd love to tell him what Kaycee has done, but I don't want to come off as whiney or like my life is full of drama.

"I dunno. She's in my first hour. I don't really know her, though."

He gives me a look like maybe he doesn't believe me, but he's too polite to prod.

"Do *you* know them?"

"Who doesn't? They're cheerleaders and on various sports teams and in drama and a bunch of other stuff. Kaycee dates the quarterback, Trent Cullen."

"You friends with them?"

"Define *friends*." He meets my gaze with a devilish grin.

"Do you hang out with them?"

"I don't hang out with anyone, really."

"You seemed pretty popular when we were coming in here."

"Well, I *know* people. But very few I'd call friends."

"Ah." But I'm not sure what he means.

"People come to me for stuff."

"Stuff?" I ask, then whisper, "Like drugs?"

"God, no." He laughs. "I do tests and reports for a lot of the … less inclined to study."

"Oh, the idiots," I tease.

He laughs. "I was trying to be diplomatic. But yeah, the *intelligence-challenged.*"

"Cool. So, you're what, some kinda genius?"

"No, but it's not like my clients are taking rocket science or anything. Pretty basic stuff."

"How do you even get into something like that?"

"In ninth grade, I was scrawny and short. Some seniors picked on me. One of the football players — Trent's older brother, actually, a dude named Steve — stood up for me. Soon, we were hanging out and people just knew to leave me alone because I was his friend. Not sure why he kept talking to me or went to bat for me in the first place, except we had the same taste in music and both played guitar. He was struggling with a class, and I offered to help him as a way of thanking him for saving my ass. People just started coming to me after that. It's a way for me to make some extra money on the side."

"Wow, that's pretty cool. You said you were scrawny and short freshman year. What grade are you in now?"

"Junior. You?"

JUNIOR?

JUNIORS NEVER DATE DOWN.

GIVE IT UP, KID.

"Sophomore." I want to change the subject. "So how many, erm, *clients*, do you have?"

He smiles. "Discretion is my number one rule. Let's just say more than a few."

"Yo, Alex."

He waves at the pair of jocks as they pass, then looks at me.

"Your turn."

"My turn? For what?"

"I told you my big secret. Now you tell me yours."

The bell rings.

I smile. "Sorry, gotta run."

Alex laughs. "Fair enough." He slides my art pad back to me. "I want to see the rest of those. Lunch tomorrow?"

I'm pleasantly surprised he wants to sit with me again, especially when he's clearly so much more popular.

But I don't want to get my hopes up.

"Maybe." I try to come off as coy but probably look like an idiot.

"You owe me a secret, young lady." As he stands, he points at me. Then he smiles and leaves.

A smile creeps across my face as I revel in the warm-and-fuzzies. God, I hope he isn't setting me up like Kaycee did.

TWELVE

The Walk Home

Mom texted she's working late, so I have to walk home.

I don't live that far away, so it's not too bad, though I wish I'd left a few books in my locker instead of carrying them all in my backpack, which now feels full of boulders.

When I turn off the main road and into my neighborhood, I hear the sound of wheels on pavement. So I turn around.

Alex is on a skateboard, rolling up on me.

"Hey!" He smiles as he comes to a stop, pops the skateboard up, then grabs it. He walks beside me. "Miss your ride?"

"My mom's working late. What about you? Thought your dad drove you."

"He only drives me to school, not home."

"What does he do?"

"Sits around and drinks mostly."

"I meant for a job," I say with a laugh.

"He doesn't work. He got hurt last year and needs a cane to get around. He's in a lot of pain." Alex has this expression I can't quite read.

"Sorry."

"Don't be. He's not a nice person."

I'm not sure how to respond to that. "What's your mom do?"

"She died when I was five."

"Oh, sorry."

"What does your mom do?" Alex asks.

"She's a neonatal nurse in Tacoma."

"Wow, that's quite a drive. Why don't you live closer?"

"Mom said the houses there were crazy expensive. Got this one for a good price."

"Yeah, I'll bet."

"What do you mean?"

He looks at me funny, then shakes his head. "Never mind. So, you owe me a secret."

"What? I thought I had until tomorrow."

"Okay, fair enough."

We walk in silence for a bit before he asks, "What about your dad?"

"He died a little over a year ago."

"Oh, sorry."

"Me, too. He was great."

"Yeah? Tell me about him."

"His name was Andrew, and he was the best."

"How did he die?"

"Car accident."

"Wow, that sucks."

"Yes. Yes, it does."

"What did he do? Was he an artist, too?"

"Well, kind of." I debate whether to tell him, but there's something about Alex I trust. "A different kind of art. He was a writer."

"Really? What kind?"

"Horror and some young adult stuff. Andrew Gray."

"Wait … *the* Andrew Gray was your father? The guy that wrote *The Lost Ones* and *The House on the Edge of Never?*"

"You know him?"

"*Know him?* I read every book he's ever written!"

"Really?"

"Yeah. Your dad was one of my favorite writers." He's staring at me with awe.

It's weird. I've never had this reaction to my father's work. People usually either act like fans but aren't or treat me differently — usually worse — because of some fame they think I had by being his daughter. I've not met anyone my age who was an actual fan.

I kind of like the way Alex is suddenly looking at me, a bit more impressed.

"Thank you."

"Have you read his books?"

YEAH, BUT NOT UNTIL AFTER HE DIED.

SHE WASN'T EVEN AS GOOD A FAN AS YOU, SOMEONE WHO DIDN'T EVEN KNOW HIM!

"Yes. I loved them."

We start talking in detail about my dad's stories, and Alex gushes like a fan boy. He seemed cool last night and at lunch, but he's totally dorking out now, and I find it wonderfully charming.

"Do *you* write?" he asks.

"A little. Mostly poems, though."

"Really? Could I read them sometime?"

"They're not that good."

A grin spreads across his face.

Before he says what I know he's going to, I interrupt. "But you like bad poetry, right?"

He smiles. "The worse, the better."

"I'll have to dig through some boxes. I haven't finished

all the unpacking yet. And then I'll have to find the least embarrassing ones to show you."

"Yeah? Lots of sappy poems about boys?"

"Totally."

He laughs. "What else are you into?"

"Photography, though I'm not good. I post photos on my LiveLyfe sometimes. Nothing great, but—"

"'Nothing great?' My favorite kind!"

I laugh.

Before I know it, we're on our block and his entire demeanor changes.

The smile is gone. His shoulders slump. He's looking down at the road instead of up or at me and is walking slow enough to look lost. Then he averts his attention to peer nervously at his house, as if afraid his father might see him or something.

I want to ask about his home life, but I don't want to pry. Or ruin the good conversation.

The silence is painful, and I'm desperate to break it. "Oh, I sent you a friend request on LiveLyfe."

"Cool. I'll check after my chores and homework."

Conversation grinds to a halt at the end of the street. His tension crushes us both. Finally, he meets my gaze again. "See ya tomorrow." And with a tentative wave, he heads to his house.

His father stands in the window. The house is too dark to see his face, but I can feel his glare.

"Bye, Alex."

THIRTEEN

Back To The Woods

I GO INSIDE MY HOUSE, get a drink, sit in the oversized living room chair, then check to see if Kris got back to me.

She finally did.

Yes!

She wrote, *It's okay. TTYL.*

TALK TO YOU LATER?

NOT AN I LOVE YOU, APPLE?

OOH, SHE HATES YOU!

At least she's not ignoring me.

Still, it feels like an obligatory text. She would've written more if she wasn't holding a grudge. Maybe included a few more details or asked how I am.

Alex hasn't accepted my friend request.

I wonder if his dad yelled at him when he got home. I should've asked if his dad had a problem with me being mixed race because it sure feels like it.

JUST BECAUSE HE GLARED AT YOU DOESN'T MAKE HIM A RACIST!

THERE ARE PLENTY OF OTHER REASONS TO HATE YOU!

But judging how Alex clammed up when I asked about his dad, and again as we got close to his house, maybe it's not a good idea to ask questions. Maybe I should wait until I know him better.

Then, because apparently I'm a masochist, I decide to check Kaycee's wall, seeing if she wrote anything about me.

She posted a bunch of photos on Sunday about her shoes from the mall. Below the photos are tons of comments from other girls complimenting the shoes, saying how beautiful she is and generally kissing her ass.

Ugh.

I see hearts from the twins, and a comment from Alice. None from Amber.

I click on Alice's name to go to her page.

It's not private, so I can view her posts and am surprised to see a few drawings — faeries, girls with long flowing hair, sketches of clothing, and lots of eyes. And her drawings are good, maybe great.

That would explain why she seemed to take an interest in my art and didn't appear as eager to join in when Kaycee and her sister dumped on me.

Maybe beneath that pretty, mean-girl facade is a kind, artistic soul.

Doesn't matter, though, since she's still friends with Kaycee.

I consider unfriending Kaycee, but decide not to. That would only prove that I was thinking about her. And besides, if her page is friends only, I can't stalk her to see what she's saying.

I shouldn't even care what she says about me. She's a horrible person. But if she starts posting crap, I want to see it so I can brace myself for whatever is coming. Maybe I'm overthinking things, but I've been the target of vicious girls before. No matter how paranoid I might seem, the sad reality is I'm probably not being paranoid enough.

After a while, I'm bored.

I remember my only other friend. Well, sorta friend. Emily. Might be nice to hang with her again.

Decision made, I go upstairs and change into black jeans and an even blacker Jack Skellington sweater. The outfit might appeal to Emily's goth sensibilities.

The necklace goes on over my sweater. Then I grab my phone before heading to the path behind my house.

I run through the woods to the treehouse, but slow to a disappointing stop. Emily isn't there.

Maybe there's something else that will occupy my time. I find a few things to photograph — birds, wildflowers. A couple macro shots of tree bark turn out kind of cool.

After a while, I climb the treehouse ladder, figuring I'll wait and see if she shows up. My heart leaps as I look through the window.

Emily is sleeping on the treehouse floor. She's wearing the same thing as last time.

I knock on the door, lightly.

She stirs, sits up, looks at me. Her eyes and nose are red, her mascara is a mess, but she kinda smiles as she motions for me to enter.

I crawl inside then sit across from her. "You okay?"

"No."

"What's wrong?"

"It doesn't matter."

I'm not sure if she means it or if she's just testing to see if I care enough to ask more questions.

"Family stuff?"

She nods. "But you wouldn't understand."

"Why not?"

"You get along with your mom, don't you?"

"Yeah, but I didn't always. We used to fight a lot."

"Why?"

I tell her how bad my depression used to be, how nobody liked me at school. About getting bullied and about my mother never really understanding — she always thought it was something I was doing, that my attitude provoked people. Even when the doctors said I needed to be medicated, she blamed me because I'd forget to take my meds or wasn't following whatever diet they insisted I go on.

My dad understood because he suffered from depression, too. Sometimes that meant he fought with mom, which made me feel worse. For a while, she accused me of manipulating him and seeking his attention. I thought she hated me.

"Did she?"

"No. I think it was my depression making things seem worse than they were. My mom loves me."

"How do you know she didn't hate you? Maybe she was jealous of your dad's attention." She looks at me as if this is perfectly obvious.

"Because she's my mother. And she's always been there for me. When I hurt, so does she. Maybe we have misunderstandings, but still, that isn't the same as *hating* someone. Even if things *were* bad, we've been closer than ever since Dad died."

"Do you think she ever blames you for his death?"

I stare at Emily, wondering why she'd ask that, wondering what she knows. Has she been looking up stuff online about my father's death? The news didn't cover what *really* happened, the *reason* my father was driving so late that night, but maybe she somehow put two and two together.

"Why would you ask that?"

"Sorry. Just sometimes the surviving parent looks for someone to blame. I didn't mean to imply anything."

Yet something in her eyes says otherwise, that she somehow *knows*.

But that's impossible. *Isn't it?*

I change the subject. "So, what happened with you?"

She rolls up her sleeves and shows me the cuts. Fresh red ones.

"My mom saw them and freaked out. Claimed the devil was inside me. Threatened to send me away to a boarding school for troubled kids. A religious boarding school, of course."

"Sorry."

"Me, too."

"Have you seen any therapists?"

"About the cutting?"

"Yeah."

"No. My family doesn't believe in therapy or any of that stuff. They think it's me not letting God into my heart. So, I guess he's punishing me. Which, if you ask me, would make God a major asshole."

"Wow."

"I tried to tell them it had nothing to do with God or the devil or any of that, that depression is a chemical imbalance. I begged them to let me see a doctor. I think my mother was close to agreeing, but then my father squashed it. Said psychiatrists were ungodly pill-pushers."

I want to ask how she gets goth clothes to piss her parents off, but seeing as I've only seen her in this one outfit, I'm guessing maybe she doesn't have too much in way of rebellious clothing. Now that I think about it, her dark dress is long and maybe it's not seen as all that rebellious since it's technically modest clothing. The only thing really gothy about her is the thick eyeliner and mascara, lipstick, and black boots with purple laces. Maybe those are the tiny freedoms she fought for and won. Or maybe she only does her makeup like this when going out.

"Do you ever wish you were dead?" Emily asks.

"There was a time I did, yes."

"Why?"

"Bullies, mostly. Made my life a living hell."

"So, what kept you from doing it?"

Again, I feel like she knows too much, like she's looking inside me at memories I don't want to relive.

"I dunno," I lie. "Did *you* ever wish you were dead?"

"Every single day."

"Why?"

"My parents are nuts, and, unlike your mom, mine do hate me. I also don't have any friends. And … I just want it to be over. It'd be easier."

She stares at the ground, hair falling in her face. I think she might be crying, but I can't tell for sure.

I put a hand on her shoulder. "You've only got another couple years. Just hold on. Then, when you're eighteen, escape."

"Escape to *where?*"

"I don't know. *Anywhere* sounds better than where you are, though. Are they sending you to college?"

"I doubt it. My dad thinks the only place for women is barefoot and pregnant."

"For real?"

"Yeah."

"So, your mom doesn't work?"

"No. She's a 'good little housewife.'"

"What does *he* do?"

"Sanitation. Which is appropriate, since he's so full of shit." Emily laughs, and I join her. She looks like she needs a hug, so I give her one.

As she embraces me, tight, a chill runs through me. I shiver.

SHE'S GOING TO KILL HERSELF.

She notices and pulls away. "You okay?"

"Just had a chill."

I'm blinking, un-thinking the horrifying thought.

Sometimes my OCD thoughts feel more like real premonitions than something that might happen.

This is one of those times.

She's not going to kill herself.

She's not going to kill herself.

She's not going to kill herself.

She's not going to kill herself.

She nods. Stays quiet.

"Listen," I say. "You don't have to suffer alone. If you need a friend, I'm here. Heck, you're the first nice person I've met. Well, first nice girl I've met, anyway."

"Really?" Her eyes well with tears, and she smiles.

"Yeah. You got a LiveLyfe account?" I pull my phone from my pocket.

"Um, no. Don't have a phone … or a computer."

"What?"

"Devil's tools, Dad says."

"You poor girl. What about TV or video games?"

She shakes her head.

"*What?*"

I consider inviting her over to expose her to all the joys she's been missing out on, but figure it's probably best not to invite someone before Mom has met them. She's overprotective, especially given all that's happened. I'm not sure how Mom will feel about Emily, especially if she sees the scars. She'll probably think Emily will be bad for me. Fear she'll trigger some of my old worst behaviors.

Emily shakes her head. "I guess you can't miss what you never really had."

"Maybe."

I look at my phone and see that it's almost time for Mom to come home. "I need to get back. Will you be okay?"

"Yes, I think so." She hugs me again. "Thank you, Cora."

I can almost feel the pain roiling off of her. Maybe my mother is right about people's despair being infectious and dragging me down. It's possible I am too vulnerable to other people's emotions.

How can I help someone without harming myself?

FOURTEEN

Tuesday

IT's POURING OUTSIDE as Mom and I rush from the house to the car without our umbrellas, which were lost in the move.

"Sorry about last night." Mom's guilty for coming home and heading straight to bed.

"It's okay. I finished the leftover pizza."

"Sorry."

"Don't be. I *like* leftover pizza, remember? You going to get some rest today?"

"I'll try. I go in at five. I'll leave you something for dinner."

"Thank you."

I never got a chance to tell Mom about Emily or ask if she could come over. But that's okay. I'm not really sure how to introduce Emily just yet, anyway.

Hey, Mom, here's a goth girl I met in the woods. She's suicidal, cuts, and hates her parents. Can she hang with us?

I've got to frame it in the right way so she knows I'm not falling in with a bad crowd. That I'm actually doing a good thing — Emily needs a friend and I want to help her.

Then Mom'll be less concerned about me slipping into my old mindset.

"You straightened your hair, I see? Didn't like the braids anymore?"

"I don't know. Just wasn't feeling them." I don't want to admit that I'm just trying to fit in, though she's too observant not to reach the conclusion herself. If she has, she doesn't say anything.

I see a familiar figure walking along the side of the road, getting soaked.

"Hey, that's Alex!"

"Who?"

I didn't get a chance to tell Mom about Alex, either.

"The kid next door."

"Why is he walking in the rain?" She pulls up beside him, rolls down my window and shouts, "Hey, neighbor. Need a ride?"

He looks into the car and I feel a punch to the gut.

Alex has a huge black circle under his left eye.

I pretend not to notice, but it's kinda hard to shift my expression before he catches it.

He looks at my Mom. "Yeah?"

"Yeah, get in."

Alex runs to the back door as Mom unlocks it. He climbs inside, sets his wet backpack on the floor, and closes the door.

"Thank you, ma'am," he says as Mom starts driving. "Sorry for getting your car wet."

"You're welcome. And don't worry, dear."

I look in the mirror at the black eye and wonder if his father did it to him. I want to ask but certainly won't in front of Mom. "Why are you *walking* in the rain?"

"I woke up late. Dad doesn't tolerate tardiness."

"But he doesn't even work. What's it matter if you

wake up a few minutes late?" I ask. "Not like he has anything else to do."

I can feel Mom wanting to say something, probably to tell me to mind my own business and not prod. Obviously, she's seen his black eye and is probably wondering about it herself, but she has manners enough to bite her tongue.

"It's the principle of the matter. Dad is strict on his rules. It's okay. I should've gotten up earlier. I've got dry clothes and shoes in my backpack. I'll be all right."

We drive in silence, each of us looking out the windows, avoiding the elephant under our passenger's eye.

Mom tries to lighten the mood, asks Alex about himself, his favorite subjects in school, what he likes to do. He opens up. Soon they're talking and laughing like long-lost friends. I don't normally like a Southern accent, but his is charming.

When we arrive at school, Alex thanks Mom again then gets out of the car.

Before I join him, I lean over and give her a kiss on the cheek. "Thanks for being cool to him."

"When am I *not* cool?" She gives me a sly smile as she pretends to dust off her shoulder.

Not sure what *that* has to do with being cool, but I laugh just the same.

I get out and join Alex, then race inside to get out of the downpour.

TODAY'S BEEN a good day because Kaycee isn't at school.

I've passed the twins twice in the hall and neither of them gave me the evil glare. Alice even half-smiled, if you can believe that. The second time I ran into her, between third and fourth period, I considered trying talking to her but didn't have time if I didn't want to be late.

I'm glad they don't seem to hate me without their leader around. Maybe once Kaycee moves on to someone else, they'll forget to dislike me.

ASSUMING SHE MOVES ON.

SHE MIGHT JUST DECIDE YOU'RE WORTH HER FULL-TIME ATTENTION.

I meet Alex for lunch, buying his meal even though he insists I don't need to pay him back. I refuse to take no for an answer, hopping in front of him and handing the cashier money enough for both meals.

We sit at the same table in the back, alone, save for three emo kids with colorful hair and dark clothing at the other end, deep in conversation, ignoring us.

"So," Alex says. "Where is it?"

"Where's what?"

"The secret."

"Oh, crap, I forgot about that."

He smiles and folds his hands on the table like he's not going to take another bite of his spaghetti until I spill my guts.

"I don't have any secrets."

"*Everyone* has secrets, Cora."

"Nothing interesting."

"*I'll* be the judge of that."

"Anyone ever tell you you're a pain in the ass?"

"Usually they say *persistent.*"

"A *persistent* pain in the ass? That's the worst kind."

He laughs. "Stop stalling."

"I'm not stalling. I can't think of anything."

He's still staring at me, expectantly.

"How about you ask me a question instead."

"Anything?"

"Sure." But I'm a little nervous. He seems too polite to ask me something embarrassing or sexual, not that I've anything to talk about on that front. I wonder if he's a virgin. If he's had a girlfriend.

MAYBE HE HAS ONE NOW.

"Do you have Tourette's?"

"What?"

"The blinking you do sometimes."

I look down, my cheeks flaming.

"Sorry. I'm not judging. My cousin had it real bad."

"No. At least, I don't think so. It's an anxiety/OCD thing. Was I blinking just now?"

"No."

And, just like that, I feel compelled to start.

He laughs. "Well, *now* you are."

"It's not funny," I say, half pouting, crossing my arms.

"Sorry. I'm not laughing *at* you. I think it's cute."

"It's not *cute*. I hate it."

"The way your nose scrunches up *is* adorable, I don't care what you say. You kinda look like a bunny."

I stare at him.

"A *cute* bunny."

"Thanks. I think."

"How long have you been doing it?"

"It started in middle school, out of the blue."

"Any other compulsions or tics?"

YEAH, SHE BURNS HERSELF.

WANNA SEE THE SCARS?

"A few. They come and go."

"Like what?"

"I only agreed to one secret."

"Okay, then *you* ask *me* something, Cora."

I like the way he drawls my name.

"Anything?" I ask with a devious smile, even though I haven't yet thought of a question to match it.

"Anything."

I shouldn't ask, but why not be bold? Tit for tat for his question about my blinking.

"Who hit you in the eye?"

He looks down, and for a moment his charming facade is a shadow of itself. Then his confident mask is suddenly back.

"Doesn't matter."

"Hey, if we're playing the Secrets Game, you've gotta answer."

"Oh, yeah? I didn't see that in the rules."

"Yeah. It's one of the first ones," I tease. "Apparently you don't read the manuals."

"Fine. I got in a fight."

"Really?"

"You don't believe me?"

Now I'm looking down. I don't want to hurt his feelings. If he's being abused and isn't ready to talk about it, I shouldn't force him.

"Never mind," I say.

He's staring, as if debating to tell me.

There's *something* he wants to say. I can feel it, heavy in the air.

"Fine." His voice lowers to a whisper. "My dad hit me. But it doesn't matter. Because nothing's gonna change until I'm far away from this place."

I flash back to Emily. The similar positions of Alex, Emily and Kris, all with domineering fathers. It feels like some weird coincidence. Or maybe fate.

Did everyone's father suck except mine?

Lots of kids have crappy, abusive parents. Probably more than you'd think. But three of my friends — pretty much my only friends — having the same situation seems like more than a horrible coincidence.

OR MAYBE YOU JUST ATTRACT MISERABLE PEOPLE WITH DRAMA.

"Why don't you tell someone?"

"Because it doesn't matter. People here think spanking your kids is their God-given right. Besides, Dad's been through enough crap without being thrown in jail. It doesn't happen that often, and the alternative is foster care, where kids get smacked around, too. The devil you know, right?"

I nod.

"Okay, my turn to ask a question. What's it like living in *that house?*"

"What do you mean *that house?*"

"What's it like living where …" He stares at me for a long moment as if I should know what he's talking about, then looks down at his hands. "Oh. You don't know, do you?"

A chill runs through me as if we're not in this cafeteria, but outside in the cold wind and rain. "Know what?"

"Nobody told you what happened there last year?"

"No. What happened?"

"Never mind. It doesn't matter."

"You can't tease me like that. What happened, Alex?"

"The girl who lived there before. She … killed her parents, then herself."

"What?"

"I can't believe nobody told you. I thought realtors were supposed to disclose that sort of thing."

"Did you know her?"

He looks down at his hands again. "Yes. We were friends."

"Oh, my God. I'm so sorry."

"Me, too. She … she had some problems, especially with her father. But I still can't believe she killed her family."

"How? Why?"

"Stabbed them in their sleep. Then hung herself in her bedroom. I guess things were worse than anybody really knew."

I wonder if my room was hers. It would almost have to be, since Dad's office is so small, and Mom's is the only other bedroom in the house.

Visions of this girl dangling from the ceiling — *my ceiling* — flash by. I shut my eyes then squeeze them tight so I don't break into a blinking fit.

My neck and cheeks grow hot despite the sudden ice water in my veins. The necklace is warm against my chest.

"I can't believe nobody told you about Emily."

"Who?"

"Emily Jordan."

Emily? As in Emily from the woods?

I can't remember if she told me her last name.

"What did she look like?"

"She was pretty, though a lot of kids made fun of her because her parents made her wear these awful long black dresses. Like she was in some 1800s religious sect. Emily got someone to buy her some makeup and she started wearing heavy eyeliner and mascara, trying to fit in with the goths because nobody else liked her. But even the goths and emos rejected her. She didn't fit in with any group. I felt terrible for her."

Goth? Just like Emily in the woods.

No, it must be a coincidence. There's got to be more than one goth Emily in this town. In a long black dress. Near my house— her old house.

There's an itch in my brain, something wrong, demanding I scratch it. "Do you have a pic?"

"Yeah, hold on." He fishes the phone from his pocket, then thumbs across the screen until he finds a pic of Emily and turns the screen to me.

My heart stops with a jolt as I stare at the familiar face.

The one I'd met in the woods.

I swallow.

No. Impossible. This can't be —

RELAX, IDIOT.

HE'S CLEARLY MESSING WITH YOU.

THEY ORGANIZED THIS, JUST LIKE KAYCEE AND THE TWINS MADE YOU MEET THEM AT THE MALL.

HE GOT TOGETHER WITH EMILY TO PULL THIS PRANK.

GOD, YOU MUST HAVE A SIGN THAT SAYS, "GULLIBLE, PLEASE TAKE ADVANTAGE OF ME!"

I laugh because what else can I do after learning Alex is a jerk, too?

"What?" he asks, playing dumb like an ace.

Should have known it was too good to be true. Like this cute, nice, witty boy *really* wanted to be friends with me. "This is some kind of joke, right? You're trying to scare me?"

"No, why would I do that?" He's almost convincingly clueless.

I want to blink, need to blink, but I resist the burning urge. I *refuse* to surrender.

I shake my head, not playing along, not wanting to give him, or anyone watching, the satisfaction of me freaking out. I might be naive, but I won't be the butt of some joke. I fully expect Emily to walk up behind me at any moment and yell, "Gotcha, sucker!" Then they'll both erupt into laughter.

Turning around, I check to see if Emily — or maybe some other group of friends, hell, maybe even Kaycee and the twins — are sneaking up to join in mocking me.

But nobody is even paying attention.

"Are you okay?" he asks.

I feel nauseous, and though I'm burning up, cold sweat trickles down my back.

"Um, no, I don't feel well." I grab my bag and stand.

"Cora!"

I ignore him and walk fast — trying not to run — to the closest restroom. When I get there, I burst through the door, rush inside, check to make sure it's empty. Thank God it is. So I shove myself into a stall, slam the door shut, slide the latch locked.

Then I grab my phone to search the Internet for Emily Jordan.

And there it is, the news story.

No, no, no.

This … this can't be real.

I'm shaking.

My heart is racing fast enough to explode.

Is this how people have heart attacks? My heart will fail right here in this stall with nobody around to save me, no one to restart it.

Scared to death. Found in a bathroom stall.

How pathetic.

I stare at the phone.

Everything is getting blurry and dark.

I try to stand. I need to find help before—

I WAKE UP CONFUSED, on the floor, slumped against the bathroom stall door.

Someone is knocking.

"Are you okay?" A girl's voice drifts through the haze fogging my brain. She sounds familiar. Worried.

As I get up, my head swims. My legs are wobbly. I lean against the wall for balance when I bend down for my phone. After I stand, I slip it into my pants pocket then open the door.

It's Alice, the nicer twin.

She steps back a bit once she realizes who I am. Looks away, like she can't possibly meet my gaze without seeing the damage she, her sister, and Kaycee have caused.

"Oh, hi."

"Hi," I mutter as I brush past her. At the sink, I splash cold water on my face then look in the mirror.

Alice is no longer avoiding eye contact. She's staring right at me, clearly worried.

I don't want her pity, or for her to say anything else.

I start blinking.

"Are you okay?" she asks again.

"I'm fine." I close my eyes and splash more water on my face, trying to figure out what happened. I've never passed out like that before. Is something wrong with me? Is this what happens when your brain overheats from anxiety?

Then I remember what caused me to freak out — Emily.

I turn to Alice. "Why do you even care?"

"What?"

"Don't act like you don't know."

She starts to say something, then shakes her head, "You wouldn't understand."

"No, I guess not." I push my way past her and leave.

FIFTEEN

Plans

I'M WALKING HOME, not yet off the school grounds, when Alex starts calling my name.

Crap.

So much for avoiding the inevitable question. Does he know why I reacted like I did? He couldn't possibly have any idea that I sometimes see things that aren't really there. It comes with my depression, especially when I'm exhausted.

AND WHEN YOU DON'T TAKE YOUR MEDS.

Shut up! I don't need this now.

I can't tell Alex any of this. Not just because I don't feel like explaining and having him think I'm a freak, but also because I don't even understand what's going on.

When I was younger, I saw things, and people, that no one else could. Sometimes I'd hear voices. Nothing scary, at first. I might see a woman standing in our yard, or a little kid talking to me in my bedroom, only to have Mom or Dad ask who I was talking to.

At first, they dismissed it as a little kid with an imaginary friend. Or several. Assumed I someone who wanted attention she wasn't getting elsewhere.

It was something they tolerated. Until they didn't.

When I was nine, I saw, and spoke with, my grandma a month after she died. When I told my parents, they thought I was having trouble coping with her passing. Then, one night after I told my Dad something grandma wanted me to tell him, he got furious with me. It was the first time I ever saw him cry. He stormed out of my room. I heard him telling Mom he refused to continue playing along with my attempts to get attention. A week later was my first visit to a shrink.

They all had different theories as to why I was seeing and hearing things, but the solutions were always the same — to medicate me. *Try this pill. No, try that one. Actually, try these.* Funny how far medicine has come, yet how much we still don't know — especially when it comes to the brain.

God, so many pills.

AND YOU HAVEN'T BEEN TAKING THE PILLS, HAVE YOU?

THAT'S WHY YOU'RE SEEING THINGS.

Funny, my critical voice usually tells me *not* to take my meds, insists I don't need them.

I'm such a mess.

And I can't stop thinking about Emily. She seemed so real. We had a long conversation. I remember it perfectly. It's not like the times I've talked to ghosts — or imaginary people — when I was younger. I don't remember much from then except there was always this fuzzy feeling when I tried to recall the exchanges later. They had a dreamlike quality, which convinced me my mind was a liar.

But this time was different.

It felt so real — no different than talking to my Mom or Alex. She was *there*.

Or was she in my head?

If so, is whatever's wrong with me back? Is it getting worse?

I should tell my mother, have her make an appointment.

NO, YOU SHOULDN'T!

YOU WANT TO GET LOCKED UP IN A LOONY BIN AGAIN?

Mom will worry. She'll put me back in a crazy place, and who knows how long I'll have to stay next time.

MAYBE THEY SHOULD'VE NEVER LET YOU OUT.

YOU ARE TOTALLY BROKEN.

Did I really see Emily? Or is this a case of me missing my meds then my mind working behind the scenes, running with some story I'd seen or heard about the murders? Kind of the way your brain constructs dreams around snippets of memory, taking random bits and weaving them into some story that makes sense until you wake up.

But I didn't know about the murders, so how could my brain have done that?

MAYBE YOU JUST DON'T REMEMBER MOM TELLING YOU ABOUT THEM.

MAYBE YOU BLOCKED IT OUT.

WOULDN'T BE THE FIRST TIME YOU CONVE-NIENTLY DID THAT.

I just need to take my meds, then everything will be all right.

I *certainly* did not talk to a ghost.

Definitely didn't talk to her twice!

Nope.

"Cora!" Alex calls out, footsteps pounding louder as he catches up to me.

I turn, pasting on the best everything-is-awesome face I can muster.

"Hey, Alex."

He's looking at me, puzzled. "Are you okay? When you didn't come back to the lunch table, I went looking for you. Where'd you go?"

"Yeah, I just felt sick to my stomach. Went to the bathroom and puked, but I'm better now."

"You sure?"

"Yes, thanks for asking."

"Did you really think I was trying to scare you?"

"I … I dunno. Sorry. People here haven't exactly been nice, so it's hard to know who to trust."

"I'm not like them."

LIKE HE'D TELL YOU IF HE WAS?

Something in his eyes strikes me — a bottomless look that makes me feel like I've known him forever even though we're practically strangers. He *isn't* like them. And he wouldn't mess with me like that.

"Sorry."

"No need to apologize. I get it."

I want to say something else, but what can I say that won't make me sound crazy?

So we walk in silence.

I can feel him looking at me, probably trying to figure me out. Hopefully he'll find something normal to talk about so I can stop dwelling on all of this Emily stuff.

Cool autumn gusts make colorful leaves scrape the pavement. I flash back to a memory of me and my parents walking near our old house on one October day just like this, me so excited for Halloween I could hardly contain myself.

I was six or seven. The first brisk breeze of fall was blowing through my hair, and I loved it. I prattled on, telling my parents about all the costumes I'd seen in the shop and trying to decide which one I'd get.

A blue Camaro full of jocks pulls up beside Alex and me, yanking me back to the present.

I don't recognize any of them, but my body tenses as I wait for a comment on my body or some other insult.

Instead, the guy in the passenger seat, a black kid wearing a Fighting Lions jacket, says, "My man, Alex. What's up?"

They shake hands, some cool bro handshake that looks way too elaborate.

"Not much." Alex looks back at me. "You all know Cora?"

The kid says, "No. *'Sup?*"

"Not much," I say.

Alex introduces them as John, the one in the passenger seat; KJ, the beefy redheaded driver; and Larry, another big dude with brown curly hair who is sitting in the back.

John says, "Just wanted to thank you on that thing. Got an A. You saved my ass."

"Don't mention it."

John reaches into his pocket then hands Alex a bag of something I can't see but assume to be drugs of some sort. "Bonus for ya."

Alex quickly stashes it in his pocket. "Thanks, man."

Does Alex do drugs? I didn't peg him as the type. Now I'm disappointed.

WHY? YOU DO DRUGS.

I *take drugs for medical reasons. Drugs I don't even want to take.*

MAYBE HIS ISN'T MEDICAL, BUT HE'S OBVIOUSLY COPING WITH SOME SERIOUS SHIT — AN ABUSIVE FATHER, A DEAD MOTHER, A NEIGHBOR WHO KILLED HERSELF AND HER FAMILY.

HELL, I'D DO ALL THE DRUGS IN THE WORLD IF THAT WAS MY LIFE!

You're right. I shouldn't judge when I don't know.

As the guys leave, John looks me up and down, giving me a wink that isn't even creepy. "Nice meetin' ya, Cora."

I'm not sure why, but when guys flirt with me, I almost always giggle or laugh. Maybe it's my default attempt at flirting back. Or it's discomfort. Probably the latter. This time, I manage to keep the giggle to a smile and wave. "You, too."

As they drive away, Alex looks at me with a grin. "Ah, John likes you."

"You think?" I wonder if he's jealous. Maybe he's curious about my type.

"Oh, yeah. But I'd steer clear."

"Why?"

"He's … he's not a nice guy."

"But you're friends?"

"He's an acquaintance. There's a distinction."

"Ah, gotcha. That's okay. He's not my type, anyway."

"No?" he asks, almost a bit too quickly. "What *is* your type?"

The look on his face could not be more laid-back, but I'm ninety percent certain he's asking because maybe he likes me.

Maybe eighty percent.

"I dunno. Never really thought about it. But I know he's not it."

"No? How do you not know what kinda guy you like?"

"Who said I even like guys?" I smile.

"Oh?" Alex arches his eyebrows. "Didn't peg you as being into girls." Then, after a moment of reflection, he adds, "Not that there's anything wrong with that."

"Thanks for your approval of whom I choose to lust after."

He looks down, cockiness replaced with embarrassment. I feel both bad and slightly pleased that he cares if I'm offended.

"Relax. I'm just messing with you. Though, I suppose if the right girl came along, I wouldn't be opposed."

I say this partly because it's true. A few times I'm pretty sure I was crushing on Kris. But I also say it to test his response. To see if he'll say something homophobic or creepy. Way too many teenage guys fetishize lesbians, and if he gets all pervy, then he'll probably never respect me.

But he doesn't really react at all.

"What's *your* type?"

"I like a smart girl. Someone quick on her feet, who doesn't just go with what everyone else does. *Sooooo* many girls like that in our school. Basic and fake. *Fasics*, I call them."

"*Fasics!*" I laugh. "Okay, what else?"

"A sense of humor is important."

"Because she's gotta look at your face," I tease.

"Exactly," he says with a laugh. "I mean, I *could* wear a bag, but eventually she's gotta see this ugly mug when I change it and whatnot."

"Of course."

"And, maybe this is the biggest one, she's gotta have a thing she's into. Not just a hobby, but a passion. Something that drives her."

"Like what?"

"I don't care, as long as it's something she pursues with all her heart. Shows me layers, that she's deeper than most."

I wonder if he's only saying these things for my benefit because he knows I like writing and photography.

"What if her passion is collecting Kardashian memorabilia? You still into her?"

"Hmm, I'd *really* have to think about that. Why, is that *your* thing, Cora?"

"Totally."

He pulls away, putting distance between us. "Nooooo!" He throws up his hands, his fingers making a cross as if warding off a demon. Eventually, he comes back. "Well, I suppose I could overlook it."

"So, you said you're into music, right? You play guitar?"

"Guitar *and* piano, actually." He raises his chin in excessive faux pride. "Do you play anything?"

"I've always wanted to learn guitar. I even have my Dad's, but haven't gotten very far. I can't get my fingers to work that way."

"I could teach you to play," he says in a delightfully-eager way that betrays his casual cool.

"Really?"

"Sure. What are you doing tonight?" He pushes his longish hair away from his face.

"Um, lemme see. Oh, yeah, nothing. My mom is working."

"I could come over after I do my chores and stuff … if you want."

If I want? Of course I want.

"That would be cool." I try not to seem too excited. Or desperate.

And just like that, I suddenly have plans.

SIXTEEN

A Change Of Plans

I SKIP DINNER. I *can't* eat anything.

I'm too excited about Alex coming over.

So, instead of making food, I make myself miserable. I spend an hour or so tidying my room presentable then trying on six different outfits.

I hate my entire wardrobe.

Finally, I decide on blue jeans and an old Foo Fighters tee my dad gave me when I showed some interest in one of his favorite bands.

I wonder if Alex likes the band.

STOP TRYING SO HARD.

YOU'LL COME OFF LIKE YOU'RE NEEDY.

But I am needy. I have no friends here. I need a friend.

STOP PRETENDING YOU ONLY LIKE HIM AS A FRIEND.

I do. I barely know him.

LIKE THAT EVER STOPS YOU.

YOU'RE THE THIRSTIEST GIRL EVER.

YOU MUST LIKE GETTING YOUR HEART BROKEN.

It's now after seven o'clock. I'm sitting on the couch

wondering how long Alex's chores take when my phone buzzes with a LiveLyfe message.

It's him.

Hey, sorry I can't make it over tonight.

I stare at the screen, disappointed, waiting for further explanation. But he isn't writing anything else.

HE HAS BETTER THINGS TO DO.

OBVIOUSLY.

HE'S PROBABLY HANGING OUT WITH SOMEONE COOLER OR PRETTIER THAN YOU.

I feel like a birthday balloon, full of helium for a canceled party. I want to ask why, but don't want to seem clingy. Or *needy*.

Best to play it cool. Like I've got better things to do, anyway.

Okay, I text back. Then I add, *No problem.*

While my self-doubt boils with dozens of potential reasons Alex could've canceled, I try and calm myself with reasonable explanations. Maybe his dad won't let him go out.

Rather than focus on the negative, I grab the pasta Mom left for me and heat it up, then head to my father's office, warm bowl in hand.

I fire up his computer and watch some videos on YouTube as I eat, trying to take my mind off of Alex and Emily.

But as darkness descends outside, an uneasiness grows within.

I keep imagining myself walking into the woods right now and seeing Emily in the treehouse, waiting.

This isn't a productive way to spend my time.

I need to take my meds.

At last, a plan. I head to my room then pause in the doorway.

My blinds are open.

I specifically remember them being closed when I went to school.

STOP FREAKING OUT.

MOM PROBABLY OPENED THEM LIKE SHE ALWAYS DOES DURING THE DAY.

How many times would she come into my room and ask, "Why do you always keep it so dark? Let some light in here," as she opened my blinds or curtains?

I cross the room quickly and close them.

Don't look outside.

Don't look outside.

Don't look outside.

Don't look outside.

I know if I do I'll see Emily there, waiting at the tree line, watching.

I'll scream for sure.

I think about the shape I thought I'd seen standing there the other night.

Was it her?

Was it my imagination?

I grab the pill bottles from my nightstand, bring them into my Dad's office, then set them on his desk — all six in a straight little line.

Next I unscrew each cap then deposit the pills one by one in another barracks-neat row.

Just as I'm about to take the first of them, a bright light interrupts me, filling Dad's office.

I get up, kill the lights. Go to the window, peer out. A car is pulling into my driveway.

Who's here?

Too early for Mom, plus it doesn't look like her headlights.

It's not her. The driver backs out of my driveway, turns

around, then parks in front of Alex's house. The vehicle ends up perpendicular to my house, and I can see it from the side just as its lights die.

KJ's blue Camaro.

At least, I think it is. It's too dark to see who's driving or if anyone else is inside it.

Why is he sitting in front of Alex's house?

I see a window open on the second story.

Alex crawls out, climbs onto the portico over his front door, then leaps down.

He lands in the grass, pops up. Doesn't even glance over his shoulder as he runs to KJ's car then gets into the back on the passenger's side.

The car pulls away slowly, not turning its lights back on until it reaches the other end of the cul-de-sac.

SO, THAT'S WHY HE SOLD YOU OUT, TO HANG OUT WITH HIS BOYS.

Maybe he's helping KJ with his homework or something.

OR PARTYING WITH THEM.

FACE IT, THE DUDE ISN'T WHO YOU THINK HE IS.

Wasn't it you who said not all drug users are druggies and I should give him a chance? Now you're trashing him.

I SAID NOT ALL, BUT MAYBE HE IS A DRUGGIE DIRTBAG.

I close the blinds, turn the lights back on, return to my dad's desk, then start screwing the caps back onto their bottles.

I'm about to take the first pill in line when the doorbell startles me.

Again, I go to the window. There isn't a car in my driveway.

Who is ringing my bell at this hour?

The portico blocks my view of the door, so I head

down to see, phone in hand just in case I need to make a quick call to 9-1-1.

I look through the peephole.

Emily.

At my door.

No.

No.

No.

No.

My heart pounds in my throat as I back away from the door.

No, she's not real.

This isn't happening.

No.

No.

She knocks.

Three raps.

"Cora?" Emily says. "Please, open up. I need to talk to you."

I say nothing.

I'm not here. Just go away!

"I know you're there," she says, as if reading my thoughts. "Please, open the door."

OF COURSE SHE'S READING YOUR THOUGHTS.

SHE'S A FIGMENT OF YOUR IMAGINATION.

FACE IT, KIDDO, YOU'VE GONE NUTS.

I can't move.

Literally paralyzed by fear.

"Come on, it's cold out here."

Cold? You're a ghost! You can't feel cold.

Then I have an idea to prove I'm not crazy.

I go to the front window, peel the blinds open just enough to aim my phone at the porch.

I see her on my phone's screen.

I snap a photo.

I move from the window and quickly check my gallery.

The photo of the door is there.

But Emily is not.

Yet she knocks again.

YEP, YOU'VE DONE LOST YOUR MIND!

MAY AS WELL OPEN THE DOOR AND SEE WHAT YOUR CRAZY FIGMENT WANTS!

No! I should not! *I should head upstairs and take my pills and ignore her. If I open the door, I'm inviting the madness. Mom will put me in another place.*

YOU CAN'T IGNORE HER, THOUGH.

SHE ISN'T GOING AWAY.

I'm walking toward the door even though I haven't made a conscious decision to do so. My body is on autopilot, obeying commands from someone else. Or some other part of myself.

FROM YOUR OTHER PERSONALITY, YOU NUT!

My hand is unlocking the door and sliding the security chain off.

What the hell am I doing?

Am I really going to open the door and let her in?

Yes, that's exactly what I do.

SEVENTEEN

The Visitor

"So, I guess you know," Emily says as she brushes past me and into my living room.

How can she brush against me if she's not real? Can I imagine a touch that feels real?

"Why are you here? You're … dead, aren't you?"

My front door is wide open, but I don't close it. Instead I turn to Emily and stare at her. She's wearing the same clothes I've seen her in both other times.

"Yes, and I've been waiting for someone to see me. You're like me when I was alive — you can see spirits."

"No, no I can't. You're not really here."

"Yes, I am, Cora. I might not be living, but I am very much *here*."

"Nope, you're in my head. And I've taken a one-way trip to Crazy Town, population me."

I close my eyes, hoping she'll be gone when I open them, desperate for my house to be empty so I can go to bed like a normal person.

She grabs my arms and shakes me hard.

My eyes snap open. I'm startled at both her touch and

the force with which she's shaking me. I don't think she's trying to hurt me so much as snap me out of denying her existence.

I can't be imagining all of this, can I?

"Let go of me!" I break free from her grip and take a step back toward the door, which still open behind me.

Can I outrun a ghost?

What would've happened if I'd never opened the door? Can she float through things, or is she bound to physics despite not being corporeal?

"We need to talk," she says.

"I don't want to talk. I don't want to even *see* you. This … this is crazy!"

I'm blinking.

YEAH, YOU OUGHTA KNOW CRAZY, BLINKY!

"I think we were meant to find one another, Cora. I think Fate brought you to this house, to find the necklace."

"My father dying brought me here. And if Fate killed my dad just to introduce us, then Fate sucks!"

"You're drawn to me. To our shared pain."

"Shared pain? You killed your parents!"

"You wouldn't blame me if you knew what they did."

"What did they do to you that could make you kill them?"

Was she protecting herself?

"I'll tell you everything. If you still don't want to talk to me after that, then I'll go away and stay there for good. But right now, I need someone to listen. You said you'd do that, remember? You said if I need someone, I could come to you. You didn't lie to me, did you, Cora?"

I shake my head, repeating, "This isn't real, this isn't real" as I blink more than I ever have before, like I'm trying to land the blue ribbon in a blinking contest.

"Would you please stop it?" she yells. "Do you need

proof I'm really here?"

"Yeah, that would be a nice start!"

"Fine. That necklace was mine. I left it in the attic before I killed myself."

I look down at the necklace and start to take it off.

"Don't." She grabs my wrists. "Take it off and you won't be able to see me."

"Great! Sounds like a plan." I try to yank free from her grip.

"That doesn't mean I'll go away. It just means you won't see me. I'll still be here, Cora. I'll still need your help."

I relax my hands, then she lets go.

"Was that you in my Dad's office knocking books over?"

She nods. "I was trying to get you to see me, to hear me. To find the necklace."

"No, no, I still don't believe you. This … this is too much."

"You want proof I'm real beyond me knowing where the necklace was? Fine, I'll show you something else."

"What?"

"You'll see. But you're going to need a shovel."

WE'RE IN THE WOODS, under the treehouse, standing over a hole Emily told me to dig.

I'm staring down at a black book wrapped in several layers of plastic bags.

"What is it?"

"Open it up."

I bend down, grab the book, balance against the shovel — just in case I need to defend myself — then start unraveling the package until I'm holding the book in my hand. The front, in gold foil print, reads, JOURNAL.

It feels oddly heavier than it should, and I'd swear there's an electricity buzzing between me and the book.

I look at Emily.

"Open it."

I do.

The first page has elaborate ink drawings of flowers and twisted tree trunks.

"You drew this?" I'm impressed. Emily is a way better artist than me.

She nods.

Beneath the drawing reads: *Emily's List. Part One: Father.*

"If I'm not here, you wouldn't have found this. Right?"

I'm shaking.

My heart is racing.

My breathing is short, rapid.

"Calm down, you're going to pass out."

"How? *How* are you here? How am I seeing you? How is *any* of this happening?"

"The necklace. It lets you see me more easily."

"Is it magic?"

"Something like that. Something very old, and you wouldn't believe it if I explained. The important thing is that you can see me. You can help."

"Help you do what?"

"Read my journal. That's the first of them."

"How much of this you expect me to read?"

She laughs. "The lists aren't that long. I broke them up by topic. Or rather, by name."

"What do you mean?"

"You'll understand when you read it."

"And then what?"

"Come find me, and I'll give you the next one."

"There are more?"

"Yes."

"And that's what you want? For me to read them?"

"That's part of it."

"What's the rest?"

She smiles. "In time, Cora."

"No, I want to know now."

Suddenly, I hear my mother shouting my name.

"Cora?"

Emily says, "You've gotta go."

I turn and shout, "I'm coming!" to keep her from finding me us. I'm not sure why, as she probably can't see her. Maybe I'm protecting Mom from Emily.

How can you trust anyone who would kill their own parents?

"Fine." I hold up the journal. "I'll read this. But I want answers next time we talk."

"Fair enough. Oh… one other thing."

"Yes?"

"Don't show anyone the journals. Or the necklace."

"Why?"

"Because she won't be happy."

"*Who* won't be happy?"

"Cora!" Mom calls, her voice closer.

"I'm coming!" I yell, annoyed by her impatience. She sounds really near, so I turn to make sure she isn't stepping into the clearing. She's not that close yet.

When I spin back to Emily to say goodbye, I find she's already gone.

Or at least, I can't see her.

I stuff the journal down the front of my pants, make sure my shirt is covering the bulge, then go to Mom.

~

EMILY'S LIST, PART ONE: FATHER

THE FIRST TIME my father made me bleed was when I was three.

I'd left the front door open and our dog, Sampson, got out. He found Sampson quickly enough, but he said he had to teach me a lesson.

He made me break a branch off the tree out back and bring it to him. Then he made me pull up my dress and lean over his lap.

He hit me ten times.

I tried not to cry, but lost it after the first swat.

He left lashes on my ass that were bleeding and bruised for weeks after.

My mother saw the damage and yelled at him, asking why he'd hit a three-year-old so hard.

His answer was to beat the hell out of her until she submitted to his God-given authority as the patriarch. Spare the rod, spoil the child, and all that other shit.

That was the last time she stood up for me.

The next morning, he called me down to breakfast. Mom was sitting at the table with a sullen face. She'd wear that expression forever.

He said he didn't mean to hurt either of us but lessons without pain never stuck. While Sampson was okay, he easily could've escaped or gotten killed. It was his duty as my father to prepare me for the world's cruelty, and that meant showing me my actions have consequences.

I asked why he hit Mother.

He said she'd forgotten her place. Then he turned to her and asked, "Isn't that right, Mother?"

She nodded. "Yes, and I'm sorry."

From that moment on, I hated them both.

They homeschooled me until Owen was born. Suddenly, Dad didn't seem to care about me either way. He had the son he always wanted. So he decided I was a lost cause.

I was finally allowed to go to public school, though they still controlled every aspect of my life, making me wear modest clothing that looked hideous, not letting me hang out with any friends that seemed too "of the world," and never letting me watch TV or listen to music that wasn't religious.

I was miserable.

Despite my father writing me off, he continued to find reasons to hit me. Missed chores, I got the belt. Smart talk, I got the belt along with a smack on the face.

But those weren't the punishments I hated the most.

No, those came when I'd "undermine his authority" by trying to get my mother to take my side in an argument.

Then he'd hit me with the belt before locking me in a pitch-black basement.

The worst was the time I told my little brother the world wasn't really a few thousand years old. Father not only hit me in front of Owen, he said if I ever tried to spread Satan's lies again, he'd take me out of school forever.

Then he locked me in the basement for four days with a bucket and two jugs of water.

At the end of the fourth day, I saw Lilith for the first time. She's really old. I was so hot and hungry, I thought I'd hallucinated her at first.

She told me it was a shame I had to suffer, and that one day she would come back to help me break free.

I didn't see her again for a long time. Not until things got really bad.

Kaycee Reece is next on the list.

EIGHTEEN

Wednesday

I WAKE up to my mom freaking out because I overslept and we're "for sure" going to be late. Specifically, *I'm* making her late.

After my shower, I put on one of the outfits my Mom ordered online — fashionably-ripped jeans and a red-and-black shirt, plaid but not too busy.

I look in the mirror, and despite not having time to do much with my makeup, I like this outfit, a lot. I liked the unicorn sweater, too, but it felt childish compared to what most of the other girls wear.

I consider slipping on Emily's necklace but then decide to leave it on my nightstand.

We drive to school mostly in silence.

"What time did you go to sleep?" Mom asks, an accusing look on her face.

"I dunno. Eleven?"

"Why were you up so late?"

I can't tell her the truth, that I was reading a dead girl's diary. Or that I was trying to call Kris because I needed someone to talk to about all this stuff but she never responded to my messages, so I basically sat up half the night weirded out and sad that my best friend seems to be ignoring me.

"I dunno, just couldn't sleep."

"Did you take your meds?"

"Yes," I say.

"Why were the pills all lined up on your dad's desk?"

Because I got distracted by KJ pulling up to Alex's house before Emily came knocking on my door.

"Oh, wait. I had a phone call and forgot."

"You can't forget to take your meds, Cora! You know what happens."

"I'm sorry. I'll take them tonight. I promise. I'm fine."

She lets out a long sigh. "Come on. We've been through this. You need to take your meds. I pulled a lot of strings to land this job and called in favors to get this house, all to give you a fresh start. I don't ask for much, I really don't. But you have to start doing your part."

I feel like crap. She's right, of course.

I'm blinking back tears, not wanting to cry, especially because she might accuse me of doing so to avoid a fight.

"I'm sorry." I wipe my face. "I promise, I'll take them tonight."

She looks at me for a moment then her voice relaxes. "Okay. So, why couldn't you sleep?"

"I dunno, sometimes I can't sleep. Not everything has to have some deep psychological reason, ya know?"

I shouldn't push back, and I didn't mean to, especially after she seemed to be easing off of me. But sometimes I can't help myself. It's like my brain knows what I shouldn't voice, but my mouth says *Screw it, let's say it!*

Mom looks at me sharply, then turns her attention to

the road. She stares quietly, giving me the silent treatment and making me stew in my guilt.

Mothers must go to Guilt School to learn this stuff because it *always* works so well.

I feel awful for snapping at her, but at the same time, I hate having every little thing in my life psychoanalyzed. I'm a teenager. Sometimes I can't sleep. Sometimes I'm moody. These are normal things, yet she always needs to find a reason, and then, of course, a cure. In pill form, more often than not.

We arrive at school fifteen minutes after first period started.

"Thank you."

"Love you." She gives me a cursory kiss on the cheek.

The thing about losing someone as close as a husband or father is that afterward, whether it's goodnight or goodbye for only a few hours, you're less likely to leave on bad terms, never knowing if that farewell will be the last one.

Rarely do we ever part in anger or silence, even when we're mad.

I think of the last time I saw my father and feel the guilt boiling up again.

"Love you." I climb out of the car.

I go to my locker, deposit my backpack, grab my English book, then head to first period where Mr. Jennings is in mid-lecture.

"Ah, glad you could join us, Ms. Gray."

Kids laugh.

I see Kaycee, back in school today, sending me a nasty smile as I head to my seat.

"The first one is free. After that I need a note or I mark you tardy," Mr. Jennings says, marking me present in the book sitting on top of his desk.

"Yes, sir." I sit down.

As he resumes talking, I find myself unable to focus on anything but Emily's journal. What will I see in the next one, the one about Kaycee Reece?

I turn back and glance at Trent and Kaycee. They're whispering back and forth.

Kaycee gives me bitch eyes. Trent gives a kissy face, then sticks his tongue between his fingers and wiggles it.

I roll my eyes in disgust and turn around to face the front of the class, wondering two things. What did Kaycee do to get on the list, and who else is on it?

I'M IN GYM. God, I hate this class.

It's third period, meaning that unless I shower — which I'm not doing in the locker room — I'll be sweaty the rest of the day. Coach Carson is also this super aggro guy who struts around in a shirt two sizes too tight. He's always spouting clichés like "there's no I in team" and "no pain, no gain" like they're not only his personal mantras, but holy proclamations all must live by.

He's both the gym coach and the varsity football coach. I haven't been to a game, but judging how he barks and yells at kids in a freaking mandatory gym class playing games for fun, he probably rides his football team like a drill sergeant suffering from abstinence.

This is the first day I had to dress out, since my uniform arrived last night — blue shorts and a gray tee that are stuck three counties away from a style. Why Mom didn't get me the brand I asked for, I have no idea. Instead, she got some formless generic knock-offs that fit uncomfortably and have some logo I've never even seen.

I'm not a brand whore, but at least get something close to what the other kids are wearing.

The shorts are baggy, making my butt and hips look way bigger than they are. I can't help but look around at all the other girls. Their uniforms are cut different — more form-fitting — so they look much better than I do in my potato sack. And, of course, we have to tuck our shirts into our shorts, making them stand out even more.

Coach Carson tells us we're going to play basketball today. He picks captains — Kaycee and Charlene, a butch girl with spiky jet-black hair — then tells them to come to the center of the court and pick their teams.

So, I sit on a bench, watching as the two teams in the center of the gym grow while the bench thins to a handful of losers nobody wants.

Soon, I am among the last three kids to be picked. The other two are Stephen, a fat, dorky curly-haired kid who acts like he's still in middle school and Millie, a tiny redhead with glasses thick enough to give her anime eyes.

Kaycee is looking at the three of us like it's the most difficult decision she's ever had to make, and I know she's doing it to make me feel insignificant. I might not look athletic, but I'm tall. Also, though she'd have no way of knowing, I played basketball with Dad in the driveway a lot before he got too busy. No, I never played on a team, but I can dribble, drive, and sink threes well enough.

She looks me up and down, blinks a couple of extra times, then points to Stephen and calls his name.

"Yes!" he shouts. Then he dabs, even though *nobody* dabs anymore, before trotting over to join Kaycee's team.

Charlene looks at the two of us and says, "The new girl."

I go to join her team as Millie, shoulders slumped and

head low, walks over to Kaycee's team. I feel bad for being happy I wasn't picked last. Bad for Millie, too. She looks so used to dejection, I can feel it wafting off of her. I find myself wanting to give her a hug, but given my luck, even she would reject my overtures.

I start the game on the bench with four other kids, watching the action.

Even hating Kaycee, I find myself admiring her basketball skill. She's fantastic. Sinking threes from deep behind the line, taking it to the rim, blowing by defenders. The only thing she hasn't done yet in the blowout is dunk.

After Kaycee makes an impossible three, the thin blonde beside me says, "Damn."

I turn to the girl. "Is she on the school's basketball team or something?"

"Yeah. Her and Charlene are on the girls' team. Scott, Duncan, and Mike are on the boys'."

I don't remember which guy is which, so I nod. I assume all the good players are on Kaycee's team, because ours is laughably bad outside of Charlene and the only other black kid in the gym, a tall guy named James. But even they aren't as good as Kaycee's team.

I sit on the bench with the blonde for most of the game, except when she swaps with a short, clumsy boy.

Finally, with three minutes to go and the other team winning by twenty-five points, Charlene calls me into the game.

"New girl."

I swap with James, who isn't happy about being taken out, and she tells me to play the five spot.

Kaycee enters the game, leaving the bench to score on me.

I'm not as good as her, but won't let her roll right over

me like most of the other kids on my team. And if I get the ball, I'll do my best to score.

Thirty seconds left, and I'm guarding the paint as Kaycee tries dishing it to the other team's center in front of me.

I anticipate her pass, step in front of it, and steal.

I'm tempted to drive it so I can score, but then I spot Charlene blowing past Kaycee.

I pass it perfectly to her and she nails an easy layup.

Kaycee glares at me.

I smile.

She calls a time out once her team has the ball back.

Charlene calls us to huddle, pats me on the shoulder saying, "good steal" then tells us to double team Kaycee — she always has the ball at the end of the game. "Hell, triple team her if you have to. We ain't gonna win, but let's show them we're not backing down."

The kids all nod, though, judging from what I've seen so far in the game, on the rare occasions they break from zone defense, they get confused and leave almost everybody on the other team open.

Game's back on.

Kaycee is back with the ball, holding it for the final shot with ten seconds left.

There's two people on her, and then three, leaving an extra pair wide open.

My head is on a swivel as I look from right to left, covering three people. I'm at a severe disadvantage, but I'm ready to take on whomever Kaycee dishes the ball to.

But Kaycee doesn't pass it.

With five seconds on the clock, she slips past three defenders and charges straight at the basket. And me.

I can either defend Kaycee and risk her passing it

behind me to someone I left open, or hang back and risk her scoring over me.

Even though she should pass the ball to one of the two other people I can't defend, I know she won't. She wants to score on me. I can see it in her eyes.

So I stay on her.

And she's moving fast, going for a layup.

I step up, plant my feet in the paint, throw up my arms to block her shot.

She should be stopping short and shooting, trying to get it over my outstretched hands.

But instead, she keeps the ball and charges right into me, her elbow slamming into my nose like a hammer.

I go down.

Embarrassingly easily, as if punched.

My nose explodes in pain, blood erupting everywhere.

She roars, finally releases the ball.

It sails in for the final basket as the buzzer sounds.

She should've been called for a foul, but Coach Carson doesn't blow the whistle.

Game over.

Kaycee runs backwards to join her team, smiling at me, nodding like she'd just won the championship game.

My nose is pulsating. It's pain unlike anything I've ever felt. Blood streams through my fingers as I work to contain it. I can't cry or let her see me wince.

"Suck it up, Buttercup," Carson barks at me.

I want to punch him in his big stupid face.

Charlene offers her hand, and I take it with my unbloodied right, thanking the girl as she helps me to stand.

"You okay?" She brings me a wad of paper towels to hold up to my nose.

"Yeah, thanks."

We head back to the locker room and I'm brought into Coach Darcy's office, where she gets me some ice and checks out my nose to make sure it's not broken.

Coach Darcy is an older woman with graying blonde hair pulled back in a severe ponytail. Her face is leather, but she has kind blue eyes that remind me of my grandma on my father's side. I wish I'd gotten her class instead of Coach Carson's.

"You okay?" I think she's asking if the hit was intentional. Maybe she'd heard something from one of the other girls.

But I'm not a narc. Being one is a sure way to get bullied even more.

"Yeah, thank you." I leave her office then head to my locker.

There's a weird silence in the hall. Everyone's attention is on me, like I'm the victim of a beatdown.

Nobody's making eye contact.

I feel an odd sense of tension, like something is about to happen.

Do they think I'm going to cry or snap or something?

I'm doing my best not to blink as anxiety starts to swell in my chest. Tension winds like a tight cord that might snap at any second.

I don't see Kaycee or any of her friends, so I'm guessing she's already changed and is off to her next class. Or maybe Coach pulled her aside to lecture her privately.

As I reach my locker, the pungent smell of vinegar overwhelms me, though I don't see a spill.

I reach for the combination lock to turn it, 21-10-16, when I see that the lock isn't there.

I look up to double check that this is, in fact, my locker.

It is.

Who broke in?

What did they do?

I open the door.

And then the tightening coil finally snaps as laughter rolls all around me.

NINETEEN

A Bad Day Gets Worse

SITTING in my locker in a damp pile are my clothes — drenched in vinegar.

Laughter erupts all around, as if everyone was in on the joke but me.

I turn and see who is no doubt the orchestrator of this — Kaycee and her friends standing at the end of the row, laughing, staring right at me.

I want to scream.

I want to hit her.

I want to hurt her.

Instead, my chest tightens until I can't breathe.

And I'm blinking like an idiot.

Damn it.

I turn, so they can't see me lose it.

They're still giggling.

I hate them.

I want them to pay.

I slam my locker shut, head to the bathroom, lock myself in a stall, then finally allow the tears to flow.

God, I cry a lot in bathrooms.

What am I supposed to do now? I can't wear those clothes. And I can't wear my baggy gym shorts and shirt the whole rest of the day. I feel self-conscious enough without having those godawful shorts on all day.

The only good thing is that I didn't bring my backpack, or phone, to gym class, and both of those are safe in my locker in the 400 building.

I wait in the bathroom for the other girls to get dressed and leave the locker room. Then I'll go to Coach Darcy, and tell her what happened, though I'm still not gonna snitch. Maybe she can help me figure out a clothing situation.

My nose is still throbbing.

I'm mad that my brand-new outfit is ruined, at least for the day. I'm still not sure how I'll get my clothes home without Mom knowing what happened. I can't tell her I'm being picked on again.

She'll either blame me and say I'm attracting the wrong attention, or she'll feel sorry for me, maybe even be sad that we moved. I don't want any of those things.

I don't think my day can get any worse.

MY DAY IS GETTING WORSE.

Alex isn't here, so I'm sitting in front of my locker, eating a peanut butter and jelly sandwich, reading a book on my phone, wearing clothes from the Lost and Found that are only slightly less awful than the gym outfit.

I'm in a dark blue cotton skirt that brushes my ankles and a godawful turtleneck that isn't just itchy, but feels designed specifically to choke a person to death. They don't go together, and neither piece is anywhere near fashionable. They must have gone missing a decade ago at least.

As I'd dressed in the locker room, I'd heard girls laughing. How many of them were in on the prank? How many watched as I went to my locker, waiting for me to see what had been done?

And, of course, my nose is still radiating pain.

I look like an idiot. The stares and giggles as I walk the halls are unbearable.

Trent and some other douche jocks passed me before lunch and one of them said, "Damn, looking hot, Blinky." Then they laughed.

I couldn't ignore the sting of an old nickname haunting me in a new school. I was *supposed* to be starting a new chapter of my life, but no matter what I do, the past won't let me turn the page.

At least Coach Darcy didn't push me to talk. She offered to take my clothes home to wash when I told her I was afraid to tell my mom.

So, at least I don't have to throw them away.

I try to focus on my book while eating, but I'm thinking about Alex and wondering why he sold me out last night. What did he go and do with KJ? And why isn't he here today? Did he get in trouble? Did his dad beat him so badly he can't go to school? Did he run away?

I'm as mad as I am worried.

MOM PICKS me up after school.

She asks about my nose right away, but I brush it off as a basketball injury, which isn't technically lying.

She doesn't say a word about my outfit, though. Other

than a bit about my nose and some small talk, she's quiet, as if her mind is on something else.

Maybe she's still mad at me from this morning.

Not wanting to worsen her mood, I stare out the window, thinking about my crappy day. About Alex. About Emily and her journal — and what the next one might tell me.

I CHANGE into jeans and a long-sleeved black tee, then go downstairs to make chicken and pasta for dinner while Mom argues with someone on the phone at the publishing house. She thinks they're underreporting sales on some of his bigger titles and screwing us, so she's threatening legal action.

I'm not sure if she's bluffing.

During dinner, Mom doesn't say a word about the call. She picks at her food and nurses her third glass of wine.

Outside, it begins to rain. My heart sinks because I might not be able to see Emily tonight. I need to talk to her and get the next journal. I want to know who else hurt her and what she wants from me.

Mom takes a call in her bedroom after dinner. While she's distracted, I slip on the necklace, don my raincoat, then head to the treehouse, hoping to find Emily there.

It's dark outside, so I turn back, duck inside to grab the flashlight, then once more head into the rainy night, walking as fast as I can without running and slipping.

Emily is sitting at the treehouse, legs swinging over the ledge, rain soaking her hair and clothing.

"Did you read it?" she shouts over the howling wind as I draw closer.

"Yes. And I'm sorry. Your father was so awful to you."

She nods and waves me up.

I climb the ladder then head inside the treehouse with her, rain battering the roof and windows as I do.

Once inside, I can't stop looking at her.

She doesn't look like a ghost. Wet hair hangs in her face, and her clothes are soaked through. I can even smell her — a sweet scent that reminds me of my childhood, but in a way I can't place.

"Do you see why I killed them?"

"I can see why you killed your father, but not your mother. Why didn't you tell someone or call the police to say he was beating you?"

"I told our pastor. He went to my father and asked if it was true. Of course, he lied, and the pastor believed him. Obviously I was influenced by Satan. They even did an exorcism."

"What?"

She laughs.

"Oh, my God. That's even a thing?"

"I told you my father was crazy religious. No offense if you are." And, after a beat, she asks, "Are you?"

"Yes," I tell her. "Well, sorta. I guess."

"I feel ya."

"It's complicated since my dad died. I mean, I believe, but a part of me needs to know what kind of God would take a girl's father away. Or allow so many horrible things to happen — like your abuse."

She says nothing.

A question pops into my mind, one I've wondered about for most of my life. Something she might be able to answer.

"*Is* there a God? I mean, you're dead, so you must know what's next. Right?"

"I don't know. I haven't been visited by angels or

anything like that since I died. One minute I was dead and everything was dark, and the next, I was here. I've been wandering around my house, well, your house, and these woods. Whenever I try to go farther, I pass out and wind up here."

"Did you leave the necklace knowing that whoever found it would be able to see and talk to you?"

"She told me to leave it. Said someone else would come, someone I could trust."

"Who told you that?"

"Lilith, the woman who gave it to me. She told me to hide it before I died. So you could find it."

"*Me* specifically?"

"I don't know. Tell me … have you always seen ghosts?"

"When I was younger. But the older I got, the more I convinced myself it was all in my head. Or, rather, the doctors convinced me. If the ones I saw after … well, after my father died, were real, then I'd prefer not to."

"Lilith said that only certain children can see spirits. Special children. But as they get older, most of them lose the ability. The necklace enhances it."

"How?"

She looks around as if spooked. Scoots over to one of the windows and looks outside, as if she's seen something that scared her.

Then, apparently no longer alarmed, she sits back down and meets my eyes.

"What happened to your nose?"

"Got hit in a basketball game. No big deal."

"You sure?"

"Yeah." I look away.

She stares at me for a moment as if chewing on her

follow-up questions. Instead, she asks, "Do you want to read the next journal?"

"Yes. I want to know what Kaycee Reece did to you."

Suddenly, I'm blinking.

She looks at me, head tilted ever-so-slightly. "What's wrong?"

"Nothing. It doesn't matter."

She reaches out and takes my hand into hers.

It's warm to the touch.

I can feel her pulse, even though a ghost shouldn't have one.

"It's okay, you can tell me. I'm here for you."

Just to hear those words from someone who can maybe understand my pain hits me hard in the feels. Even if she's dead, Emily's here, and that's more than I can say about anyone else. Yes, Mom is here for me, but I can't tell her the things that are happening as she'll only worry, or worse, get angry at me for not "trying harder."

Throw me in a mental hospital like she did for two weeks after I tried to kill myself.

I blink back my welling tears.

"It doesn't matter," I say, already trying to talk myself out of confession.

"Yes, it does. *You matter*. And I'm not just saying that because you're the only friend I have. Hell, the only person who can see me. Okay, maybe that's part of it," Emily laughs, "but still, there's a connection between us. Can't you feel it?"

"Weirdly enough, yes."

And then I tell her everything that happened at school.

After I'm done, she says, "These are the same people who picked on me."

"What?"

"Yes, Kaycee was the ringleader, and her freaky twin friends followed every little thing she did."

I don't tell her about my thoughts on Alice, because I'm still not sure about her, nor do I know if Alice is one of the names on her list.

"What's your list for?"

"The people who hurt me."

"Why did you make a list? Were you planning to kill them, too?"

"No. I want revenge, but I don't want to kill them."

"What kind of revenge?"

"Maybe you can help me think up something."

"As much as I hate Kaycee, and I might want to punch her in the face myself, I'm not going to *plot revenge!*"

Something about that makes me feel like I crossed the line from defending myself to actively trying to hurt someone. That's a slippery slope I don't want to go down.

She stares at me, then nods. "Sorry. You're right. I *should* move on. Never mind."

She gets up to leave.

She's crawling to the door.

Let her go. This can't end well. Just let her go.

"Wait!" I call out.

Emily stops and looks back.

"Maybe I can help you think of something, but … but I can't be involved in hurting anyone. I'm sorry about what they did to you, but I can't—"

"I'm not asking you to do anything you don't want to do. You're my only friend, Cora. I don't want you to get in trouble." She takes my hands and smiles sweetly. "I would never hurt you. You know that, right?"

UM, NO, WE DON'T KNOW THAT!

"Yeah, um, yes. I know that."

"Good. Listen, you don't have to do anything if you

don't want to, but you should read the journals, if only to know what your enemies are capable of."

"What are they capable of?"

"Destroying your life, making you wish you were dead."

The rain has stopped. I can hear Mom calling my name.

I open the treehouse door, then yell out to let her know I'm coming.

I'm about to ask Emily where the next journal is buried, hoping I'll have enough time to get to it before Mom comes looking for me.

But I don't need to, because the journal is in her hands, then a second later in mine.

Before I leave, she says, "Hey."

"Yes?"

"If you're ever feeling down, just wear the necklace and know you're not alone." She hugs me.

"Thank you."

It feels so good and reminds me how much I miss Kris's hugs.

As I head home, I decide not to take my meds tonight. I need to put the ones on Dad's desk back in their bottles and bring the others back to my room so Mom doesn't freak out again.

I feel guilty not taking them, but I don't need them now. After having talked to Emily, the warm fuzzies of friendship are helping me. It's something I haven't felt since Kris, and I can't stand the thought of dulling the only good thing I'm feeling these days.

~

EMILY'S LIST, PART TWO: KAYCEE REECE

. . .

KAYCEE and I became friends in eighth grade.

She was the new girl, and not yet the beautiful, popular blonde the whole school knows her as now.

No, she was short, kind of awkward, and hella shy.

We met in gym class when we were both sitting on the benches, not dressed out. She didn't seem to care that I was this moody emo chick.

We bonded over music and books, and, most of all, TV and movies.

I wasn't allowed to watch anything that wasn't "clean and Godly" so Kaycee introduced me to a ton of great TV shows and movies at her house. Like all the R-rated stuff that would give my dad a heart attack if he knew I saw it.

(Maybe THAT is one way to get rid of him!)

She had Netflix, and her parents had a giant library of movies. It was like this whole new world opening up to me. For the first time, I saw people like me in movies and TV, conflicted, angsty. In pain.

And I loved seeing people like me.

Then there's all the scary movies we watched.

I was a total wuss, a good little Christian girl terrified of anything even remotely "evil" like witches, demons, or magic. Weird how much of Dad's fear has seeped into me.

So Kaycee loved to scare me.

And, weird as it is, I loved being scared by the shows, so long as she was there on the couch or in the bed with me.

We hung out all the time.

Did everything together.

My parents even liked her, but only because she pretended to be a good Christian girl whenever she came over to my house.

THAT should've been my first warning sign that she wasn't who she pretended to be.

But she was my first real friend. Someone I THOUGHT I could trust.

She told me her secrets — how she secretly felt ugly, how her parents didn't really love each other even though they showed this perfect exterior to the rest of the world, and ... how she cut.

That was the darkest secret we shared.

We both cut to deal with the pain.

I told her I cut, too. Told her what my father did to me.

She felt sorry for me because my parents were so strict. She'd buy me soda and candy, things my parents never let me have.

We were inseparable.

She was my everything.

I never considered myself gay, nor sexual in any way, really. But I had a huge crush on her, which I kept to myself.

Then came the worst summer ever — between eighth and ninth grade.

Kaycee went away. Her family has a place in Bermuda. She was so excited to be going away for her annual vaca-tion. I was happy for her even though I knew my weeks would be hell without her.

And they were.

I told myself it was only temporary. Once school started back up, my bestie would be back and life would return to only sucking half the time.

Instead, Kaycee came back a few inches taller, hair a bit lighter, skin sun-kissed and flawless, and, oh yeah, now she had *huuuuuuge* boobs. She was absolutely beautiful, while I was still ... me.

Suddenly all the popular people, the same kids who'd

ignored her all this time, wanted to be friends. It was like she won the lottery and everyone suddenly wanted to hang out with her. They invited Kaycee to parties, dances, sleepovers, and all the other fun stuff that rich, pretty people get to do in high school.

And, just like that, she stopped talking to me.

It was subtle, at first. She was always just "busy."

But whenever I cornered her at lunch or outside school, I could tell she was embarrassed by me.

She was so much prettier, while life spent the summer hitting me with an ugly stick. I'd gotten taller and more awkward. I had acne. Even the emos rejected me for thinking I was fake, trying to get attention.

I know a lot of people are lonely, but most of them have a friend or two, someone to make life a little more bearable. Imagine having no one at all. Not even your family, the people who were *supposed* to love you.

That was me. I only had Owen, my four-year-old brother.

Life was a cold gray nothingness. I was virtually invisible at school, only to come home to a place where I couldn't hide from my father's wrath or leering eyes.

I wanted to die.

Then, during Christmas break, I got a call.

It was Kaycee, saying she felt bad that we hadn't talked in forever. She wanted me to come to her house for a sleepover.

Suddenly, my world was in color again!

I didn't know her parents were out of town until I got there. We'd be hanging out with the whole house to ourselves. It would be an exciting night filled with movies, junk food, and catching up.

Things started that way, as we watched our favorite

film together in the media room, it felt like we'd never stopped being friends.

Then the doorbell rang.

A bunch of her friends showed up with alcohol. Among them, Trent Cullen, though they weren't dating yet.

At first, I was sad our time alone was ruined. But then she handed me a beer and said, "Dude, relax. Have some drinks and a little fun for once in your life."

I felt anxious as hell, but I also saw it as a chance to be back in her life. If I partied with Kaycee and her friends and everyone liked me, maybe she wouldn't treat me like the secret friend she was embarrassed to have.

So I drank for the first time ever.

The get-together turned into a pool party.

And, for the first time in my life, I — *yes, me!* — was the center of attention, saying witty things and making the cool kids laugh. Girls I'd always seen in school but who'd never seen me suddenly wanted to talk and maybe get to know me.

They asked about the scars on my legs and arms, which I couldn't hide with my bathing suit, but nobody judged me. They seemed genuinely interested. I didn't tell them everything, of course. Only that I was "going through some things."

There was a moment when Kaycee and Trent were kissing in the pool. She looked over at me with this weird look, one I didn't recognize until a few days later as jealousy.

One thing led to another. I got drunk, passed out. When I came to, Trent Cullen and I were alone in a room, making out.

I remember asking him, "Aren't you Kaycee's boyfriend?"

He said, "It's all good."

I don't know why, but I believed him and kept kissing him.

The next thing I remember, his hands were reaching into my bottoms.

It triggered something in me.

I thought of my father touching me and freaked out. Started saying, "No, I don't think this is a good idea."

I wanted him off of me.

But he wouldn't take no for an answer.

So I screamed.

I remember the look in his eyes, the shock on his face. And I was so embarrassed.

Desperate to flee the room, I ran out in my bathing suit, stumbled down the stairs, frantically looked for my clothes. I was dizzy, crying.

I found myself in the living room where a bunch of people were hanging out, and every eye had found me.

I puked.

People started laughing.

Then Trent came down the stairs and threw my clothes at me. "Here's your clothes, you dumb slut."

Not one person asked if I was okay.

Not even Kaycee, who was sitting on the couch with the twins. Instead, her face was angry. She got up and charged at me, demanding to know what I'd done.

I didn't know what to say. Did she actually think I made a move on her boyfriend?

"He made a move on me!"

"She threw herself at me, the damned psycho!" Trent yelled.

I shook my head, "No, that's not what happened."

I'll never forget the glare in Kaycee's eyes. The pure hate.

She pointed at the door. "Get the hell out of my house, loser."

Loser?

More laughter.

I wanted to explain things, to make things okay, but not with all the most popular people in the school looking at me and laughing.

I ran out of the house, pulling on my shirt on as I left her yard, breaking down on her front lawn in hysterical sobs.

I didn't know what to do.

Couldn't go back in. Couldn't call my parents.

So I walked to the woods near my house, went up to the treehouse, and cried myself to sleep.

The next morning, I went home as if Kaycee's mom had dropped me off. And I didn't hear from her, or anyone else. I tried calling, but she never answered.

When school started back up, I was no longer invisible.

Now I was the psycho. The slut. The cutter.

So many rumors spread about me. Some by Trent, others by Kaycee. More from whoever else wanted to make up crap.

Just like that, both home and school were utter hell.

That's when I really started to wonder if I'd be better off dead. The only thing keeping me alive was knowing if I died, Dad might turn his rage on Owen.

Okay, one other thing kept me alive, but I'll get to that later.

TWENTY

Thursday

I'M EXHAUSTED. I spent half the night re-reading Emily's journal and the other half crying. I might have gotten ten minutes of sleep.

Mom wasn't feeling good this morning, so I'm walking to school. I'm wearing Emily's necklace inside my shirt, and it feels warm against my chest, comforting somehow.

I'm surprised to hear footsteps coming up behind me and Alex's voice calling, "Wait up."

I turn to see if he's sporting any new bruises. He's not. But he notices mine.

"What the hell happened to your nose?"

"Got hit playing basketball." I don't want to get into the drama. "What happened to you yesterday?"

"I woke up so sick I could hardly move. Heck, Dad didn't even argue with me, so I must've been pretty bad."

"Sorry to hear that." I wonder if he was sick from sneaking out with KJ and partying. Maybe using those drugs John gave him?

But I don't say that. I don't want him to know I saw him sneaking off. For one, I don't want him to think I'm spying on him. For two, I want to see if he volunteers the information. And last, I want to see if he has a tell when he lies, in case I decide to ask Alex why he stood me up.

Finding people's tells, what they do when they lie, is a trick I picked up from one of Dad's books.

I'd much rather trust Alex than test him, but I've been burned before.

"You okay now?" I ask.

"Yeah."

TEST HIM!

TEST HIM ON THE LIE YOU KNOW HE'S TELLING NOW OR YOU MIGHT NOT GET ANOTHER CHANCE!

"So, what happened to you Tuesday night, when you were gonna come over?"

He looks down for a moment, then meets my eyes. "My dad wouldn't let me go out."

LIAR!

And that's his tell, looking down, or looking away. I've got him.

I'm pissed, but I can't say anything without coming off like I'm way more invested in him than I should be. We barely know each other. Maybe he has reasons to lie, reasons he can't explain to me yet.

I lie every day about what happened with my dad's death, and I have good reasons. But his lie feels different, the kind someone says when they don't want to hang out with you, like when they got a better offer or when they don't really care.

Why have that in my life? I'm sick of fake people, fake friends. I need something real, someone I can trust.

"Oh, that's okay," I say, suddenly re-evaluating him. He seemed so nice and genuine, but there's also a sketchy side I probably can't trust. I need to know what's really happening with him, but how do I learn that? And is he even worth it?

It's usually best to steer clear of the drama.

At least that's what Mom always says.

I think back on how effortlessly he seems to get along with so many different types of people. He said it was because he did a lot of the popular kids' homework for them.

But maybe that was a lie.

He is probably a drug dealer!

WELL, HE'S GOT A DIRTBAG DADDY, A DEAD MOMMY, AND NO REAL DIRECTION.

CAN YOU SAY YOU'RE SURPRISED?

I hate that critical part of me wanting to see the worst in him. But at the same time, *something* is going on.

"I miss anything at school yesterday?"

I want to tell him about the locker room incident, but right now I don't trust him.

"No, just another day with a broken nose."

"Is it broken?"

"Nah, I'm sure it'll be fine."

The rest of the walk is uneasy silence and awkward small talk, both of us dancing around things we don't want to discuss. And it totally sucks.

Easy conversation was one of the things I liked most about Alex.

"Seeya at lunch?"

"Sure," I say as we go our separate ways.

I walk into first period and see Kaycee and Trent standing with some of the other kids, laughing and chatting. Kaycee glances my way and says, "Ew, what smells?"

They laugh.

I can't see them anymore without seeing them through Emily's eyes, remembering what they'd done to her. It feels almost as if they'd done it to me.

Mr. Jennings isn't at his desk yet, and most of the class is still empty.

I sit down and ignore them.

But I can feel them staring.

Suddenly, they're not *just* staring.

Trent sidles up to me then leans on my desk "So, me and a couple of guys were talking about the saying, 'Once you go black, you never go back,' with respect to black dudes. We were wondering if it's the same with black chicks."

I look up at him but say nothing. For one, I'm not sure what to say at such a racist comment. For two, I'm afraid if I *do* say anything, I'll get emotional and start blinking.

He's smiling his arrogant asshole's smile.

I think of how he treated Emily. How he'd tried to take advantage of her when she was drunk at the party, then called her a psycho and a slut and started all those rumors.

I see him and that slick smile and I want to punch him, knock his teeth down his throat.

My leg is shaking. Not a lot, and I'm not sure if he can tell, but I hate showing any signs of fear — especially to someone like him.

"Ah, I see. You're playing shy." He reaches out and touches my hair.

I flinch, push his hand away, and start blinking.

Damn it.

"Don't touch me."

"Don't flatter yourself. You ain't my type."

The necklace is warm — a token of a friend who's gone through this battle before — and I feel almost like Emily is here with me.

I meet his stare with a smile. "Why? I'm not drunk enough?"

His eyes widen. "What did you say?"

"Nothing," I say with that same screw-you smile. "Don't be such a psycho."

Mr. Jennings comes in.

Trent looks at the teacher then back at me before eventually walking away, brushing his hand hard against my shoulder as he goes by, probably trying to intimidate me.

I smile at my desk.

He mumbles something to Kaycee.

She asks, "What did she say?"

I don't turn around to acknowledge her.

I'm satisfied knowing she's angry.

KAYCEE COMES up to my desk the minute the bell rings, blocks me from standing, and says, "You got something to say to my boyfriend, Blinky?"

The necklace is warm against my chest, almost like it's vibrating. I'm about to reach for it, to see if it's only my imagination, but my attention is pulled to Trent, coming up behind her, and glaring at me.

"Nope," I say with a smile. "And by the way, you two make a *perfect* couple. You're *both* psychotic."

Kaycee looks at me like she's searching for a comeback, or maybe trying to figure out what I meant. She leans in and sniffs. "You smell like douche."

"Well, you date one, so I guess you'd know."

Her eyes widen.

Trent's too.

My heart is racing, eyes blinking, body flooding with adrenaline. My leg bouncing. I don't even care.

Part of me wants them to hit me. Even if it's Trent, and even if he'd kick my ass. I want it!

"Apologize to him, right now," Kaycee says, her voice going high enough that it's almost a dog whistle.

Mr. Jennings calls out from his desk, "There a problem, ladies?"

Kaycee looks at him with her big phony smile. "Not at all, Mr. Jennings, I was just talking with the new girl."

"Why don't you all get to your next class?"

Kaycee and Trent both leave, neither of them looking back at me.

I'm about to leave the classroom, when Mr. Jennings says, "I need to talk to you, Miss Gray."

Kaycee and Trent, waiting on just the other side of the door, take it as their cue to leave.

"They bothering you?"

"Nothing I can't handle, sir," I say, still filled with an overwhelming sense of joy from standing my ground. I'm almost cocky, something I've never felt before.

"And that bruised nose?"

"Basketball injury."

He looks at me skeptically. "It can be hard to fit into a new school. If you need someone to talk to, we have a great guidance counselor. Ms. Baxter."

"I'm good. But thank you." I'm touched he cares enough to tell me.

But I don't want to talk to anybody about what's going on. They can't help me with the kids in school. If I narc on Kaycee and Trent for picking on me, it'll only make the bullying worse.

Best to take care of it myself.

"Okay," he says, though he clearly doesn't believe me. "Have a good rest of the day."

"You, too," I say as I leave.

TWENTY-ONE

Retaliation

I CHANGE in the bathroom nearest my locker so I can avoid both having my clothes ruined *and* the locker room in general. Then I head straight to the gym, all dressed out. My stomach is nervous as I dread another confrontation with Kaycee.

Coach Carson isn't here today, so both classes are playing basketball against each other under Darcy, meaning Kaycee and I are sharing a team. However, because I'm still deemed off-the-bench material, we manage to go the whole class without ever sharing the court.

After class, Coach Darcy asks me into her office. She gives me my freshly washed clothes in a black plastic bag.

"Thank you."

"You still don't want to tell me what's going on?"

"I still don't know."

"I heard you and Kaycee Reece had a run-in on the court."

"Just a hard foul, nothing more." I'm sure it isn't convincing.

She nods. "Okay, well if she gives you any problem, let me know. I can talk to the basketball or cheer coach, and one of them can have a word with her."

"That won't be necessary, but thank you, Coach Darcy. And thanks for washing my clothes." I hold up the bag as I leave.

I pass Kaycee and her friends without looking to see if they're eyeing me. They probably think I was in Coach's office narcing on them.

I rush to my locker so I can grab my backpack, then to the bathroom so I can change into my regular clothes.

I have to wait for an open stall, and by the time one is free there's only a minute before the bell, which'll mark me late for my next class.

I get dressed in a flash, my heart racing, hoping I'm not late for history. I hate being tardy and loathe the stares even more. It's like I'm carrying a giant sign that says, *Look at me!*

So far I've managed to fly under the radar in that class, not attracting any attention from any of the popular kids, of which there are only a few. No one has pointed out my blinking. But if I come in late, blinking because I'm nervous, it could paint a target on me in there, too.

I finish changing then throw open the bathroom door.

Kaycee and the twins are standing between me and the exit.

She is chewing gum and blows a giant bubble. "So, you wanted to say something to me, *bitch?*"

Amber locks the door.

My heart is frozen.

I'm blinking.

I'M GOING TO DIE.

I'm not going to die.

I'm not going to die.

I'm not going to die.

I'm not going to die.

The necklace is warm against my chest again, as if focusing my fear into heat. What was comforting earlier now is burning.

My legs are jelly.

All the bravery I felt when I was being a smart-ass earlier is gone.

Why did I egg them on?

What was I thinking?

"I've got nothing to say to you." I walk toward the door even though no one seems willing to move.

I take the path to the left of Kaycee, where Alice is standing.

She steps sideways to block my exit and sternly meets my gaze.

"I'm talking to you, bitch!" Kaycee grabs me by the hair and yanks me back.

My backpack falls out of my hand as I yelp, less from pain than surprise. "Hey!"

I fall back against the cold, tiled wall, yet manage to stay on my feet. Anxiety presses in on all sides as this threatens to escalate into something horrible. My heartbeat thrums in my neck.

"Not runnin' your mouth now, I see." Kaycee smacks me hard across the face.

And then, just like that, she and Amber are on me, shoving me towards a stall door, punching and scratching as they push me.

I should scream to draw attention, but I'm frozen — taking the abuse as they unleash it upon me.

The lights go out as I fall back onto the toilet, the metal back hitting me hard in the spine.

A loud noise — might be blood rushing in my veins, could be the walls shaking — reverberates in my skull.

I don't know who killed the lights. But the bathroom is now pitch black, save for the slight red glow on the walls from the EXIT sign.

A shadow falls over Kaycee.

She turns to see who's standing there.

Then she's yanked backwards with a scream, right into the row of sinks.

There's a sickening CRACK as she hits them, then she collapses to the ground.

Oh, my God! Is she dead?

I don't see who violently yanked her away from me. It's just a dark shape moving too fast for me to see.

Whoever it is screams, and that's followed by what sounds like the trash can being hurled at one, or both of, the twins.

A girl shouts, "Get out!"

Light pours in as the bathroom door swings open then hits the wall with a thud, cracking the tile.

Kaycee isn't dead. She looks at me, dazed. Scrambles to her feet. Runs for the door.

The door slowly shuts, casting the bathroom back into darkness, leaving me alone with whoever scared the girls away.

Is it another student?

A teacher?

Maybe Coach Darcy?

I hear footsteps coming toward me, and even though this person just saved me, a cold chill runs through my entire body.

I'm terrified. Fear tightens like a band around my chest.

"Are you okay?" a girl's voice asks.

The lights flicker on.

And then I see my savior's face, standing over me, hand extended to help me up.

No.

Impossible.

How?

"Emily?"

"Did they hurt you?"

"How?" is all I can manage before she pulls me up and into a hug.

"I'm so sorry I didn't get here sooner. I'm not going to let them hurt you … never again."

I collapse against Emily in tears, still trying to figure out how she got here. *I'm safe now*, is my overwhelming thought while I'm still in her arms.

But even as she holds me and comforts me, another emotion is twisting forth from somewhere deep inside my brain — fear.

How powerful is Emily?

TWENTY-TWO

Like A Ghost

EMILY SAVED ME, said she'd see me later, then vanished.

I'm left shaking, stunned, and staring at the mess in the restroom — the cracks on the mirror where Kaycee hit it, drops of blood on the floor, though I'm not sure who they belong to, and the cracked tile where the door slammed into the wall.

I grab my bag off the ground, straighten myself in the shattered mirror, and as I do so, I feel something shifting. Like some part of me that would normally be freaking the hell out is stepping back and putting my body on autopilot.

I don't feel like me. I feel like a ghost going through the motions of me.

Gone is the anxious voice in the back of my head that usually torments me by hovering above and warning me of every conceivable threat. There are no more nonsensical OCD warnings telling me if I do this innocuous thing, bad things will happen. All the other ridiculous and distracting chatter — vanished.

I feel an odd calm I've not felt in a while, maybe forever. The necklace is a salve against my chest, a reminder of Emily. It almost feels as if she's still here with me, watching over me.

I wonder how she got here. Didn't she say she was stuck near the house? How did she just show up out of the blue and save me? Was she lying? Is she able to go anywhere she wants? And if so, how long has she been shadowing me?

I wonder if Kaycee or the twins were hurt bad. There's not a ton of blood, but there's enough to worry me.

A soothing voice pushes me past a fear that would otherwise eat me alive.

You're cleaned up. Now get out of here before anyone comes.

This never happened.

It's different from my normal inner voice. I don't think it's Emily. It sounds like a calmer, cooler version of me.

I go to History like nothing ever happened.

Even though I'm composed and detached, a part of me is waiting for the dean to announce my name, or even the principal herself to march into class. Maybe show up with cops wanting to know about the attack on Kaycee and the twins.

But that doesn't happen.

While the anxious part of me wonders if Kaycee or the twins saw Emily, another part doesn't even care. What are they going to do? Tell someone? Who would believe them?

They'd be ignored, maybe even mocked.

This makes me smile.

THE CALMNESS IS WEARING AWAY. Anxiety is returning like an old enemy I can't outrun.

I meet Alex in the cafeteria for lunch, stand with him in line while he gets a corn dog, Coke, and a giant chocolate chip cookie. Then we take our seats at the back of the cafeteria where I unpack my lunch — a peanut butter and strawberry jelly sandwich, a bag of baby carrots, and a Coke that's barely cold despite the ice pack in my bag.

No big deal. I can't keep my mind on anything for more than a few fleeting seconds. I keep looking back to see if Kaycee or the twins are around. Maybe Trent, or any of their usual crew.

But none of them are at their regular spot.

THEY'RE PROBABLY GOING TO THE PRINCIPAL AND TELLING HER EVERYTHING!

"You okay?" Alex asks, snapping me out of my thoughts. He might have been talking to me a bit before asking if I was okay.

"Yeah," I say, unconvincingly. "Just got a lot on my mind."

"Wanna share?"

Um, no, buddy. You wouldn't believe me if I told you.

"It's nothing."

"Yeah, okay."

"What?"

"Clearly, you've got *something* on your mind. You can talk to me."

Then I see him look behind me. I hear footsteps.

THEY'RE COMING FOR YOU!

I turn and see Trent quickly approaching the table with Kaycee in tow and the twins right behind.

HERE WE GO.

SHOWTIME!

My earlier confidence is gone. I don't want confrontation. I want to be left alone to live a normal life. Is that too much to ask?

He gets in my face. "What did you do to her?"

"What are you talking about?"

Trent rolls up Kaycee's left shirt sleeve, revealing big dark bruises in the shape of a hand on her bicep.

Alex stands and pushes himself between us. "Yo, let's take things down a notch, bro." He raises his hands as if to calm an irrational hothead.

Trent's barely able to hide his sneer, but at least he's not decking Alex — yet.

I can't sit here and let Alex fight my battles for me. "They attacked me!" I point to Kaycee. "They jumped me in the bathroom. What am I supposed to do, *not* defend myself?"

"We were just hazing you," Kaycee says. "Having fun. We do that to all the new girls."

"This wasn't hazing. She hates me. They all hate me, and I didn't do anything to any of them." My voice is an annoying, a cracking whine that I loathe even as I try to correct it into something more assertive, less victim-like.

Amber is glaring at me.

Alice says nothing.

I wonder if the scratch on her forehead is from Emily. I wonder if they even saw her. If so, they're not saying anything. They seem to think *I* did this. How I grabbed Kaycee so hard and pulled her backward while she was on top of *me*, I'm not quite sure, but whatever.

"We don't hate you," Kaycee says. "You're delusional. *You're* the one going around trash-talking us to everyone."

"What? I don't even talk to anyone!"

"So you didn't tell Kelly McCallister that I was a stuck-up bitch, or that the twins are ugly?"

"I don't even *know* Kelly McCallister! I never said any of that. And I'm not the one writing poems about me and reading them aloud. I didn't attack myself in the bathroom, hard-foul me in a meaningless basketball game, or soak my clothes in vinegar. You've had it out for me since we met, and I don't know what I did to deserve it. All I ever wanted was to be friends."

I hate how this last sentence comes out, making me feel weak for even admitting that I want friends, that I need friends, that I'd want to be friends with them.

But it's too late to take the words back now.

Kaycee laughs and rolls her eyes so hard I think they might go up into her giant forehead. "Honey, that's the problem. You don't get the hint. I tried to nicely tell you I don't want to be friends. But you keep messaging me over and over, and I'm all, *don't you get a hint?* I don't know why you're so obsessed with me, but you need to just back off."

"Back off? *Back off?* I messaged you one time!"

I'm staring at her incredulously. In what world am *I* the one going after her? Does she have some sort of victim mentality, or is she trying to make me look bad in front of everyone?

I don't even know what to say.

It feels like everyone in the lunch room is staring at us.

The necklace is warm again. I look around, wondering if Emily is back.

Then I see her at the other end of the cafeteria, headed this way.

No. No. No.

I don't need a repeat of the bathroom incident.

Not here.

Not in front of everyone.

A couple of teachers stand from their tables and start to come over. I don't need any of this. I don't want questions about what happened, or about Emily.

I'm flustered, my heart is racing, and, *great*, now I'm blinking.

"Oh, here she goes *again*, looking for attention with her blinking." Kaycee waves her arms to mimic a crazy person.

Trent looks back and sees what I saw, teachers coming.

But I also see Emily, and she looks like she's going to rip Trent's head off his body. I think about how fast she pulled Kaycee off of me and threw her backward with no effort at all. That wasn't human strength. It was something far more powerful, and who knows what else Emily is capable of.

I start shaking my head, trying to tell her to go away, I've got this.

I'm not in danger.

But she isn't looking at me.

She's twenty feet away and closing in, eyes filled with rage, locked on Trent.

He looks at Alex and shoves a finger hard into his chest. "Keep your crazy bitch away from my girl, or you and me have problems."

Alex is staring, dumbfounded.

Emily is right behind Trent, raising a hand, about to grab him. I imagine her throwing him clear across the cafeteria, maybe breaking his neck.

My heart feels like it's about to explode.

I cry out, "No!"

The lunchroom is completely silent, and everyone is staring at me.

Two teachers — a tall dorky man with an unfortunate mustache and a heavy-set redheaded woman I don't know — both rush over.

"Is everything okay?" the woman asks.

Trent and Kaycee flash their winsome phony smiles.

Trent says, "Yeah, everything's a'ight!"

Emily is right behind Trent, so close he could probably feel her. She's staring at me, eyes wide, gaze darting back and forth from me to Trent as if seeking permission to hurt him.

I shake my head.

The redhead looks at me oddly, then asks, "Are you okay?"

I'm practically frozen in fear, but manage a nod. "Yeah."

Emily also nods, pursing her lips as she shakes her head in disappointment, then turns on a heel and walks away, vanishing into a cluster of kids.

Trent, Kaycee, and the twins leave, none of them looking back at me even once.

The teachers stare at me and Alex like they're not sure if they should investigate further.

Alex nods. "It's all good, Mrs. Duncan. Promise."

"Okay." She looks like she actually believes him. The male teacher I can't read. He's either skeptical or doesn't give a damn either way. Probably the latter.

They both return to their tables.

I breathe a sigh of relief. Crisis averted.

Alex and I sit back down.

The emos at the end of the table are looking at us, whispering to one another.

Alex is staring at me. "What's going on?"

I give him a quick version, starting with the whole mall thing and ending with the bathroom assault, leaving out the part about my new ghost friend.

"I don't know what happened. She was on top of me, and I just freaked out."

"It's okay," he assures me. "You didn't do anything wrong. She's … she's a bitch."

He looks like he wants to say more but goes quiet instead. I can see the wheels spinning behind those brown eyes.

"So, what should I do? I don't want to tell anyone and have a bunch of drama, you know?"

"Yeah. Leave it to me. I'll talk with Trent."

"You *sure* about that? He doesn't look like he likes you too much, the way he poked you."

"We … we've got history. It'll be okay. I'll take care of it."

"I don't want you fighting my battles, Alex."

He smiles. "I owe you."

"For what?"

"For that car ride."

"No, you owe my mom. *I* told her to leave you in the rain."

He laughs. "Okay, is there anyone *your mom* needs me to take care of?"

I laugh.

For the moment, things feel like they might be okay. But then I think about Emily coming to school twice and trying to hurt people. While I'm thankful she pulled Kaycee off of me in the bathroom, coming after Trent in a crowded cafeteria is insane. What was she going to do to him?

What if I hadn't shaken my head to tell her no?

Again, I imagine her throwing him across the cafeteria. His neck snapping like a branch, his body going limp. The life leaving his eyes in an instant.

And again I wonder exactly what Emily is capable of.

TWENTY-THREE

Thursday Night

RIGHT BEFORE SCHOOL LETS OUT, Alex texts to say he won't be able to walk home with me today. No reason.

Disappointed, I leave school alone, glad Mom is at work because I'm not going straight home.

Instead, I head to the treehouse where Emily is sitting, waiting.

She leaps down and comes up to me, eager to talk. "Are you okay?"

I shake off her attempt to hug me. "What were you doing at school?"

"You needed me. I couldn't let them hurt you like they hurt me."

"How did you know? And how are you able to leave here?"

"I can go wherever the necklace is."

"What? You didn't tell me that."

And then it hits me — the favor she said she was going to ask after I read the diaries. Maybe she already asked, when she suggested I wear the necklace to school. I feel stupid and used as I realize she needs me to get to the kids on her list. But what is she planning to do to them? What she did to her parents?

I won't be part of that. Even if they're terrible people, but they don't deserve to die.

I meet her gaze. "What were you going to do to Trent?"

"Make him pay. For what he did to me, for what he did to you."

"*He* didn't hurt me."

"He will if you give him a chance. Trust me on that."

I shake my head. "But he *didn't*. And you could've seriously hurt Kaycee and the twins."

"Good. They're bitches. They were attacking you. If I didn't come, they would've seriously hurt *you*."

"I don't need you fighting my battles, Emily!"

I flash back on my conversation with Alex as I say this.

She stares at me, confused.

"Are you … are you *sticking up* for them?"

"Of course not. But you can't go around killing people!"

"I wasn't going to *kill* them. Jesus, don't be so dramatic!"

"So, what *were* you going to do? Break a bone or two? Maybe put them in a coma?"

"I can't believe this." Her arms are in the air. "I'm trying to *help* you."

"I didn't *ask* for your help."

"Fine," she says, turning and starting to walk away.

Now I feel bad. "Wait."

She stops, but doesn't turn around.

"Thank you for helping me today. I appreciate it. I really do. But you can't just come to school and kick everyone's ass on your list."

She says nothing as she stares into the woods. Then finally, "You're right. I'm sorry. I won't do it again."

"What do you want from me? You said you wanted help getting revenge, but if this is what you want, then I can't help you."

"We can talk after you read the rest of the journals. But … you don't have to. If you want me to go, I won't bother you anymore."

If this were anyone else, I would think she was manipulating me. But there's a vulnerability to her, in both Emily's presence and in the words on her pages that echo in my bones. A connection that compels me to give her the benefit of the doubt.

"No, I *want* to read them. I *want* you to stay."

She turns around, tears welling in her eyes. "You just saying that?"

"No. But I'm not wearing the necklace to school anymore."

"You don't have to. I really did want you to wear it so I could feel connected to you during the day. It's *sooooo* lonely. Just to feel you out there, to know you're okay, makes me feel closer to you. It's hard to explain. This is all so new to me. You're the first person who has seen me. The only person."

"What about other dead people? Do you see them?"

"Sometimes. But not often. I think most people have passed on to … well, wherever we're *supposed* to go after we die. I think people like me, and the others, we're not meant to be here. We're stuck for some reason." She shook her head. "I don't talk to them anymore."

"What do you mean?"

"They're scary, Cora. They're not … not all there."

"Like their bodies?"

"No, their minds. They're scared, haunted, and … sometimes violent."

I think about the last time we were in the treehouse, when Emily seemed frightened by something outside.

"Can they hurt you?"

"I don't know. I feel like they can, so I avoid them now."

"How does the necklace work? You can feel what I'm feeling when I'm wearing it? You're not like all up in my head and reading my mind and stuff, are you?"

She laughs. "No. Why, you've got secrets to hide?"

"If I told you, I'd have to kill you," I joke, wanting the conversation to feel normal again. Well, as much as it can while talking to a dead girl.

"When you wear the necklace, it's like we're connected on some emotional level. When you're happy, I feel your happiness. When you're scared, I feel that too. That's why I came."

"How can you feel what I'm feeling?"

"I don't know *how* it works. Like I said, Lilith didn't tell me much."

"Who is Lilith?"

"She used to live in the dilapidated house down the street."

I remember passing it when Mom and I got here, afraid it might be our new place.

"You knew her?"

"Not when she was alive. No. You'll read about her."

"She's on your list?"

"Sort of."

"Why?"

"You'll see soon enough."

"Is she a ghost?"

"She's something, but I wasn't sure what at first. Anyway, she protected me."

"From who? Your father?"

She nods.

"Wait, you didn't kill your parents?"

A branch breaks somewhere in the woods behind me.

I jump, then turn to see Mom standing at the foot of the trail to the clearing, looking at me nervously, eyes darting around.

"Who are you talking to?"

I turn around and Emily is gone.

"Nobody," I say, but she clearly doesn't believe me.

How much did she hear? The last thing I said was, "You didn't kill your parents?"

Oh, God, what must she be thinking if she heard that?

"Cora. Please. Are you … seeing things again?"

I *can't* tell her about Emily.

She'll think I've lost my flippin' mind. I don't want to be locked up.

That's where the worst spirits are trapped.

I can't do it. Not again.

"No, I'm just practicing dialogue, for something I'm writing."

She's still eyeing me skeptically.

I need to do a better job selling this lie.

She knows something is wrong and needs a branch of hope. A lie to stoke her faith. Something to prove that I'm no longer lost or trapped in the darkness again.

"I was looking through Dad's story ideas."

Her head tilts ever so slightly.

Yes, this is the thing she can take hold of, that she can believe.

I continue the lie, telling her I want to finish one of his stories, so I'm practicing dialogue between characters. It's something he used to do, sitting in his office talking out scenes until he got them right. She teased him about it, telling him he was like a kid playing with action figures, even though I could tell she found it adorable.

"What's the story about?"

I don't know how much Mom's read of his unfinished stuff. Maybe she's testing me.

"I don't wanna say too much or I won't want to write it." Dad used to say that all the time.

She looks like she might believe me.

Might isn't quite sold on the lie, though. I need to add flavor. Though I've been sitting in Dad's office back home, she knew a part of me was reluctant to read his unfinished stuff. She knows the guilt I feel for his death made it hard to read what he might have done — the stories I killed along with him.

"Do you think Dad will mind me finishing one of his stories?"

And there it is, that break in her face, a change from concern that I'm crazy to the loving gaze of a proud mother, pleased her daughter is finally embracing his stories.

"No, I think it's a lovely idea. He would be honored."

She hugs me.

I feel horribly guilty for using Dad's stories like this, and also for manipulating Mom. But I'll do anything to avoid the hospital.

We walk back to the house, and I'm a mix of too many emotions and a twitching uncertainty. I don't turn around, but I can feel Emily watching as Mom and I leave. I think about what she said about being alone all the time, except for when she sees me, and how awful that must feel.

On some level, I can relate. Because I've spent most of my time since middle school feeling virtually alone. But to actually *be* alone, where you can see people but can never be acknowledged or spoken to or touched — God, that must be awful.

Still, I can't risk taking the necklace to school, *can I?*

As Mom and I step back into the cozy house, I realize I've forgotten the next journal.

TWENTY-FOUR

In The Window

I'M in Dad's office, at his computer, reading through one of his short stories, searching for something to actually write now that I've committed to this lie.

At first, it's my way of feeling less guilty for lying to Mom. But soon I discover I love these peeks into Dad's mind, the raw state of stories before an editor's hand has changed them.

There are notes to himself and to his editor, questions about the story, including moments of revelatory self-doubt that make me wish I could go back in time and talk these scenes out with him, offer feedback, tell him how absolutely wonderful they — and his mind — are.

He died without me having read a single one. I wonder if that hurt him.

I tore through his books a few months after he died, eager for any part of him left in this world. And as I read each one, I looked for the truth within the fiction, a hint at the life he lived before I knew him.

As I'm reading this particular story, about a boy lost in

the woods with what might be metaphorical monsters, I wonder how much of the boy's painful childhood is Dad's biography versus his imaginings. Where does the story meld with the man? His stories are puzzles to assemble, a map to finding the reality of this man I lived with for so long, yet only partially knew.

I feel even more guilt for all the years I spent talking to him because it was almost always about *my stuff*. I pretty much never asked about him. I was focused on me.

That might be normal child behavior, but I feel awful, anyway. Now that it's too late to ask him anything.

So many questions he's no longer around to answer.

What things did he think about when he was my age?

What were his fears?

Who was his first crush?

Who was his first heartbreak?

How did he feel when he met Momma?

How did he deal with his OCD? What were his tics?

He had some verbal tics, and I know he counted numbers a lot, but surely he had a few he kept to himself so the world wouldn't think he was crazy.

I wonder if all those times he was "talking out his stories" he was really in the grip of some compulsion.

I remember how disappointed he was when he learned about my OCD. Like he'd passed on his curse. He never said anything to me, but I once saw him almost crying to Mom about it.

You don't know how bad it can get.

Had he kept the worst of it from even her?

I wanted to go in, hug him, and tell him it was okay. That I didn't blame him.

But I never did.

And now I never can.

Most of all, I wonder if he viewed existence like so many of his characters, as something painful to be endured. At my worst, I've felt it was a blight, something to get through, or maybe something best to end on your own terms.

At my worst, I wanted to die because it was the only way I could see out of the pain. But at my best, I've felt existence is a blessing, a gift. A responsibility to do something good with.

I find myself thinking more and more about his boy in the woods, which leads me to Emily in the woods. What *is* existence after death? Emily said she's seen other ghosts, lost ones that scared her.

Is that what becomes of everyone after we die?

Another thought comes.

One I wish I'd not had.

One I can't un-think now.

Is Dad's spirit stuck haunting our home in California? Is he all alone, wondering where we've gone? Does he feel like we've abandoned him?

This possibility rises like a wave of horror inside me. I can't reel the thoughts back in as they give rise to worse ones — him alone in our house, staring at whoever's living there now, waiting.

An endless wait. Alone and yearning.

My chest tightens.

I can't breathe.

Everything feels like it's buzzing. Chaos swelling and threatening to drown me in its madness.

I get out of the chair then pace, desperate to find *something* that might calm my mind. Sometimes I can focus on a single thing and anchor myself. A mantra or object.

But I can't think of a damned mantra, and everything I

look at feels wrong. I'm surrounded by Dad's stuff —
shelves full of books he'd spent so much of his life lost in,
the chair and desk where he lost all those hours, nostalgia-
soaked possessions it took a lifetime to collect.

All these things relegated to this museum of one.
Without him.

Dad's room usually offers comfort, but now his stuff
feels somehow angry. Like it's buzzing, shaking. Trying to
build enough momentum to fly off the shelves.

I'm dizzy, and hyperventilating. Legs are wobbly like I
might pass out if I don't get my crap together.

But I can't stop thinking of Dad's ghost watching as
Mom and I got in our car and drove off for the final time.

Him just standing there, yelling at us not to leave.
Screaming, "I'm still here."

Waiting.

Forever.

We've got to go back.

NO, MOM WILL NEVER GO BACK.

We've got to.

*OKAY, LET'S JUST SAY MOM DID GO BACK, HOW
ARE YOU EVEN GOING TO SEE HIM?*

*DOES EMILY'S NECKLACE WORK WITH EVERY
GHOST, OR IS IT LOCKED TO HER?*

*EVEN IF HE IS THERE, WE PROBABLY WOULDN'T
SEE HIM.*

I heard his voice after he died. I might have seen him.

YOU THOUGHT YOU DID.

YOU DIDN'T TALK TO HIM, THOUGH.

NOT LIKE WITH EMILY.

I heard him. I know I did.

STOP IT.

I'm shaking.

My heart feels like it's about to explode.

My mind is a thousand angry bees, buzzing with the books.

The room feels hot. The shirt is tight around my neck. I pull at it and accidentally rip the fabric.

I need to get out of here.

The walls are caving in, about to violently implode. Chunks of wood, drywall, and metal piercing my skin, burying me in debris as I slowly bleed out.

Fresh air. That's what I need.

When I open the windows, a cold breeze gusts into the office. I take deep gulps of the night air, trying to calm myself. To keep myself from screaming.

Mom can't see me like this.

God, no.

I turn around and look at the desk, all the medicine bottles lined in a row.

I unscrew them, spilling the pills, desperate to take one of each as fast as I can, before I lose my mind.

PILLS DON'T EVEN WORK THAT FAST!

SEE, THIS IS WHAT HAPPENS WHEN YOU DON'T TAKE THEM REGULARLY.

Shut up!

I swallow them, followed by watered-down Coke.

Then I look at the bottle with the tablets that work fastest — the sleeping pills — and take two.

I never take two. One usually knocks me out pretty fast.

I consider three, but am too scared that might knock me out for good.

I sit at the desk and close my eyes, waiting for the pills to kick in.

YOU NEED TO CALM THE HELL DOWN, CORA.

DAD'S PROBABLY ALREADY MOVED ON TO HEAVEN.

*REMEMBER WHAT EMILY SAID? THAT MOST OF
THE PEOPLE HAVE MOVED ON?*

*THERE'S NOT MANY STUCK HERE, THAT'S WHAT
SHE SAID, RIGHT?*

Right.

DAD WAS A GOOD MAN.

NO WAY HE'S STILL STUCK HERE.

*IF ANYONE GOT A FAST-PASS TO HEAVEN, IT WAS
HIM FOR HAVING TO PUT UP WITH YOUR SHIT.*

*You're right. Maybe he wasn't always there for me and Mom, but
there's no denying he did what he could. And … that look in his eyes
when he saw her or looked at me. A man like that doesn't go to hell,
doesn't get stuck here. No God would do that.*

*HE IS IN HEAVEN, LOOKING DOWN ON YOU,
HAPPY YOU'RE FINALLY READING HIS STORIES.*

*PROBABLY EVEN EXCITED THAT YOU WILL
WRITE SOMETHING IN HIS WORLDS, EVEN IF IT
MIGHT SUCK.*

*WE BOTH KNOW THAT'S WHAT HE WOULD'VE
WANTED, RIGHT?*

FOR YOU TO CARRY HIS TORCH?

Right … I think.

And that does make me feel a bit better.

Still, I saw him after he died.

YOU THOUGHT YOU DID.

YOU SAW WHAT YOU WANTED TO SEE, CORA.

*COME ON, YOU NEED TO STOP LYING TO
YOURSELF.*

I stare out the window, into the night, no longer sure of
what's real.

I remember desperately wanting to see him, wondering
why I saw ghosts or spirits or whatever you want to call
them as a child but couldn't see my very own father, the
man closest to me.

Would my mind have tricked me like that? Given me what I wanted because it was what I needed to get through it all?

The cold breeze is picking up, howling as it comes through my window. The room has gone from stifling hot to ice cold.

But at least the room, and my mind, have stopped buzzing. Things feel almost back to normal.

When I get up to close the window, I see Alex in his room across the street. His lights are on and he's sitting on his bed, strumming an acoustic guitar.

I focus, trying to imagine the tune. He looks so at peace, closing his eyes, *really* into the music. I'm guessing it's a song that has some meaning to him.

The sight puts my mind more at ease. Or maybe it's the pills kicking in. Whatever it is, I find myself lost in the moment, imagining being in the room with him, admiring his music. Staring, soaking him in.

Then he looks up. And before I can hide, he sees me.

No!

He puts the guitar down and waves.

Oh, God, he thinks I'm peeping on him!

I might die of embarrassment.

Cheeks burning, I manage to wave back.

COME ON, GIRL, HASN'T ANYONE EVER TOLD YOU IF YOU'RE GONNA PEEP ON SOMEONE TO TURN YOUR LIGHTS OFF FIRST?

He turns around and grabs something on his bed. A moment later, my phone is buzzing on Dad's desk.

I turn around and look at it. A message from Alex.

You creeping on me, ya' creeper?

I blush, shaking my head, and loudly laugh.

JK. I'm probably not ur type, anyway. 'Cuz I'm a guy and you have a crush on the Kardashians.

I laugh again.

Yeah, sorry, Alex, but you can't compete with them.

Damn. I guess there's no point in taking off my shirt then?

My eyes go wide, and I hope he can't see my face too well from across the street, or he'll know how excited I am by that prospect.

Well, you could try.

I can't believe I just typed that. I want to take the message back, but he's already seen it.

He's looking down at the screen, but hair in his face hides the expression.

Why isn't he responding?

PROBABLY BECAUSE THE IDEA OF YOU FLIRTING WITH HIM IS CRACKING UP.

OR HE JUST VOMITED IN HIS MOUTH AT THE THOUGHT.

And then he sets the guitar and phone down.

What is he doing? What is he—

He takes off his shirt.

Whoa!

Even at this distance, I can see his sinewy frame. His muscles, not big, but in all the right places. His six-pack abs. That V leading down to his jeans, and …

He looks up and smiles.

Adrenaline courses through me, mingling with desire and a fear that I'll get caught, even though I haven't done anything.

Yet.

He grabs his phone and starts typing.

WHAT YA' GONNA DO IF HE SAYS YOUR TURN?

I really did not think this through. I'm not gonna take my shirt off. No way.

Crap!

My phone buzzes.

I'm afraid to see his message.

I look down.

It's a smiley face.

What does that even mean? Does he want me to flash him?

I lift my shirt, quickly, high from a rush of adrenaline.

I'm wearing my bra, so it's not like he's seeing anything he wouldn't see if we went to the beach or a pool together. Yet, I feel naughty and thoroughly alive.

He messages, *You were too quick. I didn't even see anything.*

I raise my shirt again, slowly, and aim the camera at myself, taking a photo of my bra and cleavage.

I press send without thinking twice, I'm so caught up in the moment.

He looks down at the phone and I think he's smiling.

Suddenly, he turns.

And I see two things at once.

His father has come into his room, looking angry at something.

Then I see Alex's back — and the many, many lash marks.

Oh, my God.

I back away from the window, afraid his father might spot me.

I hide behind the wall, just out of sight, my mind flashing on Alex's back and the army of scars.

What the hell kind of monster is his father?

I make my way to the light switch and kill the lights, plunging my father's office into darkness.

Once I'm fairly sure his dad can't see me, I peek out my window. Alex's room is now empty.

All the adrenaline, naughty thoughts, and giddiness are swallowed by a familiar sadness, twisting into a painful knot in my heart.

And, as I go to delete the photo from my phone, I see that I accidentally got half my face in the photo.

What if his father sees it?

What if he comes over and tells Mom?

TWENTY-FIVE

Friday

I WAKE UP FOGGY, like I usually am after taking my meds, especially the sleeping pills.

Mom is shaking me. "You waking up today?"

Scared I overslept, I turn to see the clock telling me I don't need to rush. I sigh in relief, crawl out of bed, then drag myself to the shower.

Mom's in an okay mood and seems more awake than usual. She even made a real breakfast. Bacon, eggs, and bagels.

We sit and eat, Mom making small talk about work gossip and laughing.

I laugh with her, even though I'm not sure of the whole story. I don't ask for details just in case she told me before and I don't remember.

"How's your nose?"

"Okay." The bruising has mostly faded. And it no longer hurts.

"Did you get writing done last night?"

"Not much. I was reading more of Dad's unfinished stories. Have you read them?"

"I ... I can't."

"Why not?"

"They make me too sad."

Sometimes I forget that I wasn't the only one to lose someone. She lost her husband, and given how close they were, that has to be almost as bad as losing a father. I'm sure it's the reason she sometimes drinks too much. Aside from the occasional cocktail or wine, she didn't really drink when he was alive. Certainly not alone.

I want to make her feel better, but I'm not sure what to say and don't want to steer the conversation into depressing waters when she's already in a good mood.

"Are the stories good?" she asks. "I'm sure they've got to be, right?"

"Yes. I mean, they're incomplete, but you can tell that they were going to be great, like he was working up to his best stuff. It's a shame the world will never see them."

SO MUCH FOR AVOIDING DEPRESSING WATERS. YOU'RE LIKE THE CAPTAIN OF THE TITANIC STEERING INTO A BIG ASS ICEBERG OF SADNESS!

"Well, maybe *you* can finish them. I'm sure the publisher would love that."

"The publisher who is cheating us?"

"Yeah. Maybe we're better off finding someone new or publishing it ourselves."

She suggests a few options, including a smaller press run by an old friend of Dad's, someone who might be able to help us decide the best thing to do.

After breakfast, I go upstairs and look at the necklace, debating on whether I should wear it to school. I don't want Emily hurting anyone else on her list, but on the other hand, I don't like the idea of her feeling so lonely all day.

If it helps her to feel me near, what harm is there in that?

I slip it on and hide it under my shirt, its weight a comfort against my chest.

～

MOM and I are getting in the car as Alex and his dad are leaving their house.

Mom waves. "Hi."

Alex waves back.

His dad gives us a curt little nod.

Jerk.

I'm looking at Alex trying to get a feel for what happened last night after his father called him out of his room. Did he yell at him? Hit him? Make him do chores?

What if he knew that Alex was stripping for me?

What if he saw my naughty photo?

I feel sick to my stomach at the thought of anyone other than Alex seeing it, especially his father or my mother.

WHAT THE HELL WERE YOU THINKING?

ARE YOU NEW TO THE INTERNET OR SOMETHING?

Alex is barely making eye contact. His shoulders are slumped, and he looks miserable.

I nudge Mom and whisper, "Can we give him a ride?"

She looks at me, then back at Alex and his dad. "Hi. We could give Alex a ride to school."

His father looks insulted. "That won't be necessary. Thank you, anyway."

HE KNOWS.

AND HE THINKS YOU'RE A FILTHY SLUT TRYING TO RUIN HIS SON.

Alex and his dad get in the truck then practically peel out onto the street. The guy even drives like a jerk.

Mom looks at me. "What crawled up his ass?"

"I dunno, but someone needs to put a boot up it."

She laughs, then looks at me and sees that I don't like the man. "Why? What did he do?"

"Nothing."

"What is it?"

"He's … he's just not a nice guy. He hurts Alex."

Mom gets in the car and asks for more details as we drive.

I tell her only bits, not about the marks all over his back, but generally that I'm pretty sure his father beats him. I'm opening a can of worms. If Alex's father saw the photo and my mom goes over there to say something, he might just show it to her.

Oh, yeah? Well, your daughter is sending slutty photos to my son!

"He should tell someone."

"Alex said it's not that bad and nobody would probably even care. And if they did, he could be worse off being taken from his father. You never know what you're going to find in foster care. He's only one year away from leaving and is used to toughing it out."

"Well, maybe it's best to not get involved."

"What do you mean?"

"Some people you just can't help. When you try, they just drag you down with them."

"Alex isn't like that. He doesn't even really talk about his father. I had to pull it out of him when I asked about his eye. He's really positive. He even helps other kids at school get good grades. Pretty much everybody likes him. He's the kind of person you've been telling me to surround myself with."

"I'm just saying you need to make friends with healthy

people. And with a father like that? Well, he can't be too healthy. We don't need that in our lives. Be careful, Cora."

I sigh, then we drive the rest of the way to school in silence.

~

MORNING CLASSES GO WELL, mostly because neither Kaycee nor Trent are here. I wonder if they're just skipping together or if she's hurt and he's consoling her. Or perhaps they're both together somewhere conspiring on a play for revenge.

I pass the twins in the hall a few times during the day, but neither of them so much as looks at me, which I guess is an improvement.

At lunch, Alex is quieter than normal, very much in his head, barely picking at his pizza. I'm not hungry, but I finish my peanut butter jelly sandwich quickly, just mostly to keep my mouth busy. Anything to obscure the silence. Make it less painful.

He's making small talk, but barely. Every sentence is a struggle, leaving me feeling awkward, like we're on a meme-worthy first date. He seems distracted, occasionally looking up as if he's waiting for someone.

"Are you okay?"

"What do you mean?" Alex asks.

I want to comment on how he seems off now, but decide instead to ask about last night. I hope to work my way to the scars on his back, but that's probably a question better left for when we're alone.

"Well, one second you're playing guitar and texting me all happy, and the next minute your dad comes in your room and then you're gone. What happened?"

"I don't want to talk about it." He rips into his pizza as if starving.

"You can tell me. I won't say anything."

"*Please*, I don't want to talk about it. It doesn't matter." He looks away.

His eyes are glassy and I can't stand to see him cry, so I say okay. His hands are shaking. He seems to notice, as he thrusts them under the table.

What's happening with him?

Obnoxious laughter erupts behind me as John, KJ, and Larry approach. Their timing couldn't be worse for this conversation, but Alex seems almost relieved. He smiles when he sees them, stands up, exchanges bro handshakes and fist bumps. It amazes me how quickly Alex shifts from withdrawn and sad to animated and joking with the guys.

They don't take seats, and instead stand next to us.

I get a few "what's ups" and nods before John nods and Alex follows him off toward the common area. I'm not sure if they're going to a locker or the restrooms.

KJ and Larry take seats opposite me.

KJ tries to make easy conversation with a simple question. "So, where you from?"

"Los Orillas."

He's probably never heard of it but says, "Cool."

"What are you doing this weekend?" Larry asks.

"I don't know." It's a lot better than admitting I've got no friends except a ghost and *maybe* Alex.

KJ says, "You should hang out with us sometime."

Larry adds, "That would be cool."

"Sure, sounds cool."

God, this is even more awkward than sitting with Mopey Alex.

The small talk continues, but I'm too distracted wondering what's up with Alex and John to pay attention.

Finally they come back. I look at both of them, trying to gauge the nature of their conversation. Was it about some school work for hire, or maybe a drug sale? Something else I haven't considered?

The guys say goodbye, then Alex and I are left alone again. And he looks ... *different*, though I can't quite figure out what's changed.

He's a bit more animated.

He tells me a funny story about KJ passing out at some party and a bunch of his friends putting him in a dress then leaving him on his front lawn where his father found him the next morning.

Well, at least Alex is finding the story funny.

Then I notice his eyes. Pupils dark, the size of saucers.

He's high now.

I want to ask him, but the bell rings.

Alex pops up, offers to take my tray to the trash. I let him, following him as he continues his happy animation — a complete one-eighty from how our lunch started.

As we walk, he's back to the cool, happy-go-lucky kid greeting half the people we pass. Glimpses of the real Alex bleeding through the cracks are replaced by this facade that allows him to pass among others.

Is this his secret? That he's taking drugs just to get by?

Is this what it takes for him to exist? How long before it destroys him?

I remember my mother's warning. *Be careful, Cora.*

That familiar anxiety presses in, but last night's meds dull the sensation.

I can feel something bad about to happen, not to me, but to some other version of me. A version I don't have to be in. A version that can take the worst and shrug it off.

A version that feels nothing, and that's a good thing.

But if I let that version stay too long, it threatens to kick out the most important part of *me*.

And as much as I don't want to be hurt or fall into full-blown panic attacks like last night's, I also never want to lose myself to pills or a psychiatric ward again.

TWENTY-SIX

Sunday

I WAKE UP AT NOON, exhausted.

My phone says Sunday, but what happened to Saturday?

I can't remember yesterday, at all.

Did I sleep the day away?

It seems unlikely. Surely Mom would've woken me to see if I was okay.

Exhausted, I head downstairs where I find a note on the kitchen counter from Mom. She had a double and will be home late. There's twenty bucks telling me to "order pizza or something."

Nothing in the note asking how I am or hoping I feel better, which I'd expect if I'd actually slept through an entire day.

I check my phone. It's down to five percent.

I usually charge it at night. But the last thing I remember is walking home alone on Friday when Alex didn't join me.

I don't even remember coming home.

But I must've come home.

Obviously. You're here, dummy.

But what did I do Friday night or all of Saturday? Why can't I remember?

Maybe it's the pills.

I head up to Dad's office, sit at his desk, plug the phone into the outlet, then check my phone's history to see if I made any calls, chatted with anyone, or posted anything on LiveLyfe.

There's messages from me to Kris.

Friday night at 1:30 AM. I wrote: *Kris, call me. It's important.*

I don't remember writing that, nor the three messages that follow.

1:35 AM: Please, Kris. I NEED to talk to you.

1:57 AM: Kris!!!!! Where are you?

2:40 AM: Fine. Don't call me. Ever again. I HATE YOU!

THE PHONE IS SHAKING in my hand. I can't remember any of this. Kris must think I've lost my mind.

WHY HASN'T SHE CALLED OR MESSAGED YOU BACK THEN?

CLEARLY SHE DOESN'T CARE ABOUT YOU ANYMORE.

SHE'S GOT TYLER.

I scroll through to see if she called me or if she sent messages on any of my other social media accounts, and to make sure I didn't call or post anything else I don't remember.

Nothing.

What the hell?

I stare at the bottles of pills on Dad's desk. This wouldn't be the first time I had missing periods of time after taking them. But I can't remember if I've ever missed a day, let alone a day and a half. Or texted someone while out of my mind.

I'm embarrassed and scared.

I call Kris.

It goes straight to voicemail.

The words tumble out of me. "Hey, Kris. Sorry about the texts. I'm on some new meds and think they … well, I don't remember anything."

I laugh, hoping that she'll get that I'm not mad at her, that this is all just a big ha-ha whoopsie.

"Anyway, sorry about the texts. And if we did talk, hopefully I didn't say anything *too stupid*. Call me back when you get a chance. Love ya!"

I hang up, my heart racing.

It was one thing to move away from her, another to lose her altogether. We promised to stay in touch, always and no matter what. Even during the difficult times, especially after Dad died, our friendship survived. Even when I blocked her out, even when I lost my mind, she stayed right by my side. She was always there, waiting for me to come to my senses, to get better.

But now she's this vague concept of a friend, and I feel like I'm losing her for good. Once she's gone, I've officially got nobody who really knows me.

I need to shower. Or maybe a long hot bubble bath I can cry in. But I need to charge my phone a bit more, just in case Kris calls me back while I'm in the tub.

I turn on Dad's computer to see if I can find any clues to what I was doing yesterday.

On his desktop I see a note: *ReadMe.txt*

I open it.

. . .

"STOP TAKING THE PILLS! They're keeping you from seeing me.

Stop taking the pills!
Stop taking the pills!
Stop taking the pills!
Stop taking the pills!"

I STARE at the screen wondering if *I* wrote this under their influence, or … did Emily? I notice that she (or I) wrote it four times in a row — my OCD thing.

I didn't tell Emily about that, so I'm not sure how she'd know. But it's usually me un-thinking something four times, not instructing myself to do something like this.

MAYBE SHE CAN READ YOUR THOUGHTS.

SHE SAID SHE COULD ONLY FEEL YOUR MOOD, BUT MAYBE SHE LIED BECAUSE THE TRUTH MIGHT'VE CREEPED YOU OUT?

OR MAYBE SHE'S JUST ALWAYS HERE, SPYING ON YOU, PICKING UP ON THE FOUR TIMES THING.

I remember how she said that just because I couldn't see her without the necklace doesn't mean she goes away. I hate the idea of her being here without my being able to see her. It feels like a violation.

A cold chill runs through me.

I look around the room for some sign of her.

"Are you here right now?"

No response.

I go to my room, grab the necklace from my night-stand, slip it on, then look around again.

"Emily?"

I go from room to room, looking for her, calling her name. In the living room, I say, "I can't see you. Knock something over, or … *something* to show me you're here."

I wait, listening and looking.

Nothing.

I go back to my Dad's office to see if maybe she typed something on the text file still on the screen.

Nothing has changed.

I stare and wonder if I wrote it.

If I did, why? What else happened while I was under the influence of pills?

In the past, effects have ranged from me feeling a bit happier to almost maniacally gleeful; from drowsy to passing out after dinner; and from mildly annoyed to outright angry. Add the occasional hallucination, a bit of paranoia, a total loss of appetite, and a half dozen other side effects as I scratch the surface of yet another experience.

And just when we find a cocktail of drugs that work for a few months, one or a few stop working. Then it's back to the lab to find what might work this time for however long. Like riding a rollercoaster blindfolded, with ever-changing tracks.

I want to text Mom to ask her if I did anything weird yesterday, but I don't want to alarm her. I figure if I did anything too odd, she wouldn't have left me alone today.

I try to remember the last time I saw Emily.

I think it was before I started taking the pills again.

MAYBE YOU CAN'T SEE HER BECAUSE SHE'S NOT REALLY THERE!

A FIGMENT!

A SIGN OF YOUR ILLNESS!

Oh? Then how did I find the books?

THE SAME WAY YOU FOUND THE NECKLACE.

YOU'RE DRAWN TO SOME ENERGY OR SOMETHING LEFT BEHIND.

YOU'VE GOT A GIFT TO SENSE THINGS, I'LL GIVE

YOU THAT, BUT THAT DOESN'T MEAN YOU CAN TALK TO GHOSTS.

I draw a bath while the phone is charging, then slide into the tub, letting the warmth surround me in its comfort. Then I sit back, close my eyes, and wait for Kris to call or text.

God, I hope she doesn't hate me now.

After the water goes from scalding hot to barely warm, I sit up to add some heat.

I freeze when I hear floorboards creaking in the hallway.

I look at the bathroom door which I swore I'd closed.

It's cracked open.

Someone is in the house!

I swallow a lump in my throat.

Maybe it's just Emily. Relax. She won't hurt you.

But it doesn't feel like Emily. This feels different. I want to get up and close the door. I need to lock it, but I'm terrified of even moving.

The bathroom is stone silent as I strain to hear, waiting for another creak of the floorboards. In the spaces between plinking droplets from the faucet, I feel vulnerable. Especially undressed. Funny, clothes don't protect you from a knife or a gun, but without them, I feel so exposed.

I think of all the unsolved kidnappings, rapes, and murders on the news. Things that always happen to someone else.

Now they might be happening to me.

I scan the bathroom for a weapon.

My only viable options are the plunger and maybe the shower curtain rod. If someone bursts in, I'm thinking the shower rod is my best bet. Yank it down, hope I don't knock myself out, fend off my attacker with it. But if it's someone bigger or stronger, might they turn the weapon on me?

I consider calling 9-1-1.

But God, I'll feel stupid if there's nobody out there.

YEAH, BUT IF THERE IS SOME PSYCHO OUT THERE, YOU'LL BE DEAD.

CALL!

I remain silent.

No movement.

Yet I can sense someone on the other side of the wall. Waiting for me to lower my guard.

MAYBE IT IS EMILY.

CALL OUT TO HER.

IF SHE CAN PUSH A BOOK, SHE CAN DO SOME-THING ELSE TO SHOW SHE'S HERE.

THAT IT'S JUST HER.

I'd be spooked by Emily standing in my house invisibly, but she doesn't scare me like an intruder would. I can't call out to her because a part of my brain is sure that the only reason the intruder hasn't burst in here is because I *haven't* called out to him.

So long as I feign ignorance, I'm safe.

Until I'm not.

My heart is racing as I stare at the door, indecision a swelling knot in my throat.

I dial 9-1-1 and let my finger hover over the CALL button.

I stare at the door, fully expecting it to burst open at any moment.

The killer will be on me in seconds with his gloved hands and weapon.

Will he have a knife or a gun?

Will he kill me here or take me somewhere else, make me wish he'd finished me fast?

My only hope is that since I'm naked and slippery, maybe I can squirm away. Put enough distance between us to hit him in the head with the shower rod.

I can't take my eyes from the door.

A buzz rips through the silence, startling me — my phone.

It slips from my hands as I yelp, desperately bobbling it back and forth, trying not to drop it in the water before knocking it onto my chest, safe so long as the bubbles can't hurt it.

I look at the screen and see that Alex is calling.

"Hello?" I say, awkwardly, still staring at the bathroom door.

Did someone move outside it?

Did the floorboards creak again?

I'm not sure.

"You okay?"

"I think someone's in my house. Can you come over?" I say, more for the benefit of whomever might be in my hall than me actually wanting him to come over. "Please, hurry."

"Okay, stay on the phone."

I hear him running.

His breath hitches as he says, "I'm outside your house."

I continue staring at the bathroom door, waiting for it to open, waiting for the killer to force his way in. Will Alex get here in time? Even if he does, could he fight off a killer? In asking for his help, did I just get him killed?

"Cora?" He sounds confused or something.

"Yes?" I fear what he's about to say.

"Um … your garage door is open."

"What?"

"Yeah, it's open. Is it supposed to be?"

Oh, my God. Someone is *in here!*

"No! Call the police!"

I hop out of the shower, nearly wiping out on the floor. I fall forward into the door, slam it closed, then quickly turn the lock.

"I'm calling the cops!" I yell to the intruder.

Alex, in my ear, yells, "No, I'm coming in. Where are you?"

"Upstairs, in the bathroom. I was taking a bath."

"Stay put. I'm coming."

I clutch the phone, listening intently as he enters my house, one ear on the phone, the other listening for Alex ascending the steps. I press myself against the bathroom door, staring at the knob, waiting for it to rattle.

If it does, I swear to God, I will lose my mind.

"Hello!"

"I'm up here," I call back, sheepish when I think maybe he was calling out to our possible intruder.

"Cora?" He's suddenly in the hall. "You okay?"

"I'm in here."

"Hold on. I'm gonna secure the house."

Something about the way he says "secure the house" should sound ridiculous, like a teenager who's seen too many cop shows or played too many video games, but it makes me feel safe in the moment.

I wait, trying to decipher each sound, hoping I won't hear Alex getting killed.

DON'T JUST SIT HERE AND WAIT!

THERE'S TWO OF YOU AGAINST ONE OF THEM, PROBABLY.

PUT SOME CLOTHES ON AND GET YOUR ASS DOWN THERE!

I'm not sure why I'm thinking there's only one person, but it's a good point. I *should* get dressed. *I shouldn't* just sit in here waiting for fate to come to me. The odds are even now, or more so than they were when I was stuck in the tub.

I *should* go help Alex search the house.

I grab my clothes off the counter, and without bothering to dry off, throw them on. I grab the plunger's wooden handle, yank it out of the rubber end. Not even washing my hands, I seize it like an instrument of death, then head to the door.

I unlock it.

Alex is there, looking me up and down before a smile cracks across his face and he holds up his hands like I'm robbing him.

"Please, don't plunge me."

TWENTY-SEVEN

Don't Want To Be Alone

FORTUNATELY, Alex's dad is out of town for the day visiting his brother, meaning Alex is free to hang out with me after the scare, and he's incredibly relaxed.

After "securing the house," which I've since teased him about a half-dozen times, I called Mom and asked her if she'd left the garage door open. She apologized, saying the automatic door hadn't been shutting right lately, often taking several clicks of the remote to stay closed, and that maybe it opened after she'd driven away.

I didn't tell her about thinking someone was in the house. I don't want her to worry or rush home and spoil my first real alone time with Alex.

We're sitting on the couch watching a *Breaking Bad* marathon. I've never seen it and he insisted that I must. I sense him watching, waiting to see my reactions.

Nothing has shocked me so far, but it's a good show. He keeps saying how he wished we could just fast forward to Season Four. I tell him a few times that we can, but he keeps insisting that I have to watch them in order. "The good stuff isn't nearly as good without the build-up."

We make small talk between episodes. Each time I get up to grab more snacks, I come back and sit a bit closer. I'm not bold enough to sit *right* next to him, but we're close enough that he could reach out and hold my hand if he wanted.

God, I want him to!

After several episodes, all the snacks are gone except raisins that Mom keeps buying even though neither of us eat them. Alex asks if I'd still like to learn guitar.

"Of course!"

"Do you know where your guitar is?"

"Yeah," I tell him, then run up to my room to grab it out of the closet.

I lay the case on my bed the flick the clasps open with satisfying THUNKS to reveal the acoustic guitar. It's got a dark body and a light brown design on the front that always reminded me of a setting sun.

It's one of the most beautiful guitars I've ever seen. I don't know much about instruments, so I'm not sure if this is a particularly good one or how much it costs, but it has a sentimental value that makes it priceless.

I flash back to watching my dad play at my bedside when I was a little girl. In addition to whatever he made up with Sneezy, he'd sing classic rock songs from when he was a kid, which not only put me to sleep, but also gave me an appreciation for music that runs deeper than most kids my age.

Guitar in hand, I bound down the stairs two at a time then join Alex in the living room, eager to show him the guitar. I hope he likes it, even if he can't possibly see it as I do. To him it might look like a plain old guitar. He has a fancy electric, after all. He knows his music, and, likely, his instruments.

I hold it up. "Here it is."

His eyes widen immediately. "Wow. Is that—" he trails off before holding out his hands like a kid on Christmas. "Can I hold it?"

I hand it over.

He takes it gently, almost reverentially, then peers inside the guitar at the sticker. "Oh, my God, it is."

"What?"

"It's a Gibson J-1000!"

"What does that mean?"

He looks at me like I'm the village idiot. "This is a rare guitar!" He turns it back over, examining every square inch. "A Tobacco Burst beauty with a cedar front, rosewood back and sides, and one of the warmest sounds you've ever heard. May I?" He pulls the pick out of the strings.

"Yeah!" I'm thrilled he loves the guitar so much.

Alex strums, then makes a face before turning the knobs. "When's the last time you tuned this?"

"I never learned how."

He laughs. "Wow."

I look down, making a pouty face, exaggerating for effect.

"It's okay. I'll tune it." He alternates between twisting and strumming until it sounds right, then he plays the start of a song I don't recognize. It sounds sad, sweet.

"What is that?"

"Just something I've been tinkering with. Wow, I can't get over how great this guitar sounds in person."

"How do you know so much about guitars? Are you really into them?"

"I actually don't know that much. I learned everything I know on YouTube. This one girl I used to watch did tutorials, and she had this guitar. She was awesome."

"Was?"

"Yeah, she got cancer and couldn't afford treatments, so she wound up selling it. I remember how sad she was. I wished I'd had money to buy it from her just to give it back. Within three months of selling it, she died."

"Oh, my God, that's so awful."

"Yeah, it was. Death seems so arbitrary, don't you think? In what world does God decide to take my mother instead of my father? In what world does God take a man as talented as your dad? In what world do so many good people die while evil assholes seem to live forever?"

I stare at the ground not sure what to say. I don't want to talk about my father. Not now. Because if I do, then I have to talk about my part in his death. And that's not a story I can ever tell anyone, least of all someone I like as much as Alex. Nobody could ever understand. Hell, *I* can't even understand.

"I'm sorry." He shakes his head and smiles sweetly. "I didn't mean to bring you down."

"It's okay."

"Here." He hands me the guitar. "Show me what you can play."

I take the guitar, and wanting to impress him a little, I pluck a few notes from the beginning of *Stairway to Heaven*, one of the few songs I remember ... the beginning of, anyway.

Of course, I screw it up. But I play it off by laughing. "Sorry, I suck."

"Do you know any chords?"

"Not really."

"That's okay. They're not that hard once you get the hang of it."

"But my fingers don't want to cooperate when I try."

"It takes time to train your muscles, to train your brain,

whatever. But if you stick with it, you can learn how to play. It's all in the hours you put into it."

He asks me to sit next to him, then shows me where to put my fingers to play the C chord.

I mess it up, so he puts his fingers over mine, guiding them.

It's a shot of adrenaline, making me giddy in a way I've not felt in maybe forever. Or at least since he took off his shirt.

Play it cool, girl. Don't make a big deal about it.

After we run through some chords, Alex gets up to check the front window to check for his father.

It's after seven and dark outside.

"He there yet?"

"No."

"You need to go?"

"No, I think I have a while."

"Want to stay for dinner?"

"Sure, whadaya got?"

We head to the kitchen. The fridge, freezer, and pantry are bare. "I don't know, I think we ate everything worth eating. Do you like raisins? We've got raisins for days!"

"Well, as enticing as that is, I think we can do better. How about I order pizza?"

"Cool, it'll be just like our school lunch."

He orders pizza from an app on his phone, then looks around the living room oddly.

"What?" I ask.

"It's just weird being ... *in* the house."

"What do you mean? You've never been in here before?"

"No. Emily's parents were super strict. They didn't even want her talking to me. For a while we'd sneak out at night and talk, but of course that ended." He shivers, then looks at me. "It's weird. I almost feel like she's still here."

Nope. Not weird at all. She might very well be.

Of course, I can't say that out loud. He'd think I'm crazy. So I say nothing.

"When I was checking the house earlier, and I went into her room, your room, I felt her presence strongly." An uncomfortable laugh. "Do … do you believe in ghosts?"

"I don't know. Do *you?*"

"I don't know what to believe. But the realtors had a hard time selling this place. It sat here for a while. The bank fixed it up and stuff, but still, nobody bought. I wondered if it was because people knew about the murders or … if they sensed something here. Did *you?*"

"I thought I felt my dad here on the first day. But, no, I didn't sense something horrible. Which is kind of odd."

"Odd? Why?"

Crap. I said too much. I can't tell him that I sense bad things. There's no way he'd believe me.

"Well, because I probably would've sensed something … like you said."

"Yeah, I always felt like people considering the house must've sensed it. I feel something bad here. I know my Dad does, even though he's never been inside. Heck, my dad doesn't want me anywhere near the place."

"Oh, I thought he just hated me because I'm half-black."

"Well, maybe. Not because of your skin color, but because he's kind of an asshole. He didn't like Emily, either. Which is strange because she was the nicest person I knew. I mean, once you got past her gothy exterior. And … I guess the whole killing her family thing." He gives another nervous laugh before he continues. "I think the real reason he didn't like her was because she was the only person I ever told."

"Told what?"

He points to the bruise under his eye, faded, but still there.

"Ah. What happened the other night … in the window." My face flushes. "After? You were just gone. Did I scare you off with my boobs?"

YOU DID NOT REALLY JUST SAY THAT.

He laughs. "No, no, they were … are … quite nice."

Now he's blushing and can't even look at me. It's adorable. I've never made a guy blush before. I feel like I've just discovered some new power.

"My dad was mad about something."

"Oh, I thought he caught us."

"No. No."

I want to ask him if he deleted the picture, but hesitate.

He goes back to Emily. "Yeah, she was the only one who knew. I just wish I'd been there for her the same way."

"What happened?"

He shakes his head. "I … Sorry, it's hard to talk about. I feel awful. Like I could've stopped it if I'd been a better friend."

"Were you friends, or … something more?"

"Friends. Just friends. She … she had nobody."

Tears well in his eyes.

Something about seeing a strong boy cry makes my eyes tear up, makes me want to hug him.

I do.

He squeezes me tight, like he's needed someone to hug for a long time.

It's also something I've needed. Someone to hug. Someone to understand me. Someone not a ghost.

Someone to understand my greatest pain, what happened the night my father died.

YOU CANNOT TELL HIM THAT.

YOU BARELY KNOW HIM AND IF YOU TELL HIM THAT, HE WILL NEVER TALK TO YOU AGAIN.

I need *someone* to tell, though.

I wanted to tell Kris, but I was so afraid of what she'd think of me. Alex is obviously dealing with his own guilt. Maybe he's the one person who can understand mine.

I pull out of the embrace and meet his gaze.

He wipes at the tears and turns away. "Sorry."

"It's okay."

I've been waiting so long for someone to open up to, and here is this person who so kind and understanding. So perfect. I feel as if my entire past year has been leading up to this moment. A whistling tea kettle about to burst. And Alex is the one person who can understand, who can help me relieve this pain.

Maybe we can help each other.

"Alex?"

"Yeah?"

The doorbell rings.

Damn it.

"Pizza's here." He walks to the door.

I follow him, just in case it's Mom or someone for me.

The delivery boy is a lanky skater kid I recognize from school. "Dude, I didn't know you live here," he says to Alex.

They chat forever. By the time he leaves, it feels like ten minutes have passed, along with my chance to tell him.

We sit at the table and eat pizza, the conversation decidedly different, as Alex is back to Happy Alex, telling hilarious stories and being his entertaining self — oblivious that I'm not attracted to that version of him. Happy Alex is not the Alex I need right now.

But I don't want to dim the mood, so I play along as best I can, telling my own stories, keeping his laughter alive.

After a while, I'm in a much better mood. We didn't get to talk about what I *wanted* to talk about, but maybe that's not what I *needed* to talk about. Maybe I needed someone to lift my spirits and move my mind away from the darkness for a change.

He glances at his phone once the pizza is gone. "I better get home. Dad'll be home soon, and … well, you know."

"Okay." I walk him out.

He stops in the doorway. "I really enjoyed this. Anytime you get scared in the bath, just give me a call."

"Oh?" I raise an eyebrow, flirting.

He blushes again. And I love it. Again.

"That's not what I meant."

"Ah, too bad," I tease.

Now he's really turning red. It's adorable.

"Thank you for teaching me guitar, and for talking. It's been a long time since I've had someone to talk to."

There's that moment, that awkward silence when our eyes meet and I wonder if he's going to lean forward and kiss me goodnight.

He looks like he's thinking about it, and then —

He does.

It happens quick, just a peck on the lips, so fast I barely have time to register how it felt, how I feel, or how to respond before he pulls away, looking nervous, smiling awkwardly.

"Um, okay. See ya later." Then he walks into the door frame.

The light flickers on and off, making us jump.

I laugh out loud, unable to stop myself.

He turns and takes a bow, laughing, his face red.

"Goodnight, Cora."

"Goodnight, Alex."

I close the door and stare at my living room before exploding into giddy laughter.

My first kiss!

I need to call Kris.

I text her and wait for a response as I go to Dad's office and wait for her to call me back.

I line up my pills for the night.

I don't want to take them, but I'm feeling great and don't want any of the bad things to interfere with this. Don't want the lunacy of seeing ghosts that might be in my head. Just want a normal teenage life.

Alex's bedroom light goes on across the road.

He waves at me.

Then his father pulls up to the house.

Alex turns off his light.

My phone buzzes with a text.

I can't wait for our next lesson.

I text back, *Me either.*

Goodnight, Cora.

Goodnight, Alex.

I stare at the texts, happy enough to explode.

Yet, as I sit here trying to embrace this fleeting moment, I can't help but feel something terrible waiting to happen.

I take my pills, including one for sleeping, hoping it'll calm my racing fears.

TWENTY-EIGHT

Betrayal

I'm in Dad's office, unable to sleep, sitting in the dark at his desk when Alex's window lights up across the street.

I stand and go to the window to wave, then remember he can't see me. My lights are off. I'm about to turn them on when I see he's not alone.

He's talking to someone just out of view.

I wonder if it's his dad. He's smiling, so that's doubtful.

Maybe he's got a friend over.

He's laughing hard, over-the-top loud like one does when they're trying to get attention … or flirt.

He brushes the hair from his face.

Then a pair of hands are on his shoulder, in a familiar embrace. A lover's embrace.

One of the hands strokes his hair, then his face.

And then he leans just out of view, but I can tell what he's doing — kissing someone.

What the hell?

My chest tightens as I watch him, wondering who he's kissing, jealous but also knowing I don't have a right to be. It's not like we're dating.

NO, BUT YOU LIKE HIM.
Yeah, and I thought he liked me.
They're both out of the window frame.
He reappears, shirtless.
And he's taking off her shirt.
No.
No.
Anxiety floods me. Anger and feelings of betrayal, feelings I shouldn't be entitled to feel, should I?
IT WAS JUST A LITTLE KISS.
HE DIDN'T ASK YOU TO MARRY HIM!
No, but … I could feel a connection. That sort of bond that is so rare, some people go their whole lives wishing to feel it with someone.

I felt that with him. And I thought he felt something with me.

But now … he's with some other girl.
PROBABLY THE GIRL'S HOUSE HE WENT TO THAT NIGHT HE SOLD YOU OUT AND LEFT WITH KJ.
MAYBE SHE WAS IN THE BACK SEAT WITH HIM.
Then I see her naked back as she presses against him. They're dancing slowly. Her long blonde hair looking familiar.

No.

It can't be.

No. No. No. NO!
And then they turn and I see that it *is* her.
Kaycee.
She looks up, somehow straight at me even though I'm spying in a dark room from across the street and she can't possibly see me.

Can she?
She smiles, then opens her mouth to say something.
And, somehow, impossibly, I hear her.

"He's mine."

Suddenly, she's in the room with me.

Her hands are around my throat, squeezing tight, choking me.

Her eyes are dark, all black, no whites, and she's growling, "Heeeeee's mine."

I wake up gasping for air, something lodged in my throat.

I'm unable to breathe. Or move. Panic swells into a full-blown certainty that I'm going to choke to death.

I hear something next to my bed, someone stepping on the floor. But I can't turn my head.

Gasping, suffocating. Unable to see who is there.

Tears race down my face.

Whoever's next to my bed is dragging something along the floor, something heavy.

What the hell?

A voice whispers, "They all hate you. Nobody will ever love you."

I can finally move.

My arms flail out, overreacting to being still for so long, knocking my lamp to the ground.

I try to cry out for Mom as it shatters, but I'm still choking, unable to scream.

I try to reach for my mouth, but my arms are jelly, refusing to cooperate.

Somehow I manage to get out of bed. I stumble toward the door, thankful my legs still work. My vision goes dark at the edges.

Then I fall. At least I land on my side and not on my face. Finally, my arms and hands start to cooperate.

I reach into my mouth, feeling for what's blocking it.

Something slippery.

Thick and knotted, like congealed pasta stuck in one giant lump.

I tear at it, trying to get it out.

Fragments of pink stuff cake my fingers, fall onto the floor.

I can't get it out fast enough.

I'm drowning in it.

I flail, kicking at the floor repeatedly.

Momma!

But she isn't coming.

I'm going to choke to death on my bedroom floor. I imagine Mom finding my body, crying for losing me so soon after Dad. This time she won't be able to revive me.

This will kill her.

My door open.

Mom cries out. "Cora!" She flips me over, eyes wide, terrified.

And suddenly whatever was in my mouth is gone.

I suck in shallow breaths, then deep ones. Tears stream down my face, and I desperately cling to her as I pant and wheeze.

"What happened?" She's alarmed. Sympathetic.

I can't speak, still gagging on whatever was in my mouth.

And then I see it on the ground, vomit.

A pinkish-brown frothy mess with several dozens of half-digested capsules.

What the?

An empty bottle is overturned on my nightstand, its cap on the floor. I'm not sure which pills they are, but my heart races, fear constricts my throat. Did I take something that might kill me? I glance at the pile of puke. How much is still inside me?

I don't want to die.

She holds me tight. "Oh, my God, Cora, what did you do? *What did you do?*"

"I didn't do anything." My raw throat is burning. "I swear. I didn't … I didn't do anything. Please, you have to believe me. I didn't—"

"Then what are those?"

"I woke up choking, Mom. I didn't take those pills. I swear."

"We need to call someone."

"No!" I cry, getting to my feet, ignoring the vomit running down my shirt. "No. I swear, I didn't do it. I wouldn't do that to you. Not again."

She stares at me, sobbing in that horrified expression she had the first time I overdosed.

That look of total and utter realization that no matter what she did, she couldn't protect me from myself.

It breaks my heart.

"I swear, Momma, I didn't … I didn't do it. I know what it looks like, but I swear, I —"

"Come," she says, taking my hands, leading me to the shower. "We need to get you cleaned up. Then we're taking you to the hospital."

"I don't need to go to the hospital."

She snaps at me, "Do what I say!"

I obey.

TWENTY-NINE

A Promise

MOM IS PACING in the bathroom, on the phone with the hospital, telling them what happened while I'm in the shower. No, she's not sure what pills I took, and yes, she can grab them and take them with us.

I can't stop crying.

Did I really try to kill myself last night?

And why can't I remember?

Mom is never going to trust me again.

I fall to the floor of the tub, hot water raining down on me. I want to scream, but a whimper is all I have.

Mom's still talking, but her voice has changed, like she's talking to someone else, someone more familiar.

Is it Aunt Alicia?

"No, I don't know why she'd do it, honey. Clearly, she's lost her damned mind. I can't take this anymore. I really … I just can't."

Lost her mind?

No!

"Yes, we *will* have to do something. Something drastic."

No. No. No. No!

I can't go through that again.

But what choice do I have?

Clearly, I can't be trusted. I tried to kill myself.

I need to be put away for my own good. That's what Mom will say.

And how can I argue? She just found me on the floor choking up a bottle of pills.

The walls are closing in on me again. I have to get out of the shower, even if that hurries the process of us driving to the hospital and my being admitted to some psych ward or whatever.

I finish showering then partially open the curtain to grab a towel.

Mom isn't there. She's probably getting stuff ready to go. Maybe packing a few changes of clothing and whatever else I'll need.

So I slide back the curtain and step out of the shower, my wet feet soaking the fluffy mat. Then I grab a towel off the rack. It occurs to me with a pang of sadness that this might be the last time I ever dry off in this bathroom. Mom might give up on me. Or maybe we'll move again.

Suddenly, everything feels like it's slipping away and there's nothing I can do.

I step into the hallway expecting to see Mom racing back and forth hurriedly, rushing me to come on.

But the house feels quiet, like she's not even here.

"Mom?"

No answer.

Where'd she go? Where would she go? To get gas?

I only know I don't have long before she dumps me someplace — and for God knows how long this time.

MAYBE FOREVER.

YOU'RE SO DAMNED CRAZY THEY'LL JUST THROW AWAY THE KEY!

The garage door is grinding open below.

I go into my room. There's no puke. The floor's clean.

Mom probably cleaned it up. Was probably hating me the whole time, thinking how pathetic I am, what a waste of life.

I get dressed and sit on my bed, waiting for her to call me.

I check my phone to see if Kris called or texted back.

No response.

I consider telling her I'm about to go away for a while, again. But screw it. If she won't return my call, then she can wonder where I am. Maybe she'll think I'm dead.

THEN SHE'LL FEEL GUILTY!

Maybe if I go away long enough, she'll appreciate me when I come back. Maybe she'll miss me. A part of me wants her to, and I want her missing me to hurt.

Is that bad?

When Mom doesn't come up, I decide to head downstairs to see what's going on.

She's putting away groceries.

What?

Mom smiles at me. "What are you doing up before the crack of noon?"

She doesn't look like she just pulled me out of a suicide attempt. At all. She's stowing the groceries, like it's any other Sunday morning. If she was the type of mom to whistle as she did stuff in the kitchen, she'd be whistling a ditty now.

"Oh, I got you some more snacks. You must've been hungry yesterday. You're not smoking weed, are you?"

I'm confused.

I stare at her.

She laughs. "I'm kidding. I know you wouldn't touch that stuff."

What the hell is happening?

"How long have you been gone?" I look at the counter. There are far more bags than she would've had time to pick up had she just been in the bathroom with me ten minutes ago.

"Well, I went by the thrift store earlier to donate some stuff we don't need, then I went to the store, so, I don't know, a couple of hours."

A couple of hours?

Who was that up there with me?

Did any of that actually happen?

I rush upstairs, looking for any sign of vomit, either left on the floor, or paper towels used to clean it up in my trash can.

Nothing.

Then I see the bottle on my nightstand, closed, full.

I stop in my tracks.

My heart racing.

What the hell is happening?

YOU'VE LOST YOUR FLIPPING MIND, GIRL!

I remember taking one of the pills in Dad's office because I was afraid I wouldn't be able to fall asleep. So why are they in here? Did I take more?

YOU NEED TO STOP TAKING THOSE PILLS.

THEY'RE MESSING YOU UP.

I look around my room, trying to discern fact from fiction. Did I wake up choking and puking? There's no evidence of me throwing up.

In the bathroom, I search for any sign of puke on the T-shirt I took off when getting in the shower.

It's clean.

So, basically, I sleepwalked through a nightmare.

That's the only thing that makes sense.

NO, THERE'S ONE OTHER THING THAT MAKES

SENSE, BUT YOU DON'T WANT TO CONSIDER THAT, DO YOU?

What?

EMILY.

SHE'S DOING THIS TO YOU.

SHE WANTS YOU TO STOP TAKING THE PILLS SO YOU'LL SEE HER.

But how could Emily do this to me?

HOW COULD SHE DO WHAT SHE DID IN THE SCHOOL BATHROOM?

SHE CAN DO SOME POWERFUL STUFF, AND I DON'T THINK SHE'S TELLING YOU THE HALF OF IT.

There's a huge difference between her fighting off three girls and making me hallucinate. She's a ghost, yes. But, so far as I know, Emily doesn't have the power to get in my head and make me see things. But you know what does *cause me to see things, what has caused me to see things in the past? The pills.*

It's gotta be one of the pills, or some combination of them.

SO, WHAT DO YOU DO?

STOP TAKING THEM AND RISK GOING NUTS OR CONTINUE AND LOSE SIGHT OF WHAT'S REAL?

Maybe we need to change my prescription.

For now, I'll eliminate the sleeping pills.

I'M EATING lunch with Mom — a chicken Caesar salad she'd been craving for a while — and trying not to over-think what happened earlier.

But the more I try *not* to think about something, the more it pops in my head like a vagrant thought, setting up camp and refusing to leave.

She's talking about work again. I'm only half paying attention, mostly focused on the battle inside my head.

"What do you think?" she asks.

Crap. Busted.

"Um, I think you should do what feels right."

"So, I should shoot them all, you're saying?"

She smiles and I know that she's on to me.

"Ah, sorry. My mind is drifting. OCD stuff."

"Talk to me about it."

"About what?"

"Whatever's going on. You've been off ever since I got home."

As much as I'd love to tell her about Emily, there's no way she'd believe me, even if I showed her the necklace and the journals, and the news stories about what Emily did to her parents.

I could show her all of that, but it wouldn't prove that I'm *seeing* Emily.

BECAUSE SHE'S IN YOUR HEAD!

So I tell her the only other thing that might get her off the scent of what's really wrong.

"Remember Alex?"

"Yes," she says, giving me *that look.*

"Stop."

"What? I didn't say anything."

"You're giving me that look."

"What look?"

"Like you knew I couldn't stay away from him."

"Well…"

"Mom."

"Okay, what happened?"

I tell her about yesterday, how I thought someone was in the house and Alex came over to check on me.

"So, you were in the bathtub and you asked Alex to come over and check on you? Yeah, I'll bet he rushed right over."

"It's not like that. He's not a perv. He's sweet."

She nods with a smirk. "He's a teenage boy. They're *alllllll* walking hard-ons, but go ahead."

"So we hung out and watched TV and ate junk food."

"So, *that* explains where all the food went."

"And he's going to teach me to play Dad's guitar."

I then excitedly tell her how the guitar is rare and worth a lot, and how Alex was super impressed. Then I tell her about him being a fan of Dad's books. Like a real one, not the kind who says they are just because her father is famous. He's read all of Dad's stuff.

She's still giving me a skeptical eye.

"What?"

"You remember what I said about him, right? We don't need his problems to become your problems."

"They won't. He doesn't even talk to me about his father. He's not some moody depressing emo or whatever you're thinking. He's nice and funny. The only friend I've made in this stupid place."

"What do you mean? I thought you made friends with those popular girls?"

Crap. I forgot that lie.

"Um. Forget it."

"No, Cora. I want to know what happened."

"It doesn't matter."

"Yes, it does."

"It's the same thing that happens everywhere. If the kids sense you're different in any way, they'll target you. That's high school."

"Are you being bullied, Cora?"

"It doesn't matter." I get up, even though I'm only half done with my salad. I want this conversation to end before it leads to the same place these conversations always go — it's my fault, I need to make more of an effort to get along with people, I should try to get along with people I don't like because the world takes all types, and all that crap.

She's never said it's my fault that I don't have friends, but it's still what she thinks.

It's what she *doesn't* say that speaks volumes.

And I *sooooooo* don't want to hear it now.

I wrap my salad bowl with cellophane, stick it in the fridge, then grab my Coke off the table.

I'm about to leave the room when Mom stops me.

"Cora."

"What?"

She stands, puts her hands on my shoulders, looks me in the eyes with her best Sympathetic Mom expression — the look that says she understands me even when there's no way she could. Not when she only knows half the story.

"Listen, I know it's tough moving to a new place—"

"It's not just that—"

"I know. And yes, kids can kinda suck. But I need to know if you're being bullied."

"It's nothing I can't handle."

"What is it?"

"Nothing. They just call me names is all."

"What kind of names?"

"It doesn't matter."

"What names?"

"They call me bitch. They call me Blinky. They laugh when I walk by. Just one group of girls, really. But they're the popular ones."

"The ones you met at the mall?"

"Yeah, but ... when I went there, they walked by and laughed."

"*What?*"

I finally confess.

Her eyes well up. "Oh, Cora. I'm so sorry. Why didn't you tell me?"

"Because I felt like it was my fault." I want to say because *she'd* make it my fault, but I don't want to argue.

She hugs me.

I don't know why, but when I'm upset her hugs don't give me the same comfort as a friend's. They do the opposite — make me feel like I'm an utter disappointment and in need of her pity.

As we part from the hug, she says, "I know I tell you to try and get along with everyone, and that sometimes I've questioned your choices in friends—"

"*Sometimes?*"

"Anyway, I get it. Kids can be mean. I'm going to book an appointment with this doctor at my hospital. She's great with stuff like this."

"I don't want a new doctor giving me new drugs, Mom."

"She just wants to talk with you. Maybe give you some coping mechanisms to deal with this, and ... well, other stuff."

"Wait, she 'just wants to talk to me?' So, you've already been seeking treatment for me?"

"You knew we'd need to find someone to discuss your problems."

"I don't have those problems anymore."

"You need someone to talk to, even if it's about the bullying. You had a rough year, and these problems don't vanish overnight. Not without work. You *need* therapy. Okay?"

I nod. "Fine. What about Alex? Can I be friends with him? I swear, he's a good kid. He even stuck up for me."

"Oh?"

"Yeah," I alter the story a bit, avoiding the part about

Kaycee and her friends jumping me in the bathroom, basically saying that he defended me from a verbal attack.

"Okay. But promise me one thing, Cora."

"What's that?"

"If the bullying turns physical, or if Alex treats you bad in any way, you'll tell me. Will you promise me that?"

"I promise."

"Actually, I need one more. Promise me you'll keep taking the pills. I know you hate them, but they're helping. I know you don't see it, but things are a lot better now than last year. Okay? Swear that you'll keep taking them."

"I promise. Can I go now? I want to write for a bit."

"Okay, honey."

As I head to Dad's office, I feel conflicted for not telling her everything. I hate lying, especially when it took so long to rebuild her trust in me. But I can't tell her everything. She'll think I'm crazy, and I can't be locked up with monsters again.

I can do this on my own. I just need to be stronger. Need to focus.

The moment I enter Dad's office, I grow calmer. Though he's never been in this room, I still feel him among his things. I sense his energy, and today it's a comfort. After closing the door, I sit at the desk then pull up music on my phone. Broadway music, a playlist of *Hamilton*, *Phantom*, and *Les Misérables*.

I check to see if Kris messaged me, but there's still no response.

SHE'S FULL-ON GHOSTING YOU, DUDE.

GUESS WE KNOW WHO YOUR REAL FRIENDS ARE, EH?

OH, WAIT.

NOBODY.

Wrong. Alex is my friend.

So I text him. *Good morning!*

The minute I text, his online status goes from "on" to "away." And my message shows as read. So he read it, but instead of replying, he signed off.

Why would he do that?

It's gotta be a coincidence, right?

LIKE I SAID, NOBODY.

I look out the window, but his blinds are closed.

I surf the web on Dad's computer, waiting for Alex to respond, but nothing.

LOOKS LIKE EVERYONE IS GHOSTING YOU.

A chill runs through me.

Something feels off.

A document window pops up on my screen, over the browser window, even though I didn't create it.

I try to exit, but the cursor isn't obeying. I shake the mouse.

Letters start typing by themselves.

Don't trust him.

I stare at it but have no idea what to think.

More letters.

Alex told me he loved me before he broke my heart.

"Emily?" I look around the room for some sign of her presence. I'm not seeing her, but maybe I can make out some dim form, or *something*.

I take my hand off the mouse.

It doesn't move, but the letters continue to type.

One guess who he really loves.

I run to my room, slip on the necklace, return to the office. But I still can't see Emily.

There's a new word on the screen. *Kaycee.*

Then more typing.

Don't trust him. He'll hurt you, just like he did me.

I stare at the screen, shaking. "Emily? Tell me what he did."

No response.

"Emily? Please. Tell me."

Letters begin to type again.

Stop taking the pills and I'll give you the next journal.

Then the document vanishes.

The line of bottles sits there, waiting for me to take the pills later tonight.

I decide to break my promise to my mom.

THIRTY

Monday

I WAKE up to Mom shaking me.

"C'mon, you're gonna be late."

I'm aching, my eyes are bloodshot, and I feel like I've been in a wrestling match that lasted through the night.

After showering, I hurry to get dressed and put on makeup, the whole time hating myself in the mirror and wondering why I even bother. I look like the hell I am feeling.

I want to crawl back into bed and sleep the day away.

All last night I tossed and turned, thinking about the message on Dad's computer. Part of me wonders if I imagined it. Given everything else that happened yesterday morning, I can't rule out the idea. But there's another part, deep down, that knows the truth.

Emily wrote it.

Which would mean Alex lied to me.

I check my phone. Even though he was on LiveLyfe yesterday, he never responded.

HE'S GHOSTING YOU, JUST LIKE KRIS.

I don't want to believe it. It's only been one day. Maybe

he was really busy. Or maybe he had the app open on his phone but wasn't actually on. There are any number of reasons he might not have messaged me.

STILL, HE COULD'VE AT LEAST SAID GOODNIGHT, RIGHT?

YOU DON'T KISS A GIRL AND THEN IGNORE HER THE NEXT DAY.

Maybe he's playing hard to get. Maybe he doesn't want to seem desperate.

I grab my backpack and glance at the necklace on my nightstand. I consider taking it with me, but I'm not sure how long the pills stay in my system, meaning I might not see her if she shows up here, and if she's here, I'll need to see her before I can stop her from doing anything crazy.

So I leave it in the room.

Downstairs, I grab my bagged lunch from the kitchen counter then join Mom at the car. Just as I'm about to get in, I spot Alex walking down the street.

"Hey, Mom, mind if I walk with Alex?"

"Or I could give you both a ride."

"Um, I kinda want to talk."

She hesitates, then says, "Okay. Have a good day at school."

"Thanks, Momma." I close the door then quickly catch up. Fast as I can without running.

Once I'm halfway down the street, I call out for Alex to wait up.

Mom passes by just as I catch up.

They wave at each other.

"Hey, Cora. How's it going?"

"Can I ask you something?"

"Sure," he says, brow furrowed.

Now that he's looking at me, I want to talk about something happy rather than ruining our moment with an accusation.

YOU DON'T HAVE TO ACCUSE.

JUST ASK.

"Did you ever tell Emily that you loved her?"

He stares at me for way too long. "What? Who told you that?"

NOT NO, BUT 'WHO TOLD YOU THAT?'.

INTERESTING RESPONSE.

"Nobody 'told' me. I was just wondering."

"I told you yesterday that we were just friends. Where is this coming from?"

"I don't know, I guess the way you seemed so broken up yesterday, saying you wished you'd been a better friend. It seemed like maybe you felt more. I was wondering if you ever told her, thinking how nice it might've been for her to hear."

I didn't think this through, and now I'm rambling. So I shut my mouth before I make things even worse.

He's quiet after this, staring straight ahead as if angry. His chin is raised, defiant. Not a look I've seen on him before.

HE'S LYING.

HE'S A LYING LIAR!

ASK HIM ABOUT THE DRUGS.

No. I can't do that.

THEN ASK HIM ABOUT THE NIGHT HE SOLD YOU OUT.

ASK HIM!

He turns to me, wind whipping his hair over his face. "You don't believe me, do you?"

"I didn't say that."

"No, but I can tell by the way you're looking at me."

"I *do* believe you," I say, even though I'm not sure that I do.

"Mmm hmm." He stares at the street.

HE'S MAD AT YOU EVEN THOUGH HE'S THE LIAR WHO SOLD YOU OUT?

My stomach is in free fall. I hate the tension between us, and feel like I should find some way to walk all this back, to try and make things how they were before. Change the subject to something fun and light, to *anything* other than this.

But at the same time, he's acting so weirdly irritated. From zero to pissy in seconds, which only makes his lying more obvious. And I can't let that go. I'll put up with a lot, but not deception from someone I care about.

We continue walking. It's a beautiful morning — there's a cool breeze, singing birds, and a light mist of fog on the woods just past the houses — and I'm about to destroy it.

"Remember that first night you were going to come over, but you called and said you couldn't?"

"Yeah." He's got the same confused expression and annoyed voice as when I asked about Emily.

"What did you do that night?"

"Why are you asking?"

"Just curious."

"I stayed home. Dad said I was punished for not putting my laundry away in time."

"You stayed home?"

"Yes." He looks down.

HIS TELL!

"What?" he asks.

CALL HIM ON HIS BULLSHIT!

"You didn't stay home."

"What are you talking about?"

"I saw you leave with KJ."

He swallows, nods at me, purses his lips. "So, what? Now you're *spying* on me?"

I start blinking.

Crap!

"No! But you said you'd come over then you didn't, then you went out with KJ. I was working in my dad's office and happened to see him pull up in his car. I wasn't *spying* on you."

"First off, I *was* punished. I snuck out later to hang out with KJ. I needed to blow off some steam. I was mad at my dad. Second, where's this coming from all of a sudden?"

Panic courses through me.

My chest tightens.

My stomach lurches.

My eyes are blinking like crazy.

I need to puke.

I should just say I'm sorry and shut my mouth. Apologize before I destroy the only friendship I have.

I'm about to when he looks at me, cold enough to freeze me.

He's looking at me like he's disgusted.

"You know what, Cora? I don't need this drama."

"What *drama?* I was just asking you—"

"You didn't ask, you *accused*. And you're spying on me, keeping track of where I'm going and who I'm with. That's just … creepy."

"I'm not spying on you, I —"

"Maybe my dad was right."

"What?"

"Nothing," he says, walking ahead of me.

"No, I want to know what you meant," I say, catching up.

"Forget it."

"No, tell me!"

He stops, and says, "He said you had crazy eyes. Just like Emily. And to stay away from you."

And there it is.

I feel like he punched me in the gut.

I wish he had.

I'm standing here devastated, and he's glaring at me, looking way too pleased with himself.

I can't believe I was so wrong about him. I shake my head. Now *I'm* disgusted.

His eyes widen as if he's just woken from a nap and realized what he said, that he went too far.

"Cora—"

And now it's me walking away.

"Cora!"

I ignore him, walking faster toward school, trying not to cry.

Trying not to blink.

Not succeeding at either.

I walk even faster.

He could catch up if he wanted.

But of course he doesn't try.

He's done with me.

THEY ALL HATE YOU.

NOBODY WILL EVER LOVE YOU.

YOU DON'T DESERVE IT.

YOU'RE A MURDERER.

I DON'T GO to the cafeteria at lunch time.

Part of me wants to to see if Alex is there at our table waiting for me. Maybe he'll even apologize, though I'm not sure I'll accept it.

He lied to me.

I mean, technically, I don't *know* that he lied to me. Maybe his father *did* punish him. But it sure seems like he chose KJ over me. He could've snuck over to my house. And when I asked about it, he flipped out.

DON'T FORGET THE CRAZY EYES COMMENT.

EVEN THOUGH HE HAS A POINT!

HE MAY AS WELL HAVE CALLED YOU BLINKY.

I can't believe what a jerk he is. Can't believe I thought he was different.

THEY'RE ALL THE SAME.

NOBODY WILL EVER LOVE YOU.

YOU ARE AN UNLOVABLE FREAK.

I'm walking the halls, searching for a place I can sit by myself without running into anyone, specifically Alex, Kaycee, the twins, Trent, or any of their stupid friends.

I sit on the library side. As I'm heading over, four girls, two of them cheerleaders, approach, looking at me in that way that bitchy girls always do.

I look down, not wanting any of it.

As they pass, one of them bumps me, hard.

I fall, landing on my lunch, squishing the sandwich and chips inside.

They turn and laugh.

One of them says, "Watch your step, Blinky."

More giggling, then they're off.

People are looking at me, but nobody is coming to help. A few of them are laughing.

I get up, gather my squished lunch, then continue on my way, walking fast.

Eventually I find a place to sit in a dim hall where one of the lights is out. I pull out my sandwich. It's ruined, the peanut butter and jelly smeared against the plastic bag. When I open the bag of chips, I find only crumbs.

Great.

I grab the water bottle. At least *that's* not wrecked. I drink with a grumbling stomach.

I check my phone to see if Kris has responded.

Nope.

But I do have a message.

It's from someone I don't know named Mike.

All I can see are the first few words without clicking to read the whole thing, and they read, *Just so you know …*

I wonder if I should click.

It might be spam, so I don't want to, but the profile pic looks familiar. The message looks legit.

I click.

Just so you know … you don't HAVE to wear your granny's panties.

A photo is loading.

Dread builds as I wonder what it's going to be. Some meme that's supposed to look like me? A Photoshopped image?

But no, it's an actual photo.

Of me in my bra and underwear, taken in the locker room.

What the hell?

I want to scream.

More comments load.

How many people was this sent to?

No. No. No. No.

A few comments turn into dozens, including too many names I recognize from classes.

"LOL"

"LMAO"

"Gross!"

"I'd smash that."

"I'd smash it … with a hammer."

"Ew, girl, get some fashion."

"Such a bitch."

"LOL, Blinky Bitch."

"Nice tits!"

"Bet that's a huge bush under Granny's panties!"

"FR, like eighties bush!"

"Blinky Bush Bitch!"

The hate keeps pouring in and all I can do is stare in horror, my face feeling like it's going to crack.

Then another photo posts, even less flattering than the last.

I want to die.

~

I'M SKIPPING SCHOOL.

I snuck through a hole in the fence near the track then walked through the woods toward my house.

I can't do this anymore.

Tears fall — fat, ugly, snot-producing tears. If only I'd gotten my suicide right.

I can't believe someone took photos of me in the locker room then posted them online. Who does that?

BITCHES, THAT'S WHO!

By the time I get home, all I want to do is head upstairs, take a bath, wash off the wreckage of my ruined makeup.

I unlock the door, go inside, and find Mom sitting on the couch, a bottle of wine in hand and a glare on her face. My pill bottles are in front of her, lined in a row. The living room is very cold, like she'd opened the windows, even though they're closed.

Why does she have my pill bottles out?

Then it hits me.

"You promised," she says, after a long drink of wine. "You promised me you've been taking your meds. But you haven't been. I've been counting."

Oh, God, no.

"I can explain."

"You're damned right you will. Sit down."

I'm sick to my stomach as Mom levels her stare on me.

"I don't like the pills."

"Oh, you don't *like them?*" A big laugh. "Well, that's a damned good reason not to take them."

"I mean I don't like how they make me feel — empty and numb, like I'm going through the motions. It's worse than being anxious and sad."

"You don't just stop taking your meds, Cora! We've talked about this. Your doctor warned you that not taking them could cause some terrible side effects. No wonder you're having trouble sleeping and looking like hell. No wonder you're isolating yourself and not making friends. No wonder you're seeing things and talking to people that aren't there."

"I'm not—"

"Don't. Don't you lie to me, Cora."

"I'm not lying!" I lie.

I'm not even sure why I am, other than the fear that she'll put me away now if I tell her about any of the terrible stuff that's been happening to me.

"Damn it!" Mom tosses her wine glass across the room. It shatters against the front door.

What the hell?

I've never seen her this angry.

She gets up and comes over, standing there like she's going to hit me or something.

"I don't even know why I bother. Why your father or I ever bothered. You never took your doctors or your medicine seriously. We spent a fortune and went through hell to get you the best treatment we could and you 'didn't like the way it made you feel.' Well, I'm sorry that you're not always having a ball! You know what, Cora? Life isn't always a fucking party."

I feel like someone's thrown a rope around me and is hauling me toward a cliff. If I don't find a way to pull back, I'm going to be dragged right off the edge.

"Sometimes life just sucks, and you feel like crap, and that's just it. We're not *supposed* to be happy all the time! But *noooo*, you think you're entitled to be joyful twenty-four/seven. Damn the doctors and medicine! No, Cora wants to be happy! And because you didn't take your meds, what happened, Cora? Tell me what happened?"

The rope is tugging me faster, my feet scrambling to find purchase before I'm yanked into an endless void.

"What happened, Cora?" she repeats.

"I got worse."

"Ha, isn't that ironic! And it's because of your selfishness that your father is dead! It's *your* fault!"

She points a shaking finger at me, but it's not her finger I'm staring at. It's her eyes. They're not just angry, there is something inside them that I never thought I'd see in my own mother's eyes. *Hate.*

She hates me.

And right now, I hate her right back.

I stand up and get in her face. "You're right! It's my fault. I'm sorry. I'm sorry every fucking day. Sorry Dad died trying to save me, and even sorrier I didn't jump. I'm sorry every day that I wake up and he doesn't. If I could trade places, I would in a heartbeat. Especially if it means I wouldn't have to see you!"

The moment is frozen, our eyes locked.

I didn't mean to say it.

I don't even know if I meant what I said.

But it's too late to take it back.

She swings, slapping me hard across the face, letting out a high-pitched wail as she unleashes upon me. That cry expresses a bottomless hurt, and I'm responsible for it.

I collapse, not from the pain, but from the shock.

It's all my fault. I took her husband.

A part of me wants to tell her the thing she doesn't know.

But it will end her if I do. As much as I want to hurt my mother right now, I can't kill her with that secret.

She's looking at me, but I don't look back. Or say a word. Instead, I race up the stairs, storm into my room, snatch the necklace off of my nightstand.

I slip it on then march back down the stairs.

She's still standing where she was, staring at me as I walk to the front door.

"Where are you going?"

"Anywhere but here!" I scream and throw open the door.

"If you leave, you may as well never come back!"

The words cut deep. Is she really ready to abandon me?

I should turn around to diffuse the situation, but that damned rope is still pulling me toward the edge.

So I slam the door shut behind me, allowing the rope to keep dragging me into the darkness.

THIRTY-ONE

Into The Void

I MAKE my way to the woods, hoping to see Emily, but she isn't here.

I climb into the treehouse and lie on the blanket inside, waiting, just in case she's here but I just can't see her because the meds haven't yet worn off.

I check my phone to see if Kris has called or texted.

Of course not.

SHE'S DEAD.

A CAR ACCIDENT, JUST LIKE DADDY.

No, she's not dead.

No, she's not dead.

No, she's not dead.

No, she's not dead.

WHAT IF SHE IS?

YOU WOULDN'T EVEN KNOW.

NOT LIKE HER FAMILY OR TYLER WOULD TELL YOU.

THEY ALL HATE YOU.

JUST LIKE EVERYONE ELSE.

I don't want to be a pain in the ass and bother her if

she's ghosting me. But, at the same time, I need to know if she's okay.

I text, *Please just let me know if you're OK.*

I hit SEND, then immediately feel foolish.

SHE'S DONE WITH YOU.

GET OVER IT.

YOU'RE ACTING DESPERATE.

Did all those years of friendship mean so little that she's willing to dump me the minute I'm gone? Did she only like me because I was there when nobody else was? Kris never had an easy time making friends. But we got along well, so it worked.

Maybe it was only a friendship of convenience. I was someone until a better option came along. Something to occupy her time, so she wasn't alone. Maybe she never *really* cared like I do.

SHE DOESN'T NEED YOU NOW.

SHE HAS TYLER.

THEY ALL HATE YOU.

NOBODY WILL EVER LOVE YOU.

YOU KILL EVERYTHING THAT COMES ANYWHERE NEAR YOU.

I think back on the fight with Mom, trying to figure out where it went wrong. Clearly, she was already mad when I walked in the door. She'd been waiting for me to come home, stewing as she anticipated catching me in my lie, preparing to ambush me and accuse me of things.

GOOD THING SHE DIDN'T FIND THE LIGHTER!

Never even asked why I was home early. Maybe the attendance office called when I didn't show up to my later classes.

She was already determined to let me have it, to unleash everything she'd been holding on to, like blaming me for Dad's death.

That's what hurts the most, the realization that she hates me for what happened. Now I can never tell her the truth. She'll hate me even more.

WHAT'S IT MATTER?
SHE TOLD YOU NOT TO COME BACK.
SHE'S DONE WITH YOU.
EVERYONE IS DONE WITH YOU!

I should've just swallowed my pride and let her say what she had to say, but noooo, I had to hurt her for hurting me. Wish her dead out loud.

Below, I hear someone starting to ascend the ladder.

I'm not sure why, but my first thought is that Mom found me and is coming to finish our argument. The idea of going another round terrifies me, even if it might give us a chance at resolution. I'm afraid of what else we might say. But do I really want to make up after seeing how she really feels about me?

I hear Emily's voice as she climbs through the door. "Can you see me?"

"Yes!" I say, never happier to see her. It feels like ages since we were last in this treehouse, even if it's only been a few days.

She hugs me.

I missed her hugs.

"I'm sorry about your mother."

"What? You know?"

"I was there, in your room, waiting for you to come home. Then I heard the yelling. Sorry. I didn't mean to eavesdrop."

"It doesn't matter."

"What do you mean, you wish you'd died? What happened the night your father ....?"

I shake my head. "It doesn't matter."

She takes my hands. "Yes, it does. Something is haunting you, and I want to help."

"A ghost helping me with the thing that's haunting me." I laugh. "Sounds about right."

"Stop stalling. I want to know what happened."

"I haven't told anyone."

"You can tell me."

"It's awful."

"Hello." She waves her hands up and down, "you're talking to the person responsible for her parents' deaths. The girl who hung herself. I doubt you can corner the market on horrible around here anytime too soon. What happened?"

I tell her how I was going through a rough time at school, being bullied and not having any friends other than Kris. And even though I had her, she'd get grounded on weekends a lot and we didn't have any classes together anymore. So I was virtually alone. To make matters worse, my father went through these stretches where he'd hole up to work. Even when he was around, he wasn't *really* there.

I wasn't taking my meds like I was supposed to because they made me feel like a zombie. I wasn't sure which was worse, feeling such deep sorrow or nothing at all. When off the meds, at least I felt something. Those deep lows usually came with these manic highs where I felt on top of the world.

"What's that feel like?" Emily asks.

"Amazing!" I laugh. "But the lows were … well, I imagine you know how deep they could go."

She nods.

I continue.

"I tried telling my parents I didn't want to take the meds, but they thought I wasn't giving the pills a chance. They were probably right, though I didn't think so at the time. I felt like a guinea pig. The doctors didn't seem to know what was wrong with me or how to treat it. They kept throwing prescriptions at me, hoping something would stick. Eventually, I stopped taking everything. But I didn't tell them.

"Things were okay for a while. I had lots of lows and a few highs. But it felt like a normal existence — for a bullied kid without friends. It was what it was.

"But then one night, the lows got really low.

"School had been awful. Kris wasn't there, and it felt like I had a sign on my back begging people to hurt me. Kids called me names — nothing new there — but someone put gum in my hair, someone else pushed me into the lockers hard enough to bruise me in two places. I snapped, started crying in front of a bunch of people, blinking like crazy, and twitching. *Soooo* embarrassing. When I got home, Mom was in a mood. Dad was in his office writing. Like always. I hated his books for a long time because they marked all the time he wouldn't spend with me.

"I remember going to his office after dinner and trying to talk to him. I wanted to ask how he got through his OCD, how could I deal with the bullying. He and I never really talked about my mental problems because I was always embarrassed and he felt bad for passing these things onto me."

As I remember how bad the blinking got, it triggers me to start blinking even more.

God, I hate my brain!

"When I went into his office, he was typing, and he had this far-off expression as he chased his thought onto the page. I realized he wasn't listening, just nodding and saying the bare minimum, so I left him alone.

"And suddenly that low bottomed out beneath me.

"I hated myself. Hated my life.

"I didn't want to end it, though. I wanted it to change.

"So I did something horrible. Something I can never undo."

"What did you do?" Emily asks.

As my mind flashes back to that night, I start remembering little details I'd forgotten — the smell of Mom burning one of those giant Yankee Candles, the sound machine in Dad's office playing a rain track to help him write. I remember how cold my room was when I went in there, pulled the piece of paper out of my spiral notebook, then began to write.

My hand was shaking. And some part of me knew it was a horrible idea, a terrible thing to do, but I couldn't stop. I needed to do something.

"What did you do?" Emily asks again.

I try to tell her, but tears well in my eyes enough to stop me.

DON'T TELL HER.

YOU SHOULD NEVER TELL ANYONE.

SHE'LL LEAVE YOU JUST LIKE EVERYONE ELSE!

But I have to tell *someone*.

I almost told Kris so many times, always stopping short, which was probably the right choice, since now she's ghosting me.

I was going to tell Alex, but maybe it's best that I didn't, considering how weird he got with me after I confronted him on his lies.

I need to tell someone.

What a sweet release it will be to tell this painful secret I've been keeping inside for so long.

"What did you do, Cora?"

"I wrote a suicide note."

"You were going to kill yourself?"

"No."

She stares at me.

"What did you write it for then?"

"It doesn't matter."

"No, tell me."

She takes my hands again. "It's okay. You can tell me anything."

I'm full-on blinking, crying and hating it.

But I've come this far.

I may as well finish, as much as I hate what I did and myself for doing it.

"I wasn't in a good space. My mom seemed annoyed with me and my dad was ignoring me. I wanted him to choose me over his work, just once. So I wrote a suicide note saying I was going to jump off this bridge not too far from our house. A tall bridge, infamous as an option for people wanting to off themselves. I wrote that I was sorry for being such a burden to them."

I can't look at Emily to see how she's taking this. I continue.

"I slipped the note under his door, then went downstairs, and outside, running as fast as I could to the bridge. The sky opened up as I ran. It was pouring. Thunder and lightning, the whole deal, like my inner turmoil was adding to the storm. The faster I ran and the more I hated myself for what I'd done, the harder it fell and the louder the thunder got. The more lightning filled the sky.

"I was soaking wet, cold and shivering as I reached the bridge. I climbed over the railing, just like I was really going to jump. I remember staring down into the darkness, wondering if I'd survive the fall only to have the river kill me. I sat there for what felt like forever, wondering when my Dad was going to come. Wondering if he'd even seen the note. Or if maybe he saw it as the bluff it was and wasn't even going to come. I got angrier by the minute.

"As I stared down into the void and the storm swirled overhead, a part of me actually thought of ending it. I hadn't intended to, but since I was there, that eternal darkness almost seemed preferable to the waking one I was already living in.

"I started to dangle one leg off, toying with the idea. Then this loud crash of thunder and lightning came so close, I slipped and nearly fell. I somehow managed to grab the rail, hard, hurting my chest, but I held on for everything. I realized how much I wanted to live, and that even though life was sucking, it wouldn't be that way forever. My family loved me, and I had a best friend who had my back. It was more than a lot of people ever have. I started laughing. I'm not sure why, but I felt suddenly better. So I climbed back over the railing then started running home.

"Remember those manic highs? Well, I was on one of those insane highs as I raced back. I was flooded with a new outlook on life and a fresh appreciation for just how much I'd put my parents through. I saw myself from the outside, saw how I was contributing to my own problems by not taking the meds. I decided I'd fix everything once I got home. I'd go inside, hug my parents and tell them I'm sorry, let them know how much I love them. I'd do better. It wouldn't be easy, but we'd get through it.

"But every high has an equal low. That's when I found mine. I saw red and blue lights on the road ahead. A few cop cars and an ambulance. I heard a siren in the distance. A bad accident. I think you see where this is going."

Emily stares at me, tears now filling her eyes.

"Your dad?"

I nod. "He found the note and went to save me. He

was speeding, lost control in the rain. Ran off the road into a tree. He was in a coma for a while, and then he was gone. It was all my fault. He never would've been out driving in that weather if he hadn't gone to save me."

She hugs me, tight, pulling me against her.

"I'm so sorry," she says as I finally unleash my tears, shedding a weight that I've carried too long.

THIRTY-TWO

Amends

"YOU HAVE to make things right with your Mom," Emily says.

"I know. I just don't know what to say. I'm sure we'll get past it. I'll just give her the space she needs then figure out what to say."

"No, I don't think you understand. You need to make things right as soon as possible. She's already talking about sending you away."

"What?"

"I was in your house. I had a feeling something bad was happening, and I needed to know. I heard your mom talking to someone on the phone, saying she's 'sick of this shit' and that she ought to put you in a place and let them deal with you."

"She wants to give up on me?"

I thought that was the heat of a moment's fire, rather than smoldering coals.

How long has she hated me?

"What do I do? I can't be put in another place. I just can't. What if they never let me out? What if they think I can't be fixed? Did it sound like she was ready to let someone keep me forever?"

"I don't know. But if you want, I can come home with you. Maybe help you figure out what to say. Spy on your mom and make sure she isn't calling the white coats to come get you."

My mind flashes on the last time Emily tried to protect me. What she did to her family, even though the circumstances were quite different. As much as I want someone to be with me right now, and no matter how much I feel for her, I don't want her to hurt my mother.

Then again, it's not like I could stop her from coming over. It was her house and she's haunting it, whether I invite her or not.

"I'd like that," I say, meeting her smile. "However, I just need you to promise one thing."

"What's that?"

"That you won't ever hurt my mother. Even though we're going through something and she might hate me right now, she loves me more than anyone in the world. She's having a hard time with what happened to Dad, too. She doesn't deserve anything bad to happen to her. Do you understand?"

Emily nods. "I wouldn't ever hurt her. I know you love her. And I'd never want to hurt you. You're the only good thing to happen in my life since Owen. I love you, Cora."

We hug again and walk home together.

MOM IS PASSED out on the couch, an empty bottle of wine on the floor, spilled on the carpet.

I hate that I did this to her, that I've made her hate me

so much, that I've put her through so much pain. I'm an awful daughter.

I took her husband away.

My stomach's in knots as I look down at her.

Emily is staring, too. "Does she always get like this?"

I shake my head, then head upstairs where we can talk without waking her.

I grab a notepad and begin to write an apology, asking Emily if it sounds okay. She coaches me through it, offering some excellent suggestions.

A part of me hates writing an apology letter when I'm still so mad and when Mom is so obviously angry with me. But if this is what it takes to heal, or to at least not have her lock me up in some mental hospital, then I'll write as many apologies as it takes.

"I'll be right back," I tell Emily, then go to Mom's room, grab her blanket, bring it downstairs and cover her up. I situate the note on the coffee table, clean up the wine stain, then throw the bottle into the garbage.

I'm about to head back upstairs, but stop and kiss her on the forehead. "Sorry, Momma."

Then I head back up to Emily.

I'M SITTING on my bed with Emily when it occurs to me that she's been wearing the same clothes since I met her.

"Do you want to borrow some clothes?" I offer.

"No need." And now she's wearing a long blue tee and gray pajama bottoms.

"Whoa!" I touch her pants. "How? I mean, are these real clothes?"

"I don't know. Lilith showed me how to do it."

"Where is Lilith now? Is she here?"

"Oh, no. She's in her house."

"Do you still talk to her?"

"No."

"Why?"

She doesn't answer.

"Did she kill your parents?" I'm pretty sure she did, but I don't think Emily's actually admitted it. I wonder what kind of power this Lilith has over her.

"I can't talk about it."

"Why not?"

"Because she'll know. She doesn't like when I talk about her."

She's looking around the room, and same as back at the treehouse when she was talking about Lilith. Emily is afraid of her.

"Please, can we just change the subject?"

"Okay. I want to know how Alex hurt you."

"Wait until you read the diary about him."

"Why not just tell me? Why make me read any more?"

"Because … I can't remember everything."

"What do you mean?"

"My memory of the things that happened before are changing."

"What? Why?"

"I don't know. I feel like the longer I'm alone, the more I'm forgetting. I wonder how long before I'll be one of those lost souls I see wandering around. The only time I feel like my old self is when I'm with you. I think you're keeping me from fading. I want to ask Lilith what's happening, but …"

"But what?"

"Never mind. Do you want the next diary or not?"

"Yes. Where is it?"

Emily points toward the attic door.

~

EMILY'S LIST, PART THREE: MR. BARNES

IN THE SUMMER when Kaycee was gone, I needed something to do. So I begged my parents to let me go to a Christian summer camp. Father didn't want to let me go, said it was run by fake Christians. But Mother persuaded him, one of the few times she sort of stuck up for me. The only downside was that he didn't want to pay for me to go every day, so I only went on Mondays and Wednesdays.

That's where I met Alice.

I'd only known her from school where she and her twin, Amber, were super popular and super bitchy. They did chorus, cheer, and basketball. You name it, they did it well. And they were in yearbook class, which only added to their popularity. In other words, they were the kind of people who either ignored me or taunted me.

But so far, I'd been invisible enough to fly under their radar, and they weren't yet friends with Kaycee.

Amber was stuck at home with a broken leg, so Alice was on her own and away from her reputation. Quiet and sweet, she talked to me even though no one else did. We bonded over art projects. I'd always liked drawing, but I was nowhere near as good as her.

Mondays and Wednesdays became the highlights of my week. I missed Kaycee, but Alice was quickly becoming a good friend. I felt we had something in common, something beyond art, but I didn't know what it was until late in the summer.

One day, while all the other kids were outside playing, she and I were alone inside drawing. Alice asked me about my scars, then if I cut. I think it was pretty obvious that I did, but I guess you don't come right out and assume.

I told her yes. When she asked me why, I said, "It's a long story."

Then she lowered her shorts and showed me all the cuts on her hips.

I was surprised. Alice seemed to have it all. Beauty, popularity, and talent in so many areas. Until then I thought something like that was only done by damaged people like me.

That's when I realized we can't always see people's damage. Even the most perfect lives can be facades.

I asked Alice why she cut when it looked like she had everything.

"It's a long story," she said, echoing my reason with a smile.

That was also the day my Dad didn't pick me up. My mom called the camp and said Dad had a last-minute emergency. She wanted to know if I could go home with one of my friends.

I didn't think much about it at the time, figuring it was a work emergency. I loved the idea of going home with someone else if it meant not going back to my house. It was Wednesday, and the next time I'd be free from my family would be five long days away.

The counselor asked Alice if she thought I could go home with her. Alice said sure.

That's when I met the reason for Alice's cutting.

Her father, Colin, picked us up in his cruiser. He was this big, broad-shouldered, muscular cop who looked like he could kick some serious butt. He was also super charming. He smiled and joked with us the whole ride home, and all I could think of was how much I wished my dad was like this guy.

He even let me ride in the front seat and flip on the light bar and siren. But as I was enjoying the ride back to Alice's, I started to sense something was wrong from the way she looked at him.

She wasn't nearly as charmed by her father as I was. I thought, at first, that she was just embarrassed by her dad's corny jokes like a lot of kids are, but no, there was something else there.

Something I wouldn't find out about until later.

Alice at home was different from the girl I'd known at camp. Not only was she quieter, but she was less friendly to me. When Amber was around, making "funny" emo jokes, Alice never stuck up for me. Not even once. She even laughed along.

I wished I'd never gone home with them.

Everything felt wrong.

Alice's mom was nice. Typical soccer mom, I suppose. Overly friendly, kept in good shape, and gossiped a lot with Amber. But she seemed okay.

After dinner, she told me my parents weren't going to pick me up. Something was wrong with Owen and they were at the hospital overnight.

I was worried sick, wanting to know more, wondering why Mom or Dad didn't tell me on the phone. I had this horrible pit in my stomach, knowing that something was wrong.

Amber had a friend over, so they went off and did their own thing while Alice and me hung out in her room. She started to come out of her shell a little.

I wanted to ask what was going on with her, but it never felt right.

Eventually it was bedtime. Alice's Mom got the guest room ready for me, and I tried to sleep. But I kept tossing and turning, worrying about my brother.

Soon, there was a knock at the door.

Her dad came in with some hot cocoa, asking if I was okay.

He sat with me while I talked about how worried I was about my brother. He made me feel better, telling me everything would be better soon.

Then he noticed the cuts on my legs.

He asked who did it. And at first, I liked how protective he seemed. This nice father who was kind to his kids, this cop who risked his life to serve and protect. Everything my father wasn't.

The first adult to notice my scars and ask about them.

He seemed to care.

I told him I cut myself.

He asked why.

I was suddenly telling him everything about how kids were mean to me, how people hit me in the halls, and how my life generally sucked. I did not tell him about my father. I'm not sure why, but I didn't want him arrested. My father said if I ever told anyone, they'd never believe me, then he'd hurt Owen as my punishment.

So I kept that pain to myself.

Alice's father was sweet. He said I was a pretty girl and that he couldn't understand why anyone would ever be mean to me.

I feel so stupid now not seeing what he was doing, but, like I said, no adult had ever really cared. I ate all those compliments up.

He even said I could be a model.

I laughed, not believing any of it. He said he was serious, and that both his girls modeled. He knew people. He asked if he could take a few photos and send them to someone.

I laughed again, knowing and saying I looked like crap.

I had no makeup on and was ready for bed. He said not to worry, the natural look worked for me. "Trust me," he said as he went to go get his camera.

I don't remember what happened after that.

I didn't wake up until morning, and then I was groggy. My shirt was off. I didn't remember anything after he left for his camera.

I don't think he raped me. I think I'd know. Maybe? But he did *something*.

I got dressed then went downstairs for breakfast. He was all smiles as he asked if I wanted sausages and pancakes. Acted like nothing happened. I started to doubt myself. Maybe nothing happened. Maybe I took my shirt off in my sleep. That happens when I'm restless.

Everyone was acting so normal. Except Alice.

She had this look. Alice met my gaze and proved she knew something.

My parents came to pick me up alone. They told me that Owen had fallen down the stairs and was hurt pretty bad. But he would be okay.

And he was, for a little while longer.

That was the last time Alice talked to me. She ignored me at camp. She wasn't mean, just busy. But of course she was brushing me off.

I couldn't help but feel like something happened.

Colin did something, and Alice knew all about it.

THIRTY-THREE

Tuesday

I WAKE up in my warm, cozy bed to Emily spooning me.

I don't want to wake up.

I'm reminded of sleeping over at Kris's house. She spooned me, too. It wasn't romantic or anything, but I enjoyed the closeness of another person's touch.

She stirs and says, "Good morning."

"So, you can sleep?"

"Yes. I spend most of my time sleeping."

"Wow, I think you've just sold me on being a ghost."

She laughs.

"What else? Do you eat or drink?"

"No."

"Well, *that* sucks. *Can* you eat or drink? I mean you feel like you're here. You're not floating through the bed or anything. You're warm. So, you have a body, right?"

"I don't know how it works. I *can* go through things, and I can also touch them. But whenever I've tried to eat or drink, it vanishes into me, whatever I am now. I don't ever taste anything."

"Weird."

I wish I hadn't read her diary before going to sleep.

"I had the weirdest dream. I was with you at the twins' house. And I was trying to tell you not to drink the cocoa, but you couldn't hear me. It was like *I* was the ghost, somehow going back in time."

"Do you remember what he looked like?" she asks.

"Yeah, tall, broad-shouldered, like you'd written in the journal. With this big jaw and a mustache. Big brown eyes and a buzz cut. He looked like an action figure or a movie star, but goofier."

"Oh, my God. That *is* what he looks like."

"No way."

"Yeah, get your phone and look at the twins' LiveLyfe account. I'm sure they've got pics of their dad in there."

I go to Amber's profile, as she's the one more likely to have a public account. There I find a photo of the girls with a man who looks like the one in my dream.

"Is this him?" I show Emily the photo.

She nods. "That's the man you saw in your dreams?"

"Yes!" A chill goes through me. "How did that happen? How can I have seen him in my dream?"

"Maybe you picked up on my memories?"

I think back, trying to remember if I'd looked through the twins' photos when I first got onto LiveLyfe. I might have seen him, and his picture stuck in my subconscious.

That makes more sense than Emily's memories bleeding into my dreams.

YOU'RE LOOKING FOR SENSE NOW?

YOU'RE SNUGGLING WITH A GHOST!

"So, what's going on with you and Alex? You still talking?"

I tell Emily about our argument, and how he lied to my face.

"Not exactly a shocker."

"Are you going to tell me what happened with you and him or what? You must remember that, right?"

"Oh, I remember, but you've gotta wait to read the journal."

"Why?" I whine, half-joking.

"Just be patient. So, do you think you'll still talk to him?"

"I know he was a jerk, but I think he's a nice guy. I feel like we need to talk, to work things out, ya know? But I'm not sure if he'll want to. Do you think I should apologize?"

"No."

After I'm quiet, lost in thought, she asks, "Why, are you going to apologize?"

"He was so sweet to me. Maybe I messed things up by accusing him like I did. I should've asked him in a different way instead of putting him on the defensive."

"He's a liar. I say drop him."

"You weren't there. He looked crestfallen after realizing what he'd said. I don't think he wanted to hurt me. I think if we talk, we can put this behind us."

"Maybe."

Suddenly I'm uncomfortable discussing Alex with her. "Okay, I need to get ready for school. I'll be back in a few." I grab my clothes and start heading to the shower.

"Can I use your phone to watch YouTube? They still have dumb cat videos, right? Kaycee used to show me at her house back when we were friends."

"Yeah, they still have dumb cat videos." I laugh and step into the hall.

The house is quiet. Mom's bedroom door is open but she isn't in there. I put my clothes in the bathroom then head downstairs to see if she's making breakfast, or still passed out on the couch.

Nope.

There's a note on the fridge, scribbled on the back of the apology letter I left her.

Working a double. We'll talk about this when I get home. No going out today.

I grumble then head back upstairs.

Before hopping in the shower, I stick my head back into my bedroom and ask Emily if she'd like to go to school with me today.

Of course she says yes.

EMILY and I are walking down my street when we pass the old run-down house. Lilith's place.

"She's in there?" I ask.

Emily isn't looking at the house. She's staring down at the street like the place makes her nervous.

"What is it?" I ask.

"Nothing. And yes, she's in there. She's *always* in there. Shush until we get to the next street."

As we reach the end of the block, I hear Alex's father's truck approaching from behind.

I glance over, half dreading making eye contact. But I needn't have worried. Neither of them glance my way, driving by as if I'm not even here.

"Yeah, I don't think he's worth trying to talk to," Emily says.

"Just tell me what happened with you two."

"After."

"After what?"

"I need you to do something for me."

"What?"

"I'll tell you later."

"Oh, come on. Just tell me now."

"No, I'd rather wait until after school. Otherwise, you'll dwell on it all day."

"I'll dwell on it if I don't know what it is."

She scowled. "You'll chicken out."

"I already told you I'm not going to help you hurt anyone."

"I'm not asking you to. I need you to help me find something."

"What?"

"Later."

I growl.

AS WE HEAD into first period, Emily sits in the seat beside me, empty since Brian Hanlon is absent.

For the first half of the class, Mr. Jennings is talking about themes in various novels I haven't read while Emily glares at Kaycee and Trent, makes fun of them, and mumbles snarky comments whenever one of them says something stupid. She's cracking me up. Enough that Mr. Jennings gives me a look a few times before finally asking "Is everything okay, Ms. Gray?"

Emily raises her hand. "No, everything is not okay, Mr. Jennings. These two asshats in your class need to be expelled for chronic asshattery."

I bite my lip to keep from laughing, barely keeping a smile from my face. I'm used to a somber Emily and like her sarcastic side. She reminds me a lot of Kris.

"Yes, sir. Everything's okay."

"Okay, would you like to talk about faith and guilt in *The Grapes of Wrath?*"

"Um, I haven't read it sir."

"Okay, then perhaps you'll allow me to finish my lecture?"

"Yes, sir," I say, looking down at my desk.

Kaycee laughs with Trent.

Emily glares back. "Yeah, laugh it up, bitches."

I glance at her, asking her to stop with my eyes so I can finally focus.

She apologizes, then sits with an exaggerated upright posture. "How's this, Ms. Gray? Do I seem scholarly now?"

She looks down at her pajamas. "Whoops, I totally forgot to change."

She's suddenly wearing Kaycee's exact outfit, and another laugh escapes me. The more I'm not supposed to laugh, the harder it is not to.

Mr. Jennings glances at me and I cover it up with a cough.

I glare at Emily, again begging her to knock it off.

She switches to the clothes I met her in, purple and black like an ugly bruise.

~

AFTER CLASS, we're walking in the crowded hallway on our way to second period and I whisper, "You can't do that crap. I need to pass my classes."

"What does it matter, anyway? It's one day. Not like I'm gonna get you kicked out and destroy your shot at college."

"Okay, but I don't need to make things at home any worse, remember? I'm trying to stay on Mom's good side. And besides, Mr. Jennings is nice to me. I don't want to disrupt his class."

"Fine," she says, crossing her arms. "Nerd."

A couple of jocks approach me. I don't recognize

either of them, but the taller one, a pimply faced steroid case, looks me up and down, then sucks on his lips. "Hey, girl. Just wanted to say you're lookin' pretty hot. Screw what those people are sayin', I like a little cushion for the pushin'."

He smacks my ass, hard.

"Hey!" I shout.

He and his friend laugh. "Oh, don't act like you didn't like it. An ass like that needs a spanking!"

"Don't touch me!" My voice cracks.

Laughter surrounds us, bringing with it more attention.

Emily shouts, "Back off!"

But no one can hear her.

The guys walk away.

Before I realize what she's doing, or can stop her, Emily runs up behind the guy who slapped my ass and sweeps his legs out from under him.

He flails forward, hitting the ground.

Everyone looks at him now, and there's more laughter.

He gets up, nothing wounded but his pride, and glares at me.

I'm too far away for anyone to think I had anything to do with him tripping.

Yet, he's still mad, like I did it.

"Bitch!" he shouts at me.

I'm not sure why, but I enjoy his shocked expression because he thinks I did something to him. I want him to be afraid of me, even if only a little.

I give him an exaggerated laugh, then flip him off with a face-splitting grin.

His face reddens. He looks like an angry dog about to charge. But then a teacher walks by, stops and looks as if to ask what everyone is doing, and now the ass-slapper is like a snapping Doberman yanked back by his leash.

He stares daggers my way as the crowd disperses.

I continue walking to second period, Emily next to me.

I whisper, "You said you weren't going to hurt anyone."

"I didn't *hurt* him. But I'm not gonna let people abuse you. That's Trent's buddy, Adam Powell. Total freakin' pig."

"Kinda worked that part out."

"You can't let people treat you like that, Cora."

"I told him not to touch me. And he was walking away. It was over."

"Yeah, but didn't you want to get back at him?"

"A part of me did, of course."

"Don't people like that *deserve* to be hurt?"

"Maybe. I mean, yes. But … *we* can't go around doing it. I should report it, then let the teachers or police handle it."

"Yeah, how often has that worked for you in the past? I prefer taking care of things myself."

"You promised, Emily. It's not just that you're hurting people. You're going to get me in trouble. Nobody else can see you, so I'm the one people will point at. I'm the one that has to explain how some jerk got thrown across the school and broke his neck."

"Fine! I'll go find something else to do until school's out. Maybe I'll go spy on some people, dig up some dirt."

"You do that."

Emily leaves.

Even though I'm angry she intervened, part of me liked having Emily stand up for me. So long as things don't get out of control, maybe having her around isn't a bad thing. Kind of how Kris used to protect me. It's like having my own guardian angel.

YEAH, BUT HOW LONG CAN YOU KEEP HER FROM GETTING OUT OF CONTROL?

HOW LONG BEFORE SHE REALLY HURTS SOMEONE?

THE GIRL HAS ANGER ISSUES.

Who wouldn't have anger issues dealing with people like this? Hell, I have anger issues. I just bury it in self-hate, pills, and burning myself. I understand her.

But that doesn't mean I'm going to let Emily drag me down or get me to do anything bad.

I continue on to class, hoping I didn't make a mistake wearing the necklace.

THIRTY-FOUR

Asking Why?

I CAN FEEL people staring at me in second period. Sense the whispers. It's an almost quiet condemnation.

As I dash from second period to gym, I'm assaulted with lewd comments.

"Bitch!"

"Slut!"

"Blinky, freak!"

There's more ass grabbing, and one guy even gropes my boob.

But I don't turn around quickly enough to know who it was. A group of guys is running away.

I give chase, but someone trips me and I fall hard, hurting my palms as I hit the floor. As fast as I bit the dust I'm on my feet again. I feel like a trapped animal, searching for any sign of a threat. Everyone's looking at me, but I don't recognize anyone.

Why does it feel like the world is turning on me at once?

It's a spreading contagion. Everyone jumping on

board, hurting me just because it's what the others are doing.

What prompted the spread? Did someone post another photo of me from the locker room? Or maybe a pic or video from earlier when I was yelling at Adam? I want to check LiveLyfe, but I'll probably freak out when I see something. Maybe it's still just because of the first one.

I have to focus.

But I feel so paranoid, wondering who is saying what, who might hurt or manhandle me.

What the hell is happening?

I wish I'd stayed home.

Is this how it's going to be for the rest of the year?

Is this my new reality?

A target of lewd comments. Getting groped and tripped. Maybe something worse?

I'm late for gym and don't dress out because I didn't bring my shorts. Not that I mind, as I don't want to get into another basketball game where Kaycee, or someone else emboldened by my abuse, tries for a cheap shot.

I'm never getting dressed in the locker room again. I don't know who took the picture, but given how many cameras I've seen aimed my way today, I can't take any chances.

I've gotta lay low until this goes away. It'll get worse if I feed it.

In gym class, I sit alone on the back row of the bleachers with my sketchbook while the other kids play basketball. I'm the only one not dressed out, a point which the coach happily pointed out in front of everyone.

"Ah, I guess Miss Gray thinks the rules don't apply to her today."

And of course, Kaycee laughed loudest.

I'm trying to sketch, but it's hard to focus amid the

whispers and laughter, especially when I can see the sideways glances, from both the court and the benches where players are waiting.

I pretend not to notice, that I'm focused on my drawing, but it's difficult to tune them all out.

Kaycee is being extra obnoxious, screaming as she drives to the basket and fouls other kids. Her every move is another attempt at attention. It all feels directed my way, her way of saying, *I might not be able to hard foul you, but I won't be ignored.*

The coach blows the whistle for substitutions, and Kaycee heads to the bench. I make the mistake of looking down at her.

And now she's heading my way.

Shit.

My eyes are back on my drawing, and I'm actively ignoring her.

She takes a seat to my left, leans over, and looks at my drawing of a treehouse. Of *the treehouse.*

"Aw, how cute," she says, condescendingly.

I turn to a new page, not sure what I'm drawing just yet.

Still ignoring her.

"Oh, come on, don't be such a bitch."

I refuse to let her push my buttons.

"What, you too good to talk to me?"

I continue to ignore her and hope it's driving her mad.

Then it hits me, what I should draw. I start sketching quickly, wanting her to see, which means I should probably engage her so she doesn't walk away before I'm done. So, I ask the one question I have yet to figure out. "Why me?"

"What?"

"Why do you hate me? I never did anything to you."

"Aww, I'm sorry. Did I hurt your *wittle* feelings?"

"No, I'm just trying to understand what it is about me that you hate so much. Is it because I'm different? Is it my color? Or maybe because of my OCD tics? Is it that Alice complimented my drawing? Were you jealous? Or maybe it's not about me at all."

I'm still sketching, fingers gliding across the page. I don't look at her, but I know her gaze is fixed on my drawing.

"Maybe it's about *you*. Maybe someone hurt you. Or maybe you just hate yourself so much that you project all that ugliness onto others? Tell me, is that why you were such a bitch to her?"

I hold up a sketch of Emily.

Kaycee stares at it. Her eyes wide.

I've shaken her. A part of her is wondering what I know and how I know it.

I smile. "Cat got your tongue?"

Whatever momentary shock she got from seeing the drawing is now gone in the light of her glare. She leans in close and whispers, "You think you're funny, don't you? Well, the teachers won't always be around to protect you, freak!"

"Gonna take another picture of me in my underwear?"

She laughs. "Ha! Like you've got room to talk."

"What does that mean?"

"Nothing, slut." She stomps away, her feet clanging loudly on the metal bleachers.

Everybody is calling me a slut, and people are slapping my ass and groping me. All because of a locker room pic I didn't even take.

What the hell is happening?

Trapped

I WIND up going to the cafeteria because Mom didn't pack me a lunch and I forgot to do it this morning.

I stand in line for pizza and a Coke, then search for a table to sit at.

My usual table with Alex is empty, save for the emos at the other end. I take a seat, where Alex usually sits. I can keep my back to the wall and see anyone coming.

I hope Alex doesn't think I'm waiting for him to join me. I want to talk to him, but not at school. Especially not today.

And where is Emily? I thought maybe she'd find me at lunch, but I guess she's busy spying on people or something. Maybe she'll get me some information I can use to stop this crap.

It suddenly occurs to me how useful a ghost could be in school if I was the kind of person willing to engage in blackmail and manipulation. So many secrets I could find out. I could use them to root out my enemies and turn them against each other.

If I were truly ruthless, I could be the most popular kid in school.

I eat with a smile, imagining turning the tables, going from victim to—

And that's where the power dream falls apart. As much as I'd like to stop the abuse, I don't want to traffic in secrets. I don't want to manipulate or blackmail. That will never be who I am.

Yes, it would be fun to hurt the people who hurt me, but where would it end?

I just want to be left the hell alone. Is that too much to ask?

I finally see Alex, several tables away, sitting with his friends, KJ, John, and some other guys I've seen them with. He looks at me like he wants to say something, then quickly turns away. Is he still mad? Or is he embarrassed to talk to the school laughing stock, the punching bag, and somehow — despite only having kissed one guy — the slut?

As I continue to eat, I notice that the emos are looking. One of them is aiming a camera at me.

I turn at him and growl, "What?"

He sheepishly puts his camera away while his friends all laugh.

Other people are looking at me. Kids on their cameras, though it's hard to tell who is looking at stuff or chatting versus who is aiming their camera at me. Thankfully, the cafeteria is so loud, I can't tell who is talking crap. But people are. I can feel it in their eyes and in the energy of the room.

I hate wondering how many of these people have seen me practically naked. How many guys have been ogling me? How many girls have been talking crap about my body? How many people have said horrible things about me?

I stopped looking at the comments on social media because they only made me more upset.

To give myself something better to focus on — something I can use as a shield against the glares — I start drawing. My indifference to the atmosphere around me will prove that this doesn't define me.

They might want to hurt me, but I won't let them see I care.

Nothing has changed. Just drawing like any other day.

I finish my meal then head to the restroom — not the closest one but one in another part of the school, near shop class, where I'm less likely to run into anyone. Probably spend the rest of lunch reading in the least traveled hallway in school.

I'm washing my hands when I hear two guys laughing. The bathroom door opens. I see them come in via the reflection.

Adam Powell, the jerk who'd smacked my ass earlier, and his pervy little friend.

A sneer crosses Adam's face as he sets his sights on me. "Well, well, well. Fancy meeting you here."

"Get out. This is the girl's restroom."

He laughs as he approaches.

My heart is racing as I realize they must've been following me and there's little I can do except run or scream.

I refuse to be a coward. Or let them see how scared I am.

His friend stands in front of the door, blocking it. Grinning.

Adam comes closer, backing me up into the wall. "Where's that smart mouth now?"

He grabs my mouth, squeezing my lips tight.

Now I want to scream.

I also want to hit him then flee the room, but I'm paralyzed. A cocktail of metallic fear and adrenaline coats my tongue as Adam's beady eyes draw closer.

He reeks of cheap cologne or body spray. Probably both.

What's he going to do? He won't actually try something in the school bathroom, will he?

No, no he won't. I'm not going to sit here and let him intimidate me, let him scare me. Screw this, I'm out of here.

I start to push past him.

Before I make it two steps, his hand is around my neck, choking me, slamming me into the wall.

I cry out, but not loud enough to bring help.

My heart is racing. My eyes are blinking. Every fiber in my being is telling me to scream then run.

But I can't speak.

I can't move.

My chest tightens so much, I fear it might collapse, my ribs turning inward, puncturing my lungs and organs, killing me on the spot.

Adam leers as he gets right in my face, his rancid breath hot on my cheeks. "Why don't you get on your knees?"

I will my body to move, to do something. But it refuses. It's as if my brain and body are no longer connected. I feel like a helpless passenger in my own flesh as this horrible boy and his friend are about to hurt me.

Where are you, Emily?

Adam squeezes my neck even tighter. "You know easy it is to snap someone's neck? How little pressure it would take to just—" He makes a snapping sound then laughs.

His eyes are so dark. Crazy eyes, the kind you see on

photos of school shooters and women-hating men who go on killing sprees. He hates me without even knowing me. He wants to hurt me. And why? As some sort of revenge for all his hurt feelings?

Why me? I don't even know him. Why target me?

BECAUSE YOU'RE A GIRL AND GIRLS LIKE YOU SCARE HIM.

THEY WANT TO MAKE YOU PAY.

He leans closer and gives me another reason. "Kaycee says hi."

He kisses me hard on the mouth then bites my lip before pulling away.

I finally find my voice and cry out, "Please."

The word, the sound, is small and pathetic.

I hate showing such weakness, but a part of me thinks if I seem submissive, or scared enough, he'll maybe lower his guard long enough for me to hurt him and escape.

Or maybe he'll realize how horrible it is, whatever's he's got in his sick head, and come to his senses.

But no. He's still smiling like a lunatic.

"On your knees, bitch."

The bathroom door swings open, hitting the other guy.

Both Adam and his friend turn, stunned as someone enters.

At first, I think it's Emily. I hope it's her. She could hurt both of these boys, leave them in bloody heaps for all I care.

But it's Alice.

THIRTY-SIX

Alice

ALICE LOOKS AT ME, then at Adam.

"What are you doing in here?" she asks him and his friend.

Adam's demeanor changes immediately. He's almost cowering in her presence.

"Nothing, Alice. Just hanging out with Cora."

She's standing tall, shoulders back, head up, more like Amber than the timid artist.

This Alice has an icy stare and fire in her words. "Get out, both of you!"

Adam looks like he wants to say something, but his friend looks at him and shakes his head.

They leave without even looking back at me.

I'm too stunned to do anything but gape at the door as it swings shut.

"Are you okay?" Alice asks.

I nod, feeling bad for how I'd treated her the last time she'd found me helpless in a bathroom.

"Did they hurt you?"

"No. But I'm sure they were going to."

She nods. "If you want to tell someone, I'll be your witness."

"The way he was talking, Kaycee told him to do it."

"I know. I'll still be your witness."

"Why would you do this for me?"

She shakes her head. "Because sometimes I can't look the other way. Because Kaycee is wrong."

"Thank you," I say. "But it's probably not worth it."

While a part of me would love to see Adam, the other guy, and Kaycee get in trouble, maybe even arrested, there's a reason girls don't always report these things, especially when it's a gray area that's more threat than attack.

At best, they'd probably get slaps on the wrist. At worst, both Alice and me would be shunned, our names dragged through the mud. The bullying would get even worse, and she'd be a victim too.

I've seen this game too many times to play it.

After a long moment, she says, "No, probably not."

There's this awkwardness between us that I wish wasn't there. Maybe she was hoping I'd want to report it and we'd take on this fight together. But then I think about her father and what he may have done to Emily, what he might have done to her.

Alice's father, the cop.

So many reasons to let this go.

I want to hug her, to thank her for putting herself on the line like that. But I feel the distance between us, as if we're both still stuck in our roles as enemies, even after this. Obviously, she's a good person. She was nice to Emily, too. I want to say something that'll get us past this divide.

"Thank you, Alice. You saved me."

She nods, goes into the bathroom stall, then closes the door. I'm not sure if I should wait for her to finish her business or leave.

ALICE'S FATHER IS GOING TO KILL HER!
No, Alice's father is NOT going to kill her.
No, Alice's father is NOT going to kill her.
No, Alice's father is NOT going to kill her.
No, Alice's father is NOT going to kill her.

I blink with each repetition, as if it'll save her. As if any of these crazy things I do can ward off impending doom.

I want to stay and talk about her father, ask whether he abuses her. But then the bell rings. People will start coming in here any second. Whatever chance we had to transcend where we are is now lost.

"Thank you," I say again, then leave before she can respond.

I'M WALKING home after school, wondering where Emily is.

She suddenly appears, as if she'd been invisible but beside me the entire time.

"There you are!" I say.

"What?"

"Where were you? The one time I *needed* your help, needed you to beat some people up, and you didn't come."

"What happened?"

I tell her about the whole moment, about how I was paralyzed by fear and how Alice, of all people, saved me.

"I'm sorry. That sounds awful. I wish I'd been there."

"Where *were* you?"

"I went to my old art teacher's class to see if she still had a painting I'd made of Owen hanging on her wall. After everything that happened when I died, with everyone making me into this monster, I was happy to see she didn't take it down. She was the one teacher who never looked down on me, and always encouraged me."

"That's sweet."

"So I sat in her class, listening to her teach."

After a long silence, Emily adds, "Well, I'm glad Alice saved you. Oddly enough, she actually has something to do with the favor I need to ask."

"What's that?"

"I need you to bring me to her house."

"What?"

"I need to go there."

"Why don't you just go on your own?"

"I need you to be there, with the necklace."

"I really don't want to go there."

"She'll be alone. Amber and Kaycee are hanging out with Trent. Her mom is never home, and her dad is working until later."

"How do you know Amber won't be there?"

"Because I overheard Kaycee and Trent making plans with Amber, and she called her sister a loser for wanting to stay home and study."

"Why do you want to go there? You're not going to hurt her, are you?"

"No, I need to know what her father did to me. I want to check the computer in his office, to see if he has photos or videos of me, or ... of us."

"What does it matter now?"

"Because I need to know."

"Why?"

"Because if he did, then I want to get even."

"You said you weren't going to hurt anyone."

"I said I wouldn't hurt any other *kids*. But if he's guilty, then I'm stopping him."

"No. I ... I can't be a part of that."

"Why not? You want him to keep abusing Alice?"

"You think he is?"

"Without a doubt. We can help her."

"I'm not hurting him. And I'm not going there if that's what you're planning to do."

"Why are you such a coward?"

"I'm not a coward. I … I just don't go around murdering people. You're a ghost, you can do whatever you want with no fear of retribution, but if *I* go around killing people, or if I get blamed for you doing it, my life is over. You understand that, don't you? Nobody's going to think it's you. *I'm* going to get blamed."

"I'm not going to *murder* him. I'm going to *stop* him. If I see what I think I'll find on his computer, you can call in an anonymous tip or maybe convince Alice to."

"You swear you won't touch him?"

"I swear I won't touch him."

THIRTY-SEVEN

The Past Is Not Through With Us

I KNOCK on Alice's door.

There's no answer.

We're there for a while when it seems obvious that she's either not home or not answering.

"Let's go."

"No, this is even better. We go inside."

"And how am I going to do that?"

Emily slips through the front door.

Moments later, it unlocks and opens.

"Don't just stand there."

"What if he has video cameras or something inside? They'll have proof that I was in her house."

"He doesn't have any of that stuff. Doesn't even have an alarm system. The dude is oblivious. Thinks he's untouchable. Trust me."

I'm afraid to go inside.

Emily puts her hands on her hips. "You know what's far more likely to go wrong? You standing there in the doorway and a neighbor seeing you. So get inside and close the door!"

She's right.

Blinking and anxious, I follow her.

The house is big and beautiful. It's got high ceilings, and even at a glance I can tell this the place is big enough the twins to have a pair of bedrooms each. A TV the size of our kitchen hangs on the living room wall.

There's something off in here. I can sense it like I sensed something off about my home before I learned about its tragic past. This house has a past of its own, screaming to be heard.

But I don't want to hear it. I don't know if its ghosts or something else, and I don't want to. I feel an overwhelming need to turn and leave before I hear its secrets.

"We can't stay here. There's something bad."

"I didn't come all this way to turn away now. I need to know what he did to me. I need proof if you want to do this your way." A sarcastic smile spread across her face. "The humane way."

"Fine. Where's his office?" I want to get this over with then get out of the house before someone comes home.

Emily leads me upstairs.

I hear whispers I can't quite make out. Usually when I hear voices, I can sense a spirit, or spirits, nearby.

This is different. I hear only the voices. No ghosts or shapes. I want to ask Emily if she hears or sees them, but don't want to stretch this visit any longer than necessary.

She stops at the landing and turns left, into what I'm guessing is Colin's office.

I stand outside it, not wanting to go in as she locates his laptop and opens it.

"Damn it. It's password protected."

"Of course it is," I say. "Can't your ghost powers crack it?"

"Ha ha." She closes the laptop then starts searching

through his desk, tearing stuff out and tossing it frantically to the floor with no concern for her trail.

"Hurry up," I urge, blinking harder, feeling a knot swelling in my gut.

I'm about to tell her not to make such a mess when I hear a girl crying.

Is Alice home?

I follow the hallway to a room at the end but stop halfway there, a sudden piercing pain in my skull. Like someone's dug an ice pick into my brain — pure agony, sudden and intense.

I'm ten feet from the door and every part of my body is telling me to turn around and leave. The brightness of the hall is gone, replaced by the gloaming of night, as if I've stepped through some portal.

Something awful is in there. I can feel it the same way I felt it as a child when encountering the bad spirits.

Just turn around and go back to Emily. Get out.

But the girl in the room cries louder, "No, no, please, no."

There's something off about her voice, like she's crying underwater.

Is she drowning?

I can't walk away. What if someone is being hurt? I push forward, so cold my teeth are chattering.

The ice pick digs deeper.

GET OUT!

GET OUT NOW!

DO NOT GO IN THERE!

Forward through the pain until I reach the door.

I push it open.

Emily is in the bed, Colin is on top of her. It's night. Not just night, but *that* night. Somehow I'm viewing the past and seeing it unfold.

"No!" I scream.

And the scene shatters, night replaced by daylight, past with present.

I stumble back, shaken to my core, unable to get the awfulness of that moment out of my head, as if it happened to me.

I need to get out of this house, now.

I turn and run smack into a police officer.

Colin is home.

He looks down at me, beady eyes narrowing.

"Who the hell are you?" he asks, grabbing both of my arms.

The moment his hands touch me, I'm triggered, flashing back to what he did to Emily. Then I'm seeing even more — things he did to Alice, and to other girls.

I can't breathe. I need to get away.

I try to break free, but his grip is too strong. I can't stop blinking.

"What are you doing in my house?" he barks.

"I'm … I'm a friend of Alice's!" I finally manage to make words. "We were studying in the backyard but I had to use the bathroom."

He stares at me like he's trying to process, see if I'm telling the truth. Then he's looking at me funny, probably because I'm blinking like crazy. I'm sitting here trying to lie to a man who sniffs out lies for a living, and who's been living one in his personal life — a monster hiding among the hunters.

He lets go of my arms. "Sorry."

"It's okay. Sorry to startle you, Mr. Barnes."

"No problem. I'll walk you downstairs."

No. No. No. We're going to get to the back yard and Alice won't be there. Then what?

Where is Emily?

It's the second time I need her and she's not here.

I'm walking slowly, trying to figure out what to do. I can feel him looming behind me. All he would have to do is grab me and put me in a choke hold.

He could strangle me right here and nobody would ever know.

Or maybe he'll shoot me.

He could easily say I broke into his house and threatened him. That he had to use his gun. He's a cop, he knows how to set up the scene. Hell, Emily probably inadvertently lent credence to his cover by tearing apart his office like an addict looking for drugs.

Where is Emily?

YOU ARE SO SCREWED!

GET OUT!

We reach the bottom of the stairs and I see the sliding glass door in the kitchen leading out to the back yard. Maybe once we get outside, I can scream for help and run. But as we get closer to the door, I see a deck and a pool. More importantly, the large white privacy fence. No way I'll escape before he either chases me down or puts a bullet in me.

Emily!

I can't feel her, neither her presence nor the warmth in the necklace.

I'm alone with a predator — one who has both a gun and a reason to kill me.

What have I gotten myself into? More importantly, how am I going to get out of this?

We walk into the back yard and onto the deck. The smell of chlorine is overpowering. Steam rises from the hot tub.

Alice isn't back here, of course.

"Alice?" Colin calls out.

RUN!
RUN FOR THE FENCE AND JUST KEEP RUNNING!
SCREAM "RAPE!"
HE WON'T SHOOT YOU IN BROAD DAYLIGHT.

"Daddy?" I turn to see Alice coming from the kitchen where we were.

She's smiling at him, then looks at me. "Ah, there you are, Cora! Cora, this is Daddy. Daddy, this is Cora."

Why isn't Alice asking why I'm here? Why is she not at all surprised to see me?

And then it hits me — this isn't Alice.

Emily has changed her clothes. Her appearance and voice now look and sound exactly like Alice.

And ... Colin can see her.

"Oh," he says, "okay."

He looks me up and down, and I can see his suspicion. He senses something is wrong. Or maybe he knows I know.

He looks back to *Alice*, his head tilted ever so slightly. "What do you want for dinner, honey?"

He reaches out to touch her hair.

His hand goes through her.

He stumbles backward in shock, into me, almost knocking me down. Then he grabs his gun and aims it at Emily, who immediately turns back into herself.

"No. No. What the hell?"

"Run!" Emily screams at me.

I make a break for the door, but Colin grabs me by the hair. He yanks me backward and into him.

I feel the barrel of his gun, blunt against my head.

He yells, "What the hell is happening?"

"Put the gun down!" Emily pleads.

"You're ... d-d-dead."

The gun presses tighter against my temple.

I cry out, "Please. I *am* Alice's friend."

"Where is she?"

Emily's eyes narrow on him. "She's not coming back."

"What?" he says, his grip tightening on my hair.

I cry out.

What is Emily doing? She's going to get me killed.

"Here's what's going to happen next, Mr. Barnes. You are going to remove that gun from Cora's head."

"The hell I am!" He pushes it harder against me. I wonder if the barrel can poke through my skull without even firing.

"Stop!" I cry out to them both.

Emily continues, coming closer. "You will remove that gun from her head, or I will expose every filthy thing you did to me, to Alice, and to all the others. What will your wife think? What will your co-workers think once they know what a sick bastard you are?"

"I-I- d-don't know wh-wh-whhat you're t-talking about."

"Don't play dumb, Mr. Barnes. Lower the gun now, or everyone will know all about the disgusting things you do to helpless *children!*"

The gun is shaking, and I'm afraid he's going to slip on the trigger and paint the wall with my brain.

The pressure against my head lessens.

He's lowering his weapon.

"Now let go of her, Mr. Barnes."

He does.

I step away from him quickly, eager to flee. Then I stand behind Emily, even though he can still shoot me if he wants to. I figure he's more likely to kill me if I run than if I stay and stand in back of her. She's not corporeal, but she seems to be scaring him. He's shaking as if fighting some psychic battle with his body, working to regain control of himself.

Tears stream down his angry red face. If we don't get out of here, he might raise the gun and shoot us both, though the bullets will find only my body.

"Okay," I whisper to her, "let's get out of here."

"No, Cora. We came to make sure he doesn't do this to anyone ever again."

"You said you wouldn't hurt him."

"I'm not going to," Emily says, her smile twisted.

She steps closer to him, "You've got a choice, Mr. Barnes. You can turn yourself in, or you can end things the honorable way and nobody will have to know all the awful things you did. Your family will be spared. Your daughters will be spared. Your 'honor' will be spared."

Colin's not saying a word.

His gun is trembling.

Tears pouring harder.

He opens his mouth to say something, but nothing comes out.

"Your choice," Emily says. "What are you going to do?"

He raises his hand, aiming the gun at us, shaking wildly.

Oh, God. He's going to kill me.

I should have run!

He tries to say something but can only manage a cracked, shallow scream.

"Your choice. Do the right thing, or I'll bring it all down." She's smiling.

I understand Emily's need for vengeance, but this is beyond what I expected. Beyond anything I could have conceived.

Fear floods through me.

His eyes widen as he turns the gun on himself.

I can't tell if he's doing this or if somehow Emily is.

He opens his mouth and puts the muzzle inside.

Emily turns to me and says, "You might want to go for this part."

"No, just call the cops. You don't need to do this."

"If we let him live, he'll find you and hurt you, maybe even your Mom, too. He knows you know, and that makes him dangerous, Cora. Now go."

SHE'S RIGHT.

YOU NEED TO GET THE HELL OUT OF HERE.

I walk quickly through the house then out the front door. I keep walking, trying to put as much space as I can between myself and what's about to happen.

On his sidewalk, I stop and look back at the house. I should go back in. I can't let Emily do this. If she calls the cops and reports him, he won't be a danger to me or anyone. There's got to be some—

The gun goes off.

No!

I feel my face cracking.

I can't believe she did it.

Dogs are barking. People are going to start looking out their windows.

I need to get out of here.

WALK AS CALMLY AS POSSIBLE, DO NOT ATTRACT ATTENTION!

I keep walking. Something in me is broken. I want to cry, but I can't. The tears refuse to come.

As I get farther from the house, I remove the necklace and slip it into my pocket.

THIRTY-EIGHT

After

I RACE up the stairs to my bathroom, drop to the floor, then puke in the toilet.

I'm having trouble processing what happened, and I can't get it out of my mind. Not the things I saw him doing to Emily, to Alice, and to other girls. Not the vision of his hand shaking with the gun, or the sound of him shooting himself.

Emily killed him.

And I led her to his house.

I vomit again, getting some on my shirt.

I turn the shower on, set the water to as hot as it will go, take my clothes off, then get inside. After I sink to the floor of the tub, I let the water fall on me like hard rain.

As if any rain could wash this from my memory.

SHE KILLED HIM AND YOU LET IT HAPPEN.

YOU BROUGHT HER TO HIS HOUSE.

YOU BOTH KILLED HIM!

No, she saved me. He would have killed me if Emily didn't intervene.

My mind flashes on the horrible things Colin had

done, the horrible things I'd seen him do. Things the house had showed me. Now he can't hurt anyone anymore.

SHE WAS ALWAYS GOING TO KILL HIM.

WE BOTH KNOW IT.

SHE LIED TO YOU.

No, that's not how it happened. Stop it!

THE POLICE ARE GOING TO FIND OUT YOU WERE THERE.

YOUR FINGERPRINTS ARE ON THE DOOR, ON THE STAIRWAY, ON DOORS INSIDE THE HOUSE.

THEY ARE GOING TO ARREST YOU FOR MURDER.

No, the cops will see it was a suicide. They won't even be looking at fingerprints.

HEY, DUMMY, EVERY SUICIDE IS INVESTIGATED AS A MURDER FIRST.

THEY HAVE TO CONSIDER ALL POSSIBILITIES.

AND YOU LEFT ALL SORTS OF EVIDENCE.

YOU MAY AS WELL HAVE WRITTEN THEM A CONFESSION LETTER AND SIGNED YOUR FREAKIN' NAME.

I shake my head, trying to drown out the growing anxiety.

"Stop it!" I scream. "Stoooooop!"

AFTER THE SHOWER, I go to my room then consider putting the necklace on. Is Emily in my room, trying to talk to me?

WHY DOES SHE NEED THE NECKLACE FOR YOU TO SEE HER?

ALICE'S FATHER SAW HER JUST FINE!

I THINK THE NECKLACE THING IS BULLSHIT.

MAYBE SHE NEEDS IT FOR YOU TO BRING HER PLACES, BUT NOT TO SEE HER.

SHE LIED SO YOU'LL WEAR IT MORE OFTEN.

SO SHE CAN ALWAYS BE ABLE TO BE WHERE YOU ARE.

I stare at the necklace on the nightstand, unsure of what to do.

We need to talk. How am I supposed to deal with this? Did she plan on killing him all along? Did she just use me?

WOULD YOU EVEN KNOW IF SHE'S LYING?

I can't wear the necklace again until I know.

My phone is displaying a notification of ninety-eight unread messages from random people, but I ignore them and go straight to Kris's thread.

She still hasn't responded, though it says she read my messages today.

What the hell?

I type a message, *Kris I need to talk to you. I understand if you're mad at me, and I'm sorry. I just need someone to talk to. Please, text me or call.*

I press SEND.

I get a red text which reads, *The user you're trying to reach has blocked you.*

I try to press SEND again.

This is a mistake. I know I sent her a message in some drugged state or something saying I never wanted to hear from her, but surely she'd wait for me to come to my senses and apologize, right? You just don't block your best friend without at least talking it over. I certainly wouldn't.

I get the same message again.

Screw this.

I pull up her contact info and call her.

The phone rings once and goes right to voicemail.

"Why did you block me? Come on, Kris, if this is

about Tyler, I'm sorry. Please, call me back. I feel like there's been some big misunderstanding here and I need to make things right." My voice cracks on the last word, then I end the call.

I want to let all this out. I'm desperate to scream or cry or something, but there's nothing left.

I am empty.

My only real friend, my oldest friend, is now blocking me.

I've never felt so alone or unwanted.

Feels like the world is crashing in on me.

What next?

I'm going to call Alex. He's the only person I can maybe trust enough to tell about Emily.

But I see a message from Kaycee before I can text him.

I open it.

If you don't want people to think you're a slut, maybe don't send nudes.

And below it is the photo I sent Alex.

The ice pick in my brain has moved to my gut.

Did he send this to her? Why would he send this to her?

I then look at the tab of messages from people I don't know.

My heart racing, my stomach making somersaults, I click on the tab.

I want to die.

Tons of messages from people sending me the pic, asking for nudes, calling me "slut" and saying creepy things.

Why would he do this to me? How could I have been so wrong about him?

BECAUSE YOU SUCK AT READING PEOPLE!

Screw this. It's one thing for Kaycee to mess with me,

but I refuse to let Alex do this. I'm going to call him and tear his face off.

The garage door's grinding tells me Mom is finally home.

Crap. We're supposed to talk today.

I can't talk. Not now. She'll know I'm keeping something from her. The strain will be evident on my face and in my eyes. She'll ask me what I'm hiding, and there's no way I can tell her all of this, so then she'll get mad because I'm keeping something from her.

And things will only get worse.

No, I can't be here.

Not now.

I grab the necklace, slip it on, run to Dad's office, then throw open his window. I'm about to climb out when I hear Emily.

"Don't run."

I turn to see her standing inside the doorway.

"If you run, she's done with you."

"What do you mean?"

"Your mother is at the end of her rope. She's not well."

"What are you talking about?"

"She's been talking a lot to someone named Alicia. Her sister? I heard things."

"What kinds of things?"

"It doesn't matter. You just need to know that if you run, she's done. She'll pass you off to someone else."

"Like a psychiatric hospital?"

"Yes, but not short-term."

"What?"

"From this end of the conversation, it sounded like Alicia told her it might be a good idea. Said your mom is taking on too much. That she did her best, but maybe you're too much like your father."

"No. Aunt Alicia loves me."

"Maybe, but everybody has a breaking point. I don't think you realize how hard your father's death has been on your mom and how much she really blames you."

"I know she blames me. She told me."

"It's … never mind."

"What?"

The garage door is grinding closed. Mom will be inside soon. It won't be long before she comes up to talk.

"What aren't you telling me?" I ask her again.

"I shouldn't."

"Tell me, Emily!"

"You were an accident."

"What?"

"You were an accident. Your parents didn't mean to have you and … are you sure you want to know this?"

"Yes!"

"Your mother actually took something to get rid of you, but … it didn't work."

"What the hell? No. How do you know this?"

"She was really drunk and telling your aunt a lot of things. Anyway, she wonders if the medicine did something that caused your problems, wonders if she's cursed for trying to get rid of you, and that's why she lost your father."

"Did … did he know?"

"That she tried to get rid of you?"

"Yes."

"Yeah, and he said it was her call if she wanted an abortion."

"So, he was *okay* with aborting me?"

"I'm sorry."

Mom is calling me from downstairs. "Cora?"

I'm finally able to cry.

And I can't stop.

Or go down there now.

I turn back to the window, still open. "Screw this."

I hop out the window onto the portico over the front door, then leap to the ground, not sure where I'm going to go.

I have nowhere.

And no one.

Except Emily.

~

I WAS GOING to go to the treehouse, but Mom knows I go there, so I wander through the woods instead.

Emily eventually catches up. "What are you doing?"

"I can't go back there."

"So, what, you're never going home?"

"No. I'll run away."

"And go where?"

"I don't know. I haven't thought this out yet. Maybe I'll hitchhike across the country, get a job at some strip club that doesn't care if I'm not eighteen."

"Seriously, where will you go?"

"I don't know. But anywhere is better than being thrown into some mental institution. Even being homeless."

"Come on, it can't be *that* bad. Did they hurt you? Experiment on you or anything?"

"No. It was decent, but I can't be cooped up where they won't allow me to leave. Where they monitor my every movement and won't let me have access to any computers or tablets or phones. Where they strictly schedule every moment of every day. Even though it was a large place and the rooms were decently sized, I still felt like the ceiling and walls were always pressing down and in on me. It brought out the worst of my claustrophobia. I had to get out but couldn't. It was awful. They drugged me so much I felt like a zombie, even worse than the meds I take now. Huge chunks of days are missing. I can't remember anything."

"God."

"But that wasn't the worst part."

"What was the worst part?"

"The spirits in there. The people who lost their minds before dying. They were terrifying. One night, I woke up to find an old woman standing over my bed, naked, her gums chattering like she was trying to talk but nothing came out but gasps and groans. The worst part is what was in her hands."

"What?"

"Her eyes. She'd clawed them out and was holding them out to me."

"You saw this even though you were medicated?"

"Yes. These spirits were the strongest spirits I'd ever encountered. I'm pretty sure they wanted to hurt me. I woke up several times with bruises and cuts. The doctors thought I'd done it to myself, so they put me in a freaking straight jacket for forty-eight hours."

"That's worse than my dad locking me in the basement! I've seen bad spirits, so I know what you mean. I can't imagine being trapped in a hospital with them."

"I would rather die than ever go back to another place like that."

We walk for a while and talk about how awful everything is, how I'm afraid that the police will come and blame me for Colin's murder. I yell at Emily for doing that, for putting me in that situation.

"I'm sorry. I really didn't plan to kill him. I didn't think he'd even be there. But once I saw him, things came flashing back and … I couldn't let him hurt anyone else, especially you. If we let him go, he would've hurt you, probably killed you. I know it."

I'm still not sure if I believe her, but she seems so sincere. I know she cares about me. She might be the *only* person that cares about me now.

I'm getting tired of walking. I need to sit and collect my thoughts, figure out what I'm going to do. But we can't go back to the treehouse. I ask if there's anywhere else we can go to talk.

"There's a nature trail leading to a nearby park. It's usually quiet. I go there sometimes and stare at the water."

We find the trail, follow it, then sit under a pavilion looking out on the lake. The more we talk through what I should do, the more I realize just how screwed I truly am.

"Funny, just a week or so ago, my greatest fear was that Alex might not like me. Now he's sharing a private photo I sent him with the Internet."

"What?"

I tell her all about it, from us flirting in the window to all the creepy messages I got. "That must've been why everyone was attacking me at school today. Grabbing my boobs and slapping me on the ass and calling me a slut."

"People suck so much. They did the same things to me after that party."

"Are you going to tell me what happened with Alex or not? What did he do to you?"

"I was waiting until I knew you were over him. Otherwise you might, I dunno, tell him that you've seen me or something. If Alex knew you were talking to me, it could cause problems."

"What kind of problems?"

"It doesn't matter. Do you want to read the journal or not?"

"Are you going to ask me to bring you to his house to hurt him or anything?"

"No. I'm hurt by Alex, and I hate what he did to you, but I don't want to hurt him. And besides, his house is close enough to mine that I don't need your help getting inside. So, you ready?"

"Where is it?"

She reaches into her pocket and pulls it out.

It's smaller than the others.

EMILY'S LIST, PART FOUR: ALEX

ALEX WAS MY SECRET FRIEND.

For one, he was a boy, and boys were forbidden. Father always says boys are only interested in one thing. I guess he ought to know. So they were off limits, including, or maybe even especially, the boy who was my neighbor.

But Alex began talking to me late in ninth grade, a few months after Kaycee's party. I was homeschooled by that time, after my parents had been called in and told about the rumors being spread about me being a slut.

I had no friends and no social life, even at school, by this point.

Life was hell.

Our friendship began one night when my family went out to dinner without me — my punishment for disobeying. Going out to dinner was a rare treat because Dad was so "frugal." Staying home on a restaurant night was awful. I'd rather he hit me.

I was taking out the trash and accidentally locked myself out of the house. As I sat on the porch waiting for my family to get home, my fear of my father's response grew larger in my mind. He hated carelessness and would surely take the belt to me. Again.

Alex saw me sitting outside and asked if I wanted help getting back in.

I was surprised when he pulled out a library card from his wallet, slid it into the door jamb, then somehow pulled open the door — even though it was still locked.

I felt stupid, seeing how easy that was.

"Thank you. You saved my life!"

I don't know why, but I invited him inside.

I'd never had a boy in the house. If my family came home, I'm pretty sure my father would kill both me and Alex.

But I did it, anyway.

I showed him my bedroom and my drawings, and we talked for a long time. Well, it was probably more like thirty minutes, but it was the longest I'd ever talked to a boy outside of a classroom.

We got along so great.

Soon we started sneaking out of our houses almost every night, sitting in my front yard, talking for hours about everything from whether there might be alien life out there to what we wanted to be when we got older.

He never once mentioned what happened with Kaycee, and I never told him. I'm not sure if he'd never heard the gossip or if he just didn't care. We had a lot in common, and he wasn't just my only friend, but my best one.

I wasn't sure why we connected so easily until one night he confessed that his father also hit him, but even worse. He showed me the scars on his back.

Oh, God, so many scars.

I showed him what I'd done to my own flesh.

He asked why I did it.

So I told him about my father.

He hugged me that night, held me so tight that I never wanted to let him go. It was the first time anyone had ever held me or made me feel safe.

I was falling in love.

We kept meeting in secret most nights, but not all of them. Sometimes my father would be up late. Or his would. Those nights were the worst.

But on the nights we did hang out, I felt so special. He even held my hand. And once, after my father hurt me pretty bad, Alex said he loved me.

I wasn't sure what kind of love he meant, the "you're my best friend and I love you" kind or the "I want to date you" kind. I wasn't about to ask and risk ruining whatever we had.

Things were good.

Until one night when we were lying on the front lawn under the stars.

Alex leaned over to kiss me. It was my first kiss. Terrifying and awesome all at once.

Then his dad came outside and saw us on the lawn.

I don't know why his father was so mad, but he flipped out. He banged on my front door and woke my parents up, asked if they knew what their slut daughter was up to.

Our friendship was over.

Both of our parents had us on lockdown.

My father beat me every night for a week, calling me a worthless lying slut. Telling me I would be Satan's whore in hell. He locked me in the basement again.

A few weeks later, I was washing my father's car on a Saturday. Alex's dad's truck was gone. I wondered if he'd come out and wave to me or something, but even if he did, I couldn't dare talk to him. I never knew when my father might be looking out the living room window. He spent most of his weekends on the couch watching TV, but the curtains were wide open so he could look outside.

I was vacuuming the back seat. The hose got clogged, so I turned the power off. That's when I heard car doors closing.

I looked up to see KJ's car. He was with Kaycee, Amber, and John.

I didn't know Alex was friends with them.

I quickly ducked down, sinking into the back seat, praying Kaycee didn't look over and see me. Not only did I never want to see her again, I didn't want her to poison Alex against me.

As I was hiding, I heard laughter, Alex's, along with Kaycee's.

I couldn't resist the urge to peek. They were leaning against KJ's car. And he was kissing her!

I've never hated her more than that moment. At first, I hated him too. He'd told me he loved me. We had a connection.

But what was he supposed to do, wait for us both to be eighteen and out of our houses? That was wishful, childish thinking.

Mostly, though, I hated myself for feeling so jealous.

It took a while, but eventually I got over it. While I did love Alex, I missed his friendship more than whatever romantic feelings he might have had for me. I missed our late-night talks. I missed holding his hand. I missed the way he looked at me like I mattered.

About a month later, my parents went out to dinner without me.

I was taking out the trash.

I saw Alex taking his out, too, but his father was standing in front of the window, looking out, watching.

Alex nodded, then went inside.

It hurt to see him for a moment and not be able to talk. A cosmic tease from a wicked God. It felt like someone had taken part of my soul away. Taken my only reason for living other than my brother, Owen.

I was about to head inside when I saw Lilith standing in front of her house.

When Lilith first appeared in my basement, I didn't know who she was. But since then, I'd done some research and found her obituary photos in the newspaper, so I recognized her.

And for some reason, she was beckoning me from her front lawn.

Everyone always said her house was haunted and had always been empty. My parents said a relative had taken over the property, was going to fix it up and sell it, but I'm not sure what ever happened with that.

I slowly approached her.

Lilith was ancient. The oldest person I'd ever seen, with skin so leathery and thin it looked like I could peel it off if I rubbed against it too hard. She wore a long black dress, as if in mourning and would have been scary if not for her pale blue eyes.

Kindly, she asked, "Do you want your father to stop hurting you?"

I asked if she had really come to my basement.

She promised to help me escape my father.

I couldn't understand how she'd known.

Lilith said she had a gift, and that I did too. Told me I'm special and had a power inside me, strong enough to stop my father from hurting me. I just needed to do one thing — bring her a lock of hair from the person I love most in the world.

I thought she was messing with me, and I laughed like she was crazy. Then she lifted a hand and created an orb of blue light. It looked like a spinning, miniature moon.

I went home, the two sides of my mind battling over whether this woman was legit or some sort of magician messing with me. But even if she were the latter, she knew about my father hurting me.

Later that night, I snuck into Owen's room and cut a lock of his hair. Next trash day, I brought it to her.

Then the next trash day after that, Lilith beckoned me over and handed me a beautiful old necklace with a lock of my brother's hair in it. She said the necklace would allow her to help me. She could whisper advice into my head if I called on her, or she'd help if I ever really needed her.

More than ever, I was certain Lilith was crazy. But I thanked her all the same, went home, and stuck the necklace in my attic so my parents wouldn't see it or ask where I'd gotten it.

A few weeks later, I was sleeping when I heard something hit my window lightly.

I opened my window and saw Alex standing in my yard.

My heart leapt at seeing him, even though I was afraid we'd get caught. I snuck downstairs and out the front door, then met him on the side of the house.

He was bruised and bleeding. His father had really hurt him bad.

When I asked what happened, he just hugged me and cried.

I tried to convince him to run away, maybe find some shelter to stay at. Something. Anything. His father was getting worse, and I was sure if Alex didn't leave his father would eventually go too far and kill him. I made several suggestions, but he shot them all down, insisting that he couldn't leave.

I asked why. But he refused to tell me. Said I wouldn't understand. I told him I understood more than most. I had a brother keeping me here, or I would've left long ago.

Alex thanked me for listening, then ran back home, terrified.

I went inside, into my room, and put on the necklace. I didn't think it would work, but I was out of options.

"How can I help him?" I asked.

Lilith told me to sneak into Alex's house while wearing the necklace and she would tell me what to do.

The next night, I went to his house and found the door unlocked like she said it would be. Found the baseball bat just inside, exactly where she promised.

She said she'd give me instructions once I got inside. Turns out, she wasn't planning to whisper these instructions in my head. She was already here, standing in front of Alex's father, who was passed out drunk in his boxers, just as she promised.

"Now what do you wish?" she asked.

I thought of all the times I'd seen Alex hurt. The bruises. The scars on his back. The time he'd hugged me, sobbing.

I wanted his father to pay. I wanted him to never be able to hurt Alex again.

I wanted him to die, slowly.

"Break his leg," I said.

Lilith raised her hands, put them together, made a sharp breaking motion. Then the bottom half of his leg went the wrong way with a violent crack.

He woke up screaming, clutching his knee, eyes going

wide as they found me. "What the hell are you doing in here?"

I froze, scared.

I didn't expect him to wake up and recognize me. It was suddenly impossible to order his death. It's one thing to wish a sleeping monster dead, but another while staring into its eyes.

The lights flicked on and Alex was screaming, "What the hell are you doing, Emily?"

Lilith was gone, leaving me standing there all alone.

I saw me as Alex must have, the crazy girl from across the street, standing over his injured father while holding a baseball bat.

"Call the cops, son!" his father screamed.

I couldn't let him do that. The police would probably arrest me for attempted murder. I had to break his father's control over Alex.

"I'm protecting you. I'm going to make sure he can't ever hurt you again."

I raised the bat to finish the job.

Alex cried out, "No!"

"Why? He hurts you every night! You can finally run away and be free from him. We can leave together."

"What are you talking about?" Alex looked confused.

"I love you, Alex. I want to protect you."

Then he said the words that cut me more than a thousand daggers.

"Kaycee was right. You are psycho."

He was no longer looking at me like someone special, like one of his closest friends, like someone he loved.

Alex looked at me like I was totally nuts.

I dropped the bat then ran home, devastated.

I waited all night for the cops to come, but they never did. I still don't know why.

I only know that when I woke up in the morning, I'd lost my only friend, and my brother had died in his sleep.

The doctors said it was from a congenital heart defect they hadn't known about. But I knew the truth, that God had taken my brother as punishment.

I no longer had any reason to live.

That's when Lilith told me that I didn't have to suffer in this life any longer.

I could be reunited with Owen, if that was what I wanted.

THIRTY-NINE

Lilith

THE SKY IS dark with clouds and grumbling with distant thunder as I finish the journal about Alex. It's a lot to absorb, and though Emily hated him, I'm not sure I blame Alex for what he did. Yes, he went out with a horrible person, but it doesn't seem like he did it to hurt Emily specifically. He probably got sucked into Kaycee's orbit as I almost had. Even Emily herself had once been tricked.

But I don't want to say anything to upset her. Obviously, she was hurt, and I don't want to make things worse — especially since right now she's my only friend.

I still can't believe Alex dated Kaycee.

WHY DIDN'T HE TELL YOU ABOUT DATING KAYCEE, THOUGH?

HE KNEW YOU TWO HAD PROBLEMS, BUT NEVER ONCE DID HE TELL YOU OF THEIR PAST.

MAYBE HE CONSPIRED WITH HER TO GET CLOSE TO YOU, TO HURT YOU.

MAYBE HE SENT HER THE PHOTO.

"What is Lilith?" I ask.

"What do you mean?"

"What is she? Is she a witch?"

"I don't know *what* she is. Only that she has powers. She allowed me to see my brother again."

"By killing yourself?"

"Yes."

"Where is he now?"

"He's … moved on. He was too pure to stay here forever."

"So, you killed yourself for nothing?"

"It was worth it just to see him for a few days. He needed to know how much I love him and that he'd be with Mom again."

"Have you seen your mother?"

"I saw her once, hanging around the house, but I couldn't go up to her. I couldn't face her. Now she's gone on, too."

"Why did you kill her? She seems like a victim in all of this, too. Your father controlled her. Did she deserve to die?"

"Lilith said if I killed her, she could go to Heaven with Owen. I did it to reunite them. Lilith said if we didn't kill her, she would eventually kill herself, and then she might never get into Heaven. So we had to."

"What about your father? Have you seen his ghost?"

"No. I hope he's in Hell."

"So, you said your mom couldn't kill herself or she'd go to Hell. Does that mean you're going there?"

"Lilith said children aren't judged the same. Told me I could avoid judgment forever by staying here."

"Is that what you want to do?"

"I don't know. That kind of depends on you."

"What do you mean?"

"If you stay here, I will, too. But if your mother sends you away, then … I don't know. Maybe I'll stay here alone, hoping that someday someone else will be able to see me."

I hate the idea of her being by herself again, especially after all she's been through.

I suddenly remember something Emily told me about Lilith helping me see my father again. I ask her how.

"You'd have to talk to her."

"You mean … go to her house?"

"Yes."

"Why is she on your list? Why are you scared of her?"

She glances around, as if looking to see if Lilith is nearby, listening.

Then she whispers, "Because she didn't tell me I'd be stuck here. I thought I would go to Heaven with Owen. But she said I can't. My sins were too great."

"What sins?"

"That I let her kill my parents. God would never forgive me. So I'm stuck here forever. Unless I want to take my chances and be judged."

"God might forgive you. Mom says he forgives those who come to him."

"Maybe, but that was probably while I was alive. Now I'm cursed. And eventually, I'll be as lost as those damned souls you've seen in the mental hospital."

She stares off, lost in thought, then turns to me. "Do you want to see your father? She can summon spirits in the other realms."

"How?"

"Let's go and visit Lilith. She'll tell you."

WE WAIT until it's dark outside before returning to my street, just so I can avoid running into Mom.

The lights are on at my house. I wonder if Mom has called the police to report me missing. I wonder if they've run my prints from Alice's house. How long before they find me?

Lilith's house is even scarier at night. The windows are mostly broken, and the shingles are all either rotting or have fallen off. The roof will never be repaired, despite its slanting. If anyone ever buys the place, it will be torn to the ground.

Pain emanates from the house as we approach the front door, like its structure is steeped in centuries of horrible memories. The house can't be that old, but it feels ancient.

I look at Emily. "Maybe this isn't a good idea."

The door creaks open without me knocking or touching it.

She looks back at me. "Lilith is waiting."

I step across the threshold into the darkness and cold. From what I can see through the pale moonlight bleeding through the windows, the place is a wreck inside — carpet destroyed, paper peeling off the dented walls, chips of plaster and other debris on the ground, thick layers of dust covering ancient furniture.

A crackling static fills the air.

My hairs on my arms and neck are standing on end.

"Come," Emily says, taking my hand, "she's in the basement."

I follow her down unsteady wooden steps, the air downstairs a full twenty degrees colder.

The basement is pitch black. It smells of old wood and something else, like a place I once spent time as a child.

I pause at the foot of the stairs, afraid I'll trip over something.

"Hold on." Emily lets go of my hand.

In that moment, I'm terrified she might not return, that she led me down to this dark place to abandon me.

Static crackles in the air again, like a detuned radio. Listening carefully, I swear I can hear ancient voices, like those old shows that used to play in my grandparents' days.

I fully expect the door above me to slam shut.

Instead, Emily lights a lantern on a circular wooden table.

The basement is larger than I imagined, filled with shelves that run from floor to ceiling along all the walls, with several rows coming in from the edges. And they're loaded with books. It's as if someone relocated a library to this room.

That's what this place smells like — a library!

The books are all hardcover, ancient looking tomes. No paperbacks. Emily leads me to the table surrounded by three heavy looking wooden chairs.

She pulls out a seat for me.

I sit.

She sits beside me.

The lantern flickers, its shadows dancing on several stones laid out on the table. Not stones, runes, made from rock and possibly bone. They're etched with words I don't understand and archaic-looking drawings.

SHE'S A WITCH!

GET OUT!

"It'll be okay," Emily says, squeezing my hand and looking at me before turning to the room. "Lilith, this is my friend I told you about. She's special, too."

Silence. I can't see past all the shelves, but it certainly doesn't feel like anyone else is in here, despite the static and voices.

I feel painful memories. Nothing I'm picking up on in particular so much as intense grief, anger, and despair. The emotions so thick in the air, I feel like we might choke. If I stay here too long, I'll lose all hope and want to die.

Something moves beyond one of the shelves.

I jump.

Emily tightens her grip on my hand. "It's okay."

NO, IT'S NOT.

GET OUT!

NOW!

Then I see her.

At first, she's shadows within shadows, barely a form, shuffling from behind one of the shelves. Her shape is still coming into focus, blurry and moving fast, like a visual echo.

GET OUT!!

I can't move, though.

I'm frozen by curiosity more than fear.

She stops in front of the table and finishes collecting herself into the shape of an old woman wearing several layers of black. Her face is a barely-visible grayish blur beneath a black veil.

She sits across from us.

Milky blue eyes open inside that grayish blur.

"Hello, dear," she croaks, her voice as leathery as her skin.

I see something resembling a mouth, a dark maw surrounded by ancient wrinkles carved into her face like bark on a tree trunk. As if her every movement is pain that might rip her apart.

"Hello, ma'am," I say, trying to make out details, but her face is an ever-shifting, slowly-moving blur.

"She wants to talk to her father."

"Who is your father?" Lilith asks.

I start to speak, but she interrupts. "Silence. I can see him in your mind. Just think of him."

I do. I imagine him standing at the edge of my bed with his guitar in his hands, Sneezy balanced on his lap. I can see him so vividly.

There have been times over the past year when I felt like memories of my father were fading. I worried how long I had before they were gone.

But remembering him now feels like only yesterday. Or even right now.

The static crackles louder, then there's a loud POP.

"Cora?" Dad's voice fills the room.

No, it can't be. Every skeptical molecule in my body thinks this must be a trick.

"Daddy?"

"Where are you?"

Hearing his voice so clearly melts all those doubts, and it feels as if he's walked into the room.

Without any shred of doubt, I feel him here. I know this is him.

"I'm with Mom in Washington. Where are you?"

"Waiting for you. You're alive? I thought you were dead. I've been looking for you in the In-Between."

"In-Between?"

Lilith speaks, "The place between Heaven and Earth, a place our spirits go while we await our judgment."

"Yes, dear. Looking for you."

"I'm not dead, Daddy. I … I didn't kill myself. I'm still alive."

After a long silence, he says, "I'm so glad."

"You can go to Heaven now, Daddy. You can stop looking for me."

"I can't go."

"Why?"

"Because I turned down my chance. They tried to take me, but I said no, I was searching for my daughter."

"What? You can go now, Daddy. I'm fine. Mom is fine. We'll see you someday."

Lilith says, "I'm afraid he's stuck there forever."

"What?"

"You don't turn down the angels when they come. Choose to stay, and that choice is forever."

"No!"

"Cora? Is that you?"

He sounds confused, lost. And I remember what Emily said about forgetting over time if you're alone for long enough. Will Dad be doomed to eternally roam around as an insane spirit?

"Yes, Daddy. It's me."

"When are you coming, dear?"

"I don't know, Daddy."

The crackling stops.

"Dad?"

"He's gone," Lilith says.

"What? How do we get him back?"

"We have to wait until he's ready."

"What can I do to help him get into Heaven?"

"You can't. He's stuck."

"So what happens to him now?"

"Exactly what you were thinking would happen. He will be lost."

I turn to Emily, then back to Lilith. "How can I save him?"

"You can join him."

"You mean die?"

"Yes," she says matter-of-factly, like it's a routine procedure.

"How would that even work? He died in California. I thought you were stuck where you died. If I die here, then how would we be together?"

"Your death will bring him here. He'll feel the pull."

"How do you know all this?"

She waves her layered arms at the books around us. "I spent my life researching these things. It's how I brought back Ada."

Another form appears, though I can barely see it, behind Lilith.

"Is … is that her? Why can't I see her?"

"There are many spirits here. I can't expect you to see them all. Most people don't even see those closest to them. Do you want to be with your father again? Your whole family can be reunited."

IS SHE SUGGESTING WHAT I THINK SHE IS?

I feel as if she hit me with a hammer. "You mean … kill my mother?"

"No. I mean you and your father can stay with her. Perhaps I can get her to see you both again. Then, someday, she will pass and you can all be here eternally."

Emily squeezes my hand. "We can be friends forever. Literally."

The look in her eyes, the hope, reminds me of how lonely she's been. And how she was afraid that once I was gone she might disappear altogether.

JUST LIKE YOUR FATHER.

"I … I don't know. I don't want to die."

"Why not?" Emily asks. "You've got nothing left here. For all you know, the police will blame you for killing Colin and throw you in prison. If you saw ghosts in a mental hospital, I can only imagine how horrible the ones in prison would be. All the murderers, rapists, and other monsters locked up there. The pain would be unbearable."

"Why can't we just go back to California? Now that I know he's stuck In-Between, we can just go there."

"Did you see him before?" Lilith asks.

"I ... I think so. Once."

"That's not strong enough. And I can't help you there. I'm stuck here. This is the only way I know to keep him from becoming one of the damned."

I imagine my father lost, looking for me all that time. Damned because of me and my selfish lie. I can't leave him to an eternity as one of those wretched souls without any memory.

Now that I know I can save him, it would be selfish not to.

YOU'RE TALKING ABOUT SUICIDE, THOUGH!

WHAT IF THESE PEOPLE ARE WRONG?

OR WHAT IF THIS IS ALL IN YOUR HEAD?

It can't be in my head. Stop that. We've seen too much for you to be playing that card now.

YOU'RE TALKING ABOUT ENDING IT ALL.

THAT IS GOING TO KILL YOUR MOTHER.

YOU CAN'T DO THAT.

She hates me anyway. Maybe she's better off without me.

I think about the hateful look in her eyes.

I think about how she never wanted me.

I think about my father's voice just now. It was him, I know it was. He was ... so lost.

I can't afford to be selfish again.

"Okay. I'll do it. But I need to go home and write my mom a letter first."

FORTY

Confrontation

I WALK across Lilith's lawn, eager to get home.

Emily is right behind me. "You're actually going to go home first?"

"I can't just disappear."

"Your mom is still up, though. She's going to see you. She'll want to know what's going on. She might even have people waiting to take you away."

"I'll tell her that we'll talk after I shower. I'll get paper and a pen, write it in the tub, then slit my wrists. I just need to think of something so Mom will understand this isn't her fault and it's not a bad thing."

"Maybe write hateful things in the letter so she'll be mad enough at you that it won't hurt her as much."

"Maybe." I'm trying not to talk too much about it. I'll lose my nerve if I do.

MAYBE YOU SHOULD THINK ABOUT IT!

THIS COULD ALL BE SOME CRAZY DELUSION AND YOU'RE ABOUT TO DO SOMETHING YOU CAN'T FIX!

I ignore the voice.

I need to focus.

I'm on my lawn, approaching the front door and bracing myself for whatever Mom will hit me with. Emily's right, she *will* want to talk, and it'll probably be difficult to keep my resolve if I have to sit through it.

I need to cut her off, be a bitch if necessary.

As I reach the front door, Alex walks out of it.

"Cora?" he says, eyes wide.

"What's he doing here?" Emily yells.

"What are you doing here?" I ask.

"Cora!" Mom calls from behind him. She runs out and hugs me. "Oh, my God. I was *soooo* worried about you."

As she's squeezing me tight, I can't help but remember all the awful things she said to me and the things Emily told me she'd said on the phone.

She wanted to abort me.

I pull away from the hug. "I need to go shower."

"Wait!" Alex grabs my arm.

I spin around. "What?"

"I wanted to say sorry."

"For what, sending my nude photo around?"

It wasn't nude, of course. I was in a bra, but calling it a nude will piss Mom off, so I do it. May as well go full-bore and alienate everyone before saying goodbye.

"What? I didn't send your picture around. I thought you did."

"Why would *I* send my photo around? Yeah, I love being called a slut and having dudes sexually assault me in the halls in school. It's freaking awesome!"

"I don't know. But I swear, I didn't send it to anyone. I would never do that to you."

"Then what *are* you apologizing for?"

"For how I reacted when you accused me of lying. You

were right, I was lying. I went out to get pills for my Dad. He's been hooked ever since his accident."

Emily yells, "He's a liar. They were for him! Just go upstairs and get this over with. Don't even listen to him."

I should, but I can't just drop the argument with Alex. I still don't believe him on the photo, and I want to tell him that I know about Emily.

"You mean when Emily hurt him?"

He stares at me. "What? How did you know?"

"She told me."

"What are you doing?" Emily screams. "Don't tell him I'm here! Don't tell him we're talking!"

I turn to her. "Why not? Why not get this all out in the open, call these fucking liars out on their lies? I'm sick of all the lying."

Mom is staring at me, "Who are you talking to?"

Alex's eyes are wide. "She's here now?"

I nod. "Yes, and she's told me all the lies you guys have been telling, especially you, Mom."

"What are you talking about? Who is Emily?"

Alex interrupts. "You can't listen to her, Cora. She's a liar. Whatever she's telling you, it isn't true. She just wants you to stay here with her."

Emily screams, "Liar!"

She shoves Alex fifty feet across the lawn, straight into the road.

Mom screams, runs to Alex, helps him up.

"What was that?" she asks.

I yell at Emily, "Don't hurt him!"

Mom and Alex come over. He's rubbing his head, dazed, not saying a word.

Mom is pulling my arm. "Come inside, you two."

Emily grabs my other arm. "Let's go, Cora. Screw leaving a note. These people don't deserve it."

Mom looks confused. "Come on, Cora. Stop pulling. Let's all go inside."

"I'm not pulling. She is."

"Who?"

"Emily," Alex says. "She wants you to kill yourself, doesn't she?"

I stare. "How do you know?"

"She tried to get me to kill myself. Said we belonged together. Whatever she's telling you, I swear it's a lie."

Emily moves toward him.

I jump between them.

She stops just short of slamming into me. She meets me eyes, "Don't listen to him, Cora. He's a liar. He, Kaycee, your Mom — they're all liars."

"She'll try to push you from your friends. She'll say anything to convince you you need her. She tried to do the same thing to me. But I rejected her. I thought she'd faded away, but I can see that was only wishful thinking."

"He's a liar!" Emily screams. "Come on, Cora. Don't let him pull you into his lies."

"What's going on?"

Alex turns to Mom. "Your daughter is being haunted by a ghost. My guess is she's turning Cora against everyone with lies. Maybe even sent that photo."

I turn to Emily. Her eyes go wide, unable to mask the guilt.

"Did … did *you* send the photo?"

"No. He's crazy! Come on, Cora. Let's get out of here. Your father is waiting."

I step back from her and pull my phone out of my pocket.

Emily goes to grab it.

I yank it away. "Don't touch my phone!"

She steps back. "Come on, Cora, they're just trying to confuse you. I'm your friend."

I look through my sent files. Find proof that *I* sent the photo to Kaycee and Trent this morning — the exact time I was in the shower and Emily was using my phone to watch YouTube.

"You … you lied to me."

"I didn't do it," Emily cries. "It was you when you were on your meds!"

"No, this was when I was in the shower. What else did you do?"

I remember Kaycee saying I'd sent her several messages when I'd only sent one.

I search my old messages to her.

More than a dozen, me being needy in all of them.

I shake my head, anger cracking my throat as I speak, "Why?"

"I was trying to show you what these people are like. I was only trying to protect you. I swear."

I can feel Alex and Mom staring at me, Mom probably thinking I've lost my mind along with Alex, but she's not saying anything. Maybe she *can* sense Emily.

Emily says, "These people are horrible. I swear, everything I put in those journals was true. Ask Alex about any of it. They hurt me. They'll hurt you, too. They're all horrible. I just needed you to see it, so I gently nudged a couple of things."

Then it hits me.

SHE DID ALL OF THIS!

I'm blinking, chest tightening, thinking of all the shit that's happened to me in the past few weeks — and Emily was the architect of most, if not all, of it.

I can't even look at her. I feel like I'm going to crack

wide open and scream, cry, or some horrible combination of both.

"You sent those texts to Kris, didn't you?"

Emily swallows, saying nothing.

"You chased away my only friend! She wasn't like these people. She never did anything to me. She loved me!"

"She was leaving you for Tyler!"

"What about Mom? Did she really say those things?"

"What things?" Mom asks.

"She said you were going to send me away forever, that you told Aunt Alicia you never wanted me. That you wanted to abort me."

"What? I never said any of that!"

Alex shouts, "Emily's a liar! Whatever good was inside her was twisted up by that Lilith woman."

"You know about Lilith?" I ask him.

"Yes, she told me after she died. When she came back. She said that Lilith would save me, and we could all live together in that wretched house forever. Even said she could bring my mother's ghost back. And … I almost did it. But after I went inside and saw some of the runes, I did some research and found out what Lilith really was."

I glare at Emily, then say to Alex, "She said she can unite me and my dad. Said if I killed myself he would come here. He'd be in limbo forever if I didn't, eventually going insane. He even spoke to me."

"What?" Mom says. "You were going to kill yourself?"

"I thought it would save him. She said we could all be together."

"It wasn't your father. Lilith lies. She's a kind of hag, trying to trick you like she did Emily. She told Emily she'd bring Owen back, but she couldn't. Now she has her soul."

I turn to Emily. "Is this true?"

She's crying, still not speaking.

I'm insistent. "Is this true?"

She finally nods. "I only lied because she told me we could be together forever. I love you, Cora. You're the first good—"

"Stop!" I shout, then turn to Alex. "How do I get rid of her?"

"No!" Emily shouts. "*Please*. If you leave me, I'll be all alone. I'll fade to madness, just like your father."

"Don't you ever mention him again."

"Do you have anything of hers?" Alex asks. "She gave me a necklace, but I gave it back to her."

"Is this it?" I ask, ripping the necklace off of my neck.

"No!" Emily cries out. "Please, don't break it."

"Break it," Alex says.

Emily screams, launching herself at my mother, moving so swiftly. One second she's in front of me, and the next mom is on the driveway with Emily behind her.

She has my mom in a chokehold, gripping her head in one hand and her chin in another as if she's about to snap her neck. I have no doubt she could.

"Give me the necklace or I'll kill her."

Mom's eyes widen as she tries to wiggle free. "Don't do it."

"You heard her?" I ask.

Mom, squirming, says, "Yes, she said to give her the necklace."

"Do it!" Emily demands. "I'll kill her just like you killed your father."

"What?" Mom asks.

"Oh, she didn't tell you?" Emily asks, flashing a smile at me.

I can't believe how quickly her love has turned to hate, how she wants to inflict pain on me. How she's drawing pleasure from its well.

"Don't believe her!" Alex calls out. "Come on, Emily. Let her go. You're not going to kill Cora's mother."

"I don't want to, but I will if you don't give me that necklace."

SHE'S GOING TO KILL HER!

She's not going to kill her.

She's not going to kill her.

She's not going to kill her.

She's not going to kill her.

I meet Emily's eyes, hardly able to reconcile the person I thought was my friend with what she's done. "You say you love me, yet you did so much to keep me from everyone I knew and care about, and now you threaten my mother?"

"I *do* love you. I was almost completely faded when you came. If you leave me now, I'll become nothing. These people don't care about you. Not like I do. I understand you, Cora. I love you."

"Break it!" Mom shouts.

But I can't let Emily kill my mother. I'm not sure what will happen if I hand her the necklace. Will she continue to haunt this house? Will she try to hurt us? I don't think so, but I also know I never want to see her again.

She hurt me in ways I can never forgive. She made me doubt everything, including my sanity. I want to break the necklace, if only to ensure I never see her again, to make sure she doesn't hurt Momma.

"Fine, you want it, let her go," I say holding the necklace out.

Emily lets go of my mom.

So I throw her the necklace, praying this isn't a mistake and once Emily has it, she won't kill us both.

Mom snatches it, throws the thing to the driveway, then stomps it with her heel.

Emily screams as she dives for it.

Halfway through the dive, she vanishes.

We all stare as Mom lifts her heel and reveals the crushed glass.

"Where's this Lilith?" she asks.

FORTY-ONE

One Last Thing

It's three in the morning and nobody else is out on our street.

Mom, Alex, and I stand in Lilith's backyard, emptied gas cans dangling from our hands.

Mom looks at us both, then holds up a box of matches. "Who wants the honors?"

I raise my hand.

She hands them to me.

I take one out of the box. "One, two, three, four." Then I strike it, watching as the fat red tip blazes, surrounded by a small flame.

I drop it to the ground where it ignites a larger flame, then races toward the house to destroy Lilith's home once and for all.

None of us are sure if it'll get rid of her, but it seemed like a good idea.

As the house erupts into flames, Mom looks at us both. "I think we should all get home before someone calls the fire department."

MOMMA and I are sitting in the kitchen across from one another drinking hot tea to help us relax as the sun rises outside.

Lilith's house burned to the ground. The firefighters were unable to salvage it. I'm not sure what will happen next or if Lilith, or Emily, are really gone.

But at least Mom and I have cleared the air.

I've already told her everything that's happened, save for the one thing Emily threatened to tell her — the unforgivable secret.

She's taken it all well so far, promising to listen and find the right therapists who can help me get over this — ones who aren't just looking to push pills on me.

I've promised to take my meds and follow the rules. If things get rough, with bullying or anything else, I'll come to her.

This time, I mean it.

"We'll get through this, together," she says holding my hands across the table. "I'm sorry I didn't believe you before … about seeing ghosts. Being a nurse, I've always looked for a medical reason. Something psychological. It's what makes sense, you know?"

I nod.

She's crying. "I'm so sorry, baby. I … I hate that you had to feel scared in your own house. I think of all the times you'd said you'd seen ghosts, how terrified you were, and I never believed you. I thought you wanted attention or that maybe something was wrong with you. You must've felt so alone. Oh, God, I'm so sorry."

She keeps saying the same things, and it keeps on hurting the same amount. But it also feels good.

I'm crying, tears of sadness and relief that finally someone — finally my mother — believes me.

Mom shakes her head. "I think I was so frustrated with your father's OCD and his mood swings that sometimes I … I was projecting my frustration with him onto you. And sometimes it felt like you two were ganging up on me with your OCD stuff. I should have listened, Cora. I'm so sorry."

She gets up, comes over to me, and holds out her hands.

I stand and we hug.

Tight.

I'm blinking and crying.

"It's going to be okay," she says.

"There's something else."

"What is it?"

She hasn't asked me yet what Emily meant. Maybe the chaos helped her forget. But I have to tell her.

I've been holding the secret too long.

I always thought I just needed to tell someone, but that wasn't the truth. Only one person can help me with this secret — her.

"I need to tell you something."

DON'T DO IT. SHE'LL NEVER FORGIVE YOU!

I have to tell her. She will forgive me.

I have to tell her. She will forgive me.

I have to tell her. She will forgive me.

I have to tell her. She will forgive me.

"The night I left the suicide note …"

She pulls away, looks at me. Her expression is one of openness, of love, and I'm about to smash it with the ugly truth.

"What?" she asks.

I'm sniffling and wiping at tears.

DON'T DO IT! SHE WILL NEVER FORGIVE YOU!

"I ..."

"What is it?"

DON'T!

"I wasn't going to kill myself."

"What?"

I can hardly look her in the eyes. I don't want to see them the moment she realizes what I'm saying. That Daddy died because I lied. For attention.

The moment will crush her.

But I have to come clean.

DON'T!

Only way to do it is to rip the bandage off!

"I wrote the note because I needed Dad but he always so busy. I felt like I had something serious to say but he didn't have time for it. I needed him to notice me, and ... when I got there, to the bridge, I suddenly realized I was being stupid. I ran home, wanting to apologize, wanting to get the note before he even saw it, but then I saw the ambulance lights and ..."

I crumble into tears and snot and apologies.

"If it weren't for me, he'd still be here. I'm so sorry, Momma."

Silence.

I can't look up. I'm terrified to see the hurt in her expression.

The disappointment and hate. Evidence of my betrayal.

"Cora."

I shake my head.

"Cora."

I look up.

But there is only love in her eyes.

She holds out her arms and takes me into them again.

Epilogue

SEVEN MONTHS LATER...

MOM and I pull into McCarthy's parking lot.

The steak house is the fanciest place in town, and she's taking me here for my seventeenth birthday dinner. The place is packed, which I guess is to be expected on the weekend.

I can't wait to try the food, but my happiness is dulled because Alex has to work and won't be joining us. He's only been a shift manager at Nan's for a month and it was his responsibility to cover shifts if someone called in sick. And, of course, someone did tonight.

I'm trying not to sulk.

Alex and I have come a long way since the night we burned Lilith's place to the ground. At first, things were odd between us, then one day he showed up at my house with his guitar, under the pretense of needing to finish our lesson.

It was sweet, and he had this big goofy grin. We made up.

More than made up, I guess, considering we've been dating for four months now.

"I really wish Alex was here tonight." I sigh.

I don't want to ruin the night, especially when Mom is in such a great mood.

"I'm sorry, honey. We'll still have fun, though, right?" She smiles.

"Yep" I flash a thumbs-up.

Mom and I have been way better, too. And I don't want to return to my moody old self just because Alex isn't present for my birthday.

We head inside and up to the hostess where Mom gives her our names. "Reservation for two. Gray."

The hostess, a short redhead rocking a hipster haircut, looks at the computer, her brow furrowing. "Hmm, Gray, you said?"

"Yes, Mary Gray."

"I don't have anything here. Are you sure you made reservations?"

"Yes, I made reservations. It's my daughter's birthday. I made them last month."

"I'm sorry, I don't see anything here. Hold on, let me get a manager."

Mom sighs, already impatient.

A line of people is forming behind us. At least twenty people are sitting on nearby couches waiting for their tables.

I'm feeling anxious.

I start blinking.

Even though I've finally found a medicine and a few coping mechanisms to help me with the worst of the compulsions, I'm still a hot blinky mess sometimes. My therapist says I might grow out of it or replace it with another compulsion, but so long as it doesn't interfere with my life, I shouldn't worry too much.

"Maybe we should go somewhere else," I suggest. "Maybe Nan's."

"I love your boyfriend, but we're not eating ice cream for dinner."

A tall blonde comes over and says, "I'm sorry about the confusion. We have a table in the back, if you'll please follow me."

She leads us toward a walled-off room in the rear.

The manager opens the door, and I follow Mom inside.

It takes a moment to recognize what's happening. At first, I think we're in the wrong place. The room is filled with friends from school. It's a small room, but I don't have that many friends. There are HAPPY BIRTHDAY balloons everywhere.

Everyone shouts, "Surprise!"

I finally realize it's for me.

Alex hugs and kisses me.

"I thought you were working!" I cry.

"Yeah, I lied. Don't tell my Dad, though."

Alex's dad has been a lot better since he joined a 12-step group and stopped drinking. He's even lightened up a bit regarding us dating. But he'd still be mad that Alex was blowing off work to spend time with me. He's still a bit of a hard ass, but at least he's no longer abusing Alex.

Alex says someday I might even like the man, though I doubt that'll happen anytime soon.

I look beyond him to take in the rest of the room. Alice, whom I've gotten close to in the past few months. Stephen and Millie from gym. And three new friends from the Art clique — a group I finally feel like I belong in — Kayla, Curtis, and Maggie.

Alice comes up and hugs me, "Happy Seventeenth, Cora."

I hug her tight. "Thank you for coming."

Then I see the last person in the world I expected to see — Kris, standing in the corner.

I scream. We both scream as we run to each other.

"Oh, my God! I didn't know you were coming!"

"I wouldn't miss my Apple's birthday!"

We hug, and though we haven't seen each other since California, it's suddenly as if no time has passed at all.

"I'm so sorry about all that drama," I say.

I'd had to set up a new LiveLyfe account so I could beg her to call me, then we talked on the phone for almost three hours, but this is the first time I've seen her in person, and I still feel guilty for how I reacted to her dating Tyler again. I was worried about her, but some of it was my insecurity.

"I get it," she teases. "You love me and couldn't stand the thought of Tyler and me being together forever."

"Yep, you got me," I joke back. "Just please don't ever go back to him."

I'm teasing. I know she wouldn't go back to him after she caught him with not one but two other girls.

"Damn, I was really looking forward to settling down in his mom's basement."

We laugh, just like old times.

I look around the room. For the first time in forever, I don't feel like a freak.

I feel like I belong right where I am.

Mom is talking with Kayla and Curtis. She sees me looking over and smiles.

"Thank you," I mouth.

"I love you," she mouths back.

~

THE NEXT MORNING ...

I WAKE up to Kris's hand in my face.

I forgot what a bed hog she is.

It's freezing. I climb out of bed then throw on a sweater over my pajamas.

A glance at the clock tells me it's only seven-thirty. Mom's working early, and I know Kris won't wake up until at least ten or eleven.

I've got time to grab a hot tea downstairs then head to Dad's office to work on my book.

His old friend who runs the small press loves the draft I sent him and offered me an advance.

Now I just have to finish the story.

It's been fun writing in Dad's world, and it's somehow made me feel even closer to him than I ever imagined.

When I get to his office, I wake his computer. I'm just about to open the doc when I see a new file on the desktop.

README.TXT

A CHILL RUNS THROUGH ME.

No. I haven't heard from or seen Emily since the night she nearly destroyed my life.

I figured she was probably out there, somewhere. But I haven't felt her.

Is that why it's so cold in here?

I click open.

· · ·

I KNOW *you don't want to hear from me. I just wanted to say two things.*

First, I'm sorry for everything.

Second, happy birthday.

I'm not sure how long I've got. Memories are getting harder to remember each day. But I wanted to tell you one other thing.

Lilith said she couldn't really contact your father because he was in Heaven. She'd felt his presence around you, but she couldn't communicate with him. She says that only happens when people are in Heaven.

Again, I'm sorry for everything I did. I never had a better friend than you and I screwed it up, trying to protect you. And partly I didn't want to let you go. I didn't want to be alone, forgotten.

I really do love you, though, and wish I'd shown it in some better way.

I hope you find the happiness you deserve, Cora.

–EMILY

THE END

Author's Note

Emily's List is a personal story, the kind that is a bit harder to sell/market because it's not a big concept sci-fi, post-apocalyptic, or thriller series like we usually do.

It's a quieter standalone novel. I wanted to write something that made me feel how *Let The Right One In* made me feel. Something about friendship, feeling alone, but also about family.

It's the kind of story we love to tell, because these are the sorts of stories that helped me (Dave) through some rough school years. Helped me realize that no matter how much of a freak I felt like, how much I was bullied, I wasn't alone.

Like the main character, Cora, I suffer from OCD. And while I did my best to hide my tics and compulsions, kids are perceptive. And when you're different, they notice.

And, like Cora, I hated feeling so different. I was ashamed and tried to hide to avoid the bullies.

Unlike Cora, I would've *loved* to have had a ghost friend who beat the hell out of my bullies. I would've gladly added names to that list!

But *that* probably wouldn't have ended well for anyone.

So, I turned to writing as my escape.

Thankfully, I had a few close friends who encouraged my writing and my eventual acceptance of my OCD. A few people who let me know that being different isn't a curse. They accepted me for my differences, and helped me to accept myself.

At its core, *Emily's List* is about just that — accepting yourself. It's also about the love between a mother and daughter, and about the danger of feeling alone and the things isolation can do to your mind. It made Cora vulnerable to Emily's influences and it turned Emily into a twisted version of herself.

We hope this story helps someone feel a bit less alone in the world. Or, if they need help, it'll help them reach out to loved ones and/or seek professional help.

There's no shame in being different. No shame in being bullied. Don't let others silence you. You might feel alone, but you don't have to stay that way.

BEFORE YOU GO

I have a quick favor to ask. I hate asking you for anything. You already bought our book and read our story. And that's all we ever really want — for you to enjoy what we write.

However, if you've got a couple of minutes, we'd love your help.

As indie writers it's tough to get attention for quiet stories like this.

If you enjoyed *Emily's List*, we'd love it if you could take the time to leave a review wherever you bought the book.

Reviews help get word out about our books. They help us sell more books so we can continue to write more quiet, personal stories like this.

Once *Emily's List* gets 100 reviews, we'll write a special free standalone short story set in this world and send it out, absolutely free, to everyone on our mailing list.

Thank you for reading,
Dave (and Sean)

Noella's only happiness comes in her dreams of a world where her father is alive and a mysterious stranger protects her from the monsters of her nightmares. Then those monsters walk into her waking life. Is Noella losing her mind, or is she linked to a hidden word, destined to be normal ForNevermore?

GET FORNEVERMORE

BEFORE YOU GO

I have a quick favor to ask. I hate asking you for anything. You already bought our book and read our story. And that's all we ever really want — for you to enjoy what we write.

However, if you've got a couple of minutes, we'd love your help.

As indie writers it's tough to get attention for quiet stories like this.

If you enjoyed *Emily's List*, we'd love it if you could take the time to leave a review wherever you bought the book.

Reviews help get word out about our books. They help us sell more books so we can continue to write more quiet, personal stories like this.

Once *Emily's List* gets 100 reviews, we'll write a special free standalone short story set in this world and send it out, absolutely free, to everyone on our mailing list.

Thank you for reading,
Dave (and Sean)

About the Authors

Sean Platt is an entrepreneur and founder of Sterling & Stone, where he makes stories with his partners, Johnny B. Truant, and David W. Wright, and a family of storytellers.

Sean is the bestselling author of over 10 million words' worth of books, including the Yesterday's Gone and Invasion series. Sean is also co-author of the indie publishing cornerstone, Write. Publish. Repeat. and co-host of the Story Studio Podcast.

Originally from Long Beach, California, Sean now lives in Austin, Texas with his wife and two children. He has more than his share of nose.

David W. Wright is the co-author of edge-of-your seat thrillers including the best-selling post-apocalyptic series *Yesterday's Gone*, the paranoid sci-fi *WhiteSpace* series, and the vigilante series, *No Justice*, as well as standalone thrillers *12*, and *Crash* which was recently optioned for a movie.

David is an accomplished, though intermittent, cartoonist who lives in [LOCATION REDACTED] with his wife and son [NAMES REDACTED.]

He is not at all paranoid.

He is "the grumpy one" on the *The Story Studio Podcast* with fellow Sterling and Stone founders, Sean Platt and Johnny B. Truant.

David writes about books, TV shows, movies, and

video games he enjoys; his struggles with anxiety and OCD; writing; and posts the occasional drawing at his personal blog at davidwwright.com

You can email him at david@sterlingandstone.net

We swear, he almost never bites. Unless you feed him after midnight.

For a full list of his most recent books visit sterlingand-stone.net.

Also By David W. Wright

ForNevermore

ForNevermore Season One

ForNevermore Season Two

ForNevermore Season Three

Hidden Justice

Hidden Justice

Hidden Honor

Hidden Shame

Hidden Virtue

No Justice

No Justice

No Escape

No Hope

No Return

No Stopping

No Fear

Karma Police

Jumper

Karma Police

The Collectors

Deviant

The Fall

Homecoming

Yesterday's Gone

October's Gone

Yesterday's Gone Season One

Yesterday's Gone Season Two

Yesterday's Gone Season Three

Yesterday's Gone Season Four

Yesterday's Gone Season Five

Yesterday's Gone Season Six

Tomorrow's Gone

Tomorrow's Gone Season One

Tomorrow's Gone Season Two

Tomorrow's Gone Season Three

Available Darkness

Darkness Itself

Available Darkness Book One

Available Darkness Book Two

Available Darkness Book Three

WhiteSpace

WhiteSpace Season One

WhiteSpace Season Two

WhiteSpace Season Three

Stand Alone Novels